"Will you be okay on your own with the baby for a minute?" Darcy asked.

Ridge smiled wryly at her concern. "I haven't broken the baby yet."

She nodded. "Fair enough. I'll be right back."

Ridge waited until Darcy had left, then looked down at the baby in his arms. She slept peacefully, curled up like a little shrimp against his chest.

Her mouth turned up in an impossibly sweet smile, and he felt the weight of responsibility slam down on his shoulders. Even though he wasn't related to this child and had no idea where she had come from, she was his now.

"I don't know who left you on my doorstep," he said softly. "But I promise, I will take care of you."

It was his calling to take care of the lost—the reason he'd gone into search and rescue in the first place.

He leaned down and pressed a kiss to the soft hair on the top of the baby's head. "I'll keep you safe," he whispered.

Lara Lacombe earned a PhD in microbiology and immunology and worked in several labs across the country before moving into the classroom. Her day job as a college science professor gives her time to pursue her other love—writing fast-paced romantic suspense with smart, nerdy heroines and dangerously attractive heroes. She loves to hear from readers! Find her on the web or contact her at laralacombewriter@gmail.com.

Books by Lara Lacombe

Harlequin Romantic Suspense

The Coltons of Grave Gulch

Guarding Colton's Child
Proving Colton's Innocence

The Rangers of Big Bend

Ranger's Justice
Ranger's Baby Rescue
The Ranger's Reunion Threat
Ranger's Family in Danger

The Coltons of Mustang Valley

Colton's Undercover Reunion

Deadly Contact
Fatal Fallout
Lethal Lies
Killer Exposure
Killer Season

Visit the Author Profile page at Harlequin.com for more titles.

TEXAS GUARDIAN

LARA LACOMBE

Previously published as *Colton Baby Homecoming*

Special thanks and acknowledgment are given to Lara Kingeter for her contribution to The Coltons of Texas miniseries.

ISBN-13: 978-1-335-74492-0

Texas Guardian

First published as Colton Baby Homecoming in 2016.
This edition published in 2022.

For questions and comments about the quality of this book, please contact us at CustomerService@Harlequin.com.

Harlequin Enterprises ULC
22 Adelaide St. West, 41st Floor
Toronto, Ontario M5H 4E3, Canada
www.Harlequin.com

Printed in U.S.A.

TEXAS GUARDIAN

For A—you are my heart.
Thank you for letting me write this book!

Chapter 1

Ridge Colton climbed behind the wheel of his truck and tried to rub away the gritty, sandpaper feeling from his eyes. He'd been up and at it since before dawn, searching the woods around Granite Gulch with the rest of his team, courtesy of a middle-of-the-night phone call made by a resident. Archie Johansen, a retired school bus driver, had been woken by the sound of footsteps on his porch. A curmudgeon to his core, Archie had grabbed his shotgun and thrown open the door, determined to scare off whoever dared to trespass on his property. As Archie described it, the second he opened his door a dark figure scrambled off his porch and hightailed it for the nearby trees. The old man swore up and down the intruder was carrying a rifle, which had prompted his call to the police. The people of Granite Gulch were normally pretty tough, but with the Alphabet Killer still on the loose, suspicions were running high.

And so Ridge had been dragged from his nice warm bed to comb the area, looking for any signs of an armed and possibly dangerous person skulking around in the woods that surrounded the town.

They hadn't found anyone, which wasn't a huge surprise. Secretly, Ridge thought the older man had actually seen an animal snuffling about in search of dinner rather than an armed threat. After all, Archie hadn't been wearing his glasses at the time, and he hadn't bothered to turn on his porch light before flinging open the door to do battle. It was hard enough to see in the dark, and Ridge knew from experience that heightened emotions often made people see things that weren't really there. Still, they couldn't afford to take any chances. One of these days the Alphabet Killer was going to make a mistake and Ridge wanted to be there to bring him down.

I'll have to fight the others for the privilege, though, he thought with a small smile. With the exception of his brother Ethan and his youngest sister, Josie, all his siblings had gone into law enforcement and were currently focused on this case.

In a way, it was kind of nice they were all working together, even if the circumstances of their reunion were less than ideal. Normal families didn't need the hunt for a serial killer to bring them together. But then again, their own father had been a serial killer, so *normal* wasn't exactly a word that had ever applied to them.

With a sigh, Ridge pushed aside thoughts of his father. Matthew Colton had no place in his life, and he refused to waste energy thinking about the man. It had taken him years to move past his issues with his parentage, and dwelling on a fact that couldn't be changed wouldn't do him any good.

A gentle touch on his arm snagged his attention, and he turned to find his partner, Penny, staring up at him with her soulful, dark brown eyes. "I'm okay, girl," he said, reaching over to scratch behind her ears. Penny, a chocolate Lab, was the best search and rescue dog on the team, and she was always very attuned to Ridge's moods. In truth, Ridge often felt closer to her than to other people. She didn't care who his father was, didn't whisper behind his back or ask awkward questions. She just stayed by his side, a true and loyal friend. She'd melted his heart the moment he'd found her as a lost and abandoned puppy, and he'd do anything for her.

"Ready to head home?" he asked. It had been a long day for her, as well, but she never complained.

She let out a soft "ruff" in response, and he started the truck. Keeping one hand on Penny's head, he idly stroked the velvety softness of her ears as he drove. "How about a bath tonight?" After spending all day in the woods, they both smelled pretty bad, and he needed to check her over for ticks and other unfriendly critters. Might as well kill two birds with one stone.

Her ears pricked forward at the word *bath*. True to her breed, Penny loved the water. While she'd much rather swim in the lake or splash through a stream, she tolerated a bath and its accompanying shampoo with the long-suffering patience of a martyr.

His mood lifted as he pondered the evening's activities. First, cleanup for him and Penny. Then he'd build a nice fire so she could warm herself while he threw a steak on the grill. And after dinner, he'd get back to his book. Yes, that sounded like the perfect way to wrap up a disappointing day.

It took about twenty minutes before he turned down the long, single-lane road that led to his cabin. His older sister, Annabel, made no secret of the fact that she thought he was too isolated from everyone, but Ridge liked his solitude. It was peaceful out here with his cabin nestled up to the edge of the woods. And he much preferred the soothing sounds of the forest to the grating noise of town. Even though Granite Gulch wasn't a huge metropolis like Houston, it was a growing city complete with traffic, construction and plenty of people. He knew it was only a matter of time before the urban sprawl began to creep into his oasis, but Ridge was determined to enjoy the quiet while he still could.

He pulled up next to the cabin and shut off the engine, then opened the door for Penny. She jumped out with a graceful leap, but Ridge could tell by the set of her ears and the look in her eyes she was just as tired as he. A nice, relaxing evening would do them both a world of good.

After grabbing his bag and locking up the truck, he started for the back door. It took him a few steps to realize Penny wasn't with him. She'd stayed behind, her nose lifted as she sniffed the spring air.

Probably a raccoon, maybe a squirrel, he thought, pausing to watch her. Penny was a highly trained and very skilled search and rescue operator, but she was still a dog. When she was working, she maintained a laser-like, almost unshakable focus, but when she was off duty, she was just as susceptible to the taunting of small woodland creatures as any other dog. He'd give her a few minutes to enjoy herself outside, but then they really needed to get cleaned up.

He expected her to take a quick roll in the grass and rejoin him, but she kept her nose in the air. It was the same behavior she exhibited when she'd found the scent trail of a human, and Ridge felt the skin on the back of his neck tighten. Had someone been near his cabin lately? He had no neighbors for miles around, and there was no reason anyone should have come looking for him today. Why then was Penny acting as if she'd caught a trail?

After what seemed like an eternity, Penny dropped her head and met his gaze. She let out a short, sharp yip and cocked her ears forward, the signal she used to let him know she was on to something. Intrigued, Ridge gave her the command she wanted: "Find it."

She took off, racing around the corner of the house. Ridge followed at a slightly slower pace, but he wasn't worried about her running away. Penny would stay put once she'd found the source of her interest, and her bark would tell him exactly where she was.

As it turned out, he didn't have to go far. He rounded the corner of the house just in time to see her jump onto the front porch. She headed straight for the wooden bench that sat overlooking the drive, plopped her butt down on the weathered boards, and began emitting her characteristic "I found it!" bark with all the gusto of an opera singer.

Ridge bounded up the steps and joined her, placing his hand on her head to let her know he was there and she could stop barking. She immediately quieted, but kept her gaze fixed on the floor behind the bench. Ridge leaned forward, squinting into the shadows. The front porch faced east, and the thunderclouds threatening overhead obscured the last rays of the setting sun, making it nearly impossible for him to determine what Penny had discovered. He dug a flashlight out of his bag and flicked on the light, then nearly dropped it when he realized what he was looking at.

"Oh my God," he breathed, hardly daring to believe his eyes.

One of those big plastic carriers sat on his porch, the kind people used when driving around a baby. There was a blanket draped over the top, so he couldn't tell if the seat was occupied. But Penny wouldn't have signaled if the thing was empty...

Ridge reached forward, his heart in his throat. He pushed the covering aside and bit back a curse.

How in the world did a baby wind up on his front porch?

What the hell?

Ridge stared down at the infant, now safely inside and sleeping peacefully. The little one had stirred at the sound of Penny's barking, but had drifted off again when Ridge had picked up the carrier and moved it into the cabin. He didn't know much about infants, but it seemed odd that this one was so quiet. Weren't babies supposed to cry a lot?

He glanced down at Penny, but she offered him no guidance. She looked from him to the baby and back again expectantly, and he realized he'd forgotten to reward her for her find. A spike of guilt pierced through his shock, and he moved quickly to dig her favorite toy out of his bag. "Good girl," he crooned as he presented it, giving her some extra ear scratches. Search and rescue dogs were motivated by positive reinforcement, and he'd never before forgotten to treat her right away after she'd done her job.

Of course, he'd never encountered a baby on his front porch, either.

"Where did you come from?" he murmured.

There had been no signs of anyone around his cabin, so he had no way of knowing how long the baby had been out there. His stomach twisted at the thought of the helpless infant left to the mercy of the elements, and a flash of anger warmed his chest. Who in their right mind left a baby on a stranger's porch? What kind of parent did that to a child? He glanced outside, noting the rotten-egg-green color of the sky. Bad weather was coming. A thunderstorm for sure, maybe even hail and a tornado. If he hadn't made it home when he did…

He shuddered, refusing to consider the alternative. Fortunately, he had come home. And even better, Penny had been there. Ridge didn't make it a habit to check his front porch, so there was no guarantee he would have found the child if not for his partner.

"Seems like your guardian angel is working overtime," he said, shaking his head at all the things that could have gone wrong tonight.

Ridge reached out and peeled down the light green fleece blanket to reveal an impossibly small body strapped into the car seat. The baby sported a pink long-sleeved, footed outfit, complete with small mittens. "I guess this means you're a girl," he said softly.

It took him a second to figure out how to extract her from the harness, but after a few fumbling attempts he was able to gently lift her from the carrier. Her head lolled back at the movement and she emitted a small squeak of distress, which sent his heart racing. Had he hurt her? What if she was already injured—was he making things worse? Sweat broke out on his palms, and he feared she would slip right out of his hands and onto the floor.

"Don't drop the baby," he told himself, tightening his grip on the little torso. He could feel her heartbeat under his fingers, fast as a hummingbird's wings. Was that normal? Maybe she was stressed or sick.

He brought her to his chest and held her against his heart, his large hand spanning her entire back and extending to her head. She squirmed a little against him, and he was gratified to feel the warmth of her body through his shirt. Not too cold then. That was something, at least.

Now that he'd taken her out of the carrier, he noticed a folded piece of paper that had been left behind. It was slightly wrinkled and a little damp from its stay under the baby, but the message was still legible. *Please take care of her until I can come back.—F*

Okay, then. It wasn't much to go on, but at least it was something.

If the note was to be believed, the baby's mother intended to come back for the child. So what kind of circumstances forced a woman to stash her baby on a stranger's front porch? Why not take the little one to the police station, or the hospital? After all, there was no guarantee the baby would be found, so the mother had to be truly desperate to resort to such an action.

Based on the signature, if an initial could even count as a signature, the mother's name started with the letter *F.* Was this woman worried she was the next target of the Alphabet Killer? Did she think she was in mortal danger, and had left the baby in a last-ditch attempt to save her?

It was possible, he mused. So far, the killer had targeted women in alphabetical order of their names. The latest victim's name had started with

E, which meant an *F* name was next on the list. Maybe this mother knew the killer and had good reason to suspect she was the next target.

The baby wriggled against him, and he brought his other hand up to secure his hold on her. He lifted her off his chest and was rewarded with the sight of two dark eyes squinting up at him. Her movements had knocked her cap askew, so he tugged it off her head to reveal a light dusting of dark brown hair.

Just like the Alphabet Killer's previous victims.

A tingle raced from his fingertips to his chest. Was he holding a clue to the identity of the killer? If they could identify this baby and somehow find her mother, would that lead them to the Alphabet Killer? Maybe this was the break they'd all been waiting for.

"But why are you here?" he asked the baby. She smacked her lips together as if she was trying to respond, but otherwise gave no indication she'd heard him. Was her mother somehow connected to the mysterious armed subject he'd been hunting all day? Perhaps the Alphabet Killer had been playing hide-and-seek with the unknown *F*, and the mother had taken the first opportunity she'd found to get the baby to some kind of safety. That still didn't explain why Archie Johansen had heard someone on his porch, but it would account for why the baby had been left on his property.

The little girl was now emitting an increasingly loud series of grunts and squeaks, and Ridge felt his heart begin to pound as he realized he had no idea what was wrong with the baby or what to do about it. Apparently dissatisfied with his response, or lack thereof, the baby opened her mouth to emit a piercing wail. Penny dropped her favorite toy and stared up at Ridge, her expression saying more than words ever could. *Are you going to deal with this?*

"Ah, it's okay," he said, awkwardly patting the baby's little back in what he hoped was a comforting cadence. "Don't cry. You're fine."

This did not have the desired effect. The baby settled into a rhythmic cry that made it clear she had needs and he was failing to meet them. *She's probably hungry*, he realized belatedly. *Who knows how long it's been since her last meal?*

But what did you feed a baby? There was definitely nothing in his pantry suitable for an infant. And he couldn't very well run down to the grocery store for formula—he had no idea what kind to get, nor did he have any bottles. He was hopelessly out of his depth here. Time to bring in a professional.

He tucked her back into the car seat and carried her out to the truck, dodging the big fat raindrops beginning to fall from the sky. Not about to be left behind, Penny followed him and hopped onto the floorboard of the passenger seat, keeping a watchful eye on the now red-faced and squalling baby.

"So much for my quiet night," he muttered to himself as he threw the truck into gear. "Hang in there, little one," he said, a bit louder. "We're going to get you checked out, and I'm pretty sure they have baby food at the hospital." And maybe, just maybe, he'd get lucky and there would be a record of her birth there, too.

Stranger things had happened.

Chapter 2

Doctor Darcy Marrow leaned forward and tied off the last stitch, then offered her patient a smile.

"You did a great job," she assured the little boy.

He stared up at her, his blue eyes wide with amazement. "I didn't feel a thing!" he exclaimed.

"That's good," she told him, pushing back from the bed and setting her tools on the nearby metal tray. "That means the medicine worked."

"Am I going to have a scar?" He sounded hopeful about the possibility, which triggered a sigh from his mother.

Darcy hid a smile as she started gathering up empty wrappers and used instruments. "Maybe," she said. “It’s important you keep the stitches clean and dry for now. And I can promise you, once the medicine starts to wear off, your arm is going to ache.”

“That’s so cool!”

She met his mother’s gaze and shrugged slightly. “You’ll want to take him to his pediatrician in a week, and they can remove the stitches. In the meantime, if he starts to run a fever or the wound looks infected, bring him back in.”

“Thank you,” the woman said. She was clearly exhausted, and no wonder. She’d come home from work and had started to cook dinner, only to be interrupted by the crash of the glass coffee table breaking into a million pieces. Apparently little Johnny had decided to practice his karate moves while waiting, a decision that was all the more mysterious seeing as how the boy hadn’t taken a single karate lesson in his life.

“No more kung fu movies for you,” his mother said as the pair shuffled out of the exam bay.

“But, Mom,” the boy protested, their voices growing softer as they walked away.

Darcy shook her head and silently wished them well. The injury itself hadn’t been too bad, but given the boy’s enthusiasm and appetite for adventure, it probably wouldn’t be his last scrape.

She pulled the curtain back and stepped out into the main bay of the emergency room. The facility was shaped like a giant U, with the exam rooms set up on the periphery to orbit a large central workstation where the nurses and doctors could order tests, access lab results or maybe even drink a cup of coffee when things were slow.

Like now.

One of the nurses gave her a friendly smile when she sat down. "I take it Johnny is all fixed up?"

Darcy nodded. "He'll be back in action in no time, which I'm sure will drive his mother nuts."

The woman laughed. "He is a handful."

"Is it just the two of them?" She didn't remember seeing a father's name listed on the chart, but then again, she hadn't really been focused on it.

"Yeah. Her husband took a job out in Odessa when the oil boom got started a couple of years ago. Called her up a few months later and said he wasn't coming back. As far as I know, she hasn't seen or heard from him since."

"That's terrible," Darcy replied, feeling even more sorry for the beleaguered woman. No wonder she'd looked so tired! "Is there anything we can do to help her? Maybe some kind of babysitting program, or something like that?"

The nurse eyed her curiously. "She's on a wait list for an after-school care center. But I have no idea how long it'll take before Johnny's name comes up."

"Maybe I can call them and get it bumped up a little," Darcy mused.

"Maybe you could," the nurse agreed. "But I didn't think you were sticking around long enough for things like that."

Darcy felt her face heat at the observation. It was true, she was only filling in at the Granite Gulch Regional Medical Center for a few weeks as a favor to her father. He was the chief of staff at the hospital, and when he'd found out her position in New York didn't start until May, he'd suggested she moonlight in Granite Gulch for the time being.

"To keep your skills sharp," he'd said, his tone suggesting she was in real danger of forgetting everything she'd ever learned if she took a few weeks of vacation.

His implied criticism of her skills had stung, but she'd shrugged off his remarks. It wasn't as if she had a warm, loving relationship with her parents. Growing up, her doctor father had been absent more often than not, and her socialite mother was always more interested in playing the part of the wealthy doctor's wife, fluttering from one charity obligation to another with little regard to her daughter at home. As a consequence, family conversations were always rather formal, stilted affairs.

Especially after Darcy had started dating Ridge Colton. They'd met in high school, and she'd been immediately drawn to his quiet intensity. He projected a calm confidence that said he didn't care what other people thought of him, and coming from a family obsessed with appearances, that attitude both intrigued and attracted her in equal parts. She'd known about his family's past—everyone did—but his connection to the notorious Matthew Colton hadn't bothered her. Ridge had a gentleness about him, and as she'd talked to him and gotten to know him, she realized the quiet air everyone mistook for an aloof arrogance was actually a defense against the pain of gossip and rejection. Ridge was so used to people judging him by his father's deeds that he had stopped trying to reach out and connect with others. Once he'd decided to open up and trust Darcy, he'd let down those walls and his true, amazing personality had shone through.

Around her, at least.

Her parents had hit the roof when they'd found out about the relationship. It was the one time in her life Darcy could remember them taking an actual interest in her activities and friends. They had insisted she break up with Ridge right away, but Darcy had refused. Her obstinacy had led to a further cooling of their relationship, and even though she'd eventually walked away from Ridge, she and her parents had never really warmed to each other. It was part of why she'd chosen to take the temporary job in Granite Gulch. While she knew her parents would never really understand her choices, she didn't want to start her life in New York without at least attempting to mend some fences here.

Shaking off those thoughts, Darcy returned her focus to the nurse. "I know I won't be here for very long, but I do want to try to help while I can."

The woman nodded, a small smile playing at the corners of her mouth as if Darcy had just confirmed one of her suspicions. "Give me just a minute—I'll look up that number for you."

"Thanks." Darcy turned to the computer, pulling up the list of patients still waiting to be seen. They'd been triaged according to illness or severity of injury when they'd walked in the door, and since no one was in immediate danger of dying, she'd see them in the order in which they'd arrived.

She'd just pulled up the file on her next patient—a young woman with flu-like symptoms—when she heard the faint wail of a baby's cry. "Someone's not happy," she murmured, pausing to listen. It was a regular, rhythmic cry of a hungry baby, not the piercing wail of pain or the heartbreakingly weak cry of illness, so she turned her attention back to the computer screen.

The sound of urgent voices drifted back from the waiting room, along with snippets of the conversation.

"Sir, you can't—" said Carol, the receptionist, her distress plain.

"Not leaving her—" This was a low rumble of a voice, most likely the baby's father. Who was he refusing to leave behind?

"Simply not allowed—" Carol was getting frustrated now, her tone becoming challenging. Darcy could picture the woman leaning forward, her glasses sliding down her nose as she glared up at the man who dared to defy her. Carol wasn't much to look at physically, but she ran the front desk of the ER with a drill sergeant's precision and she didn't take crap from anyone. Whoever was out there was going to have to bend to Carol's will, and the sooner he did it, the better.

"Service animal—" The words were clipped and formal, effectively ending the conversation.

Well, *that* was interesting. By law, they couldn't refuse entry to a service animal—something Carol would already know. However, most service animals wore a distinctive harness or other clearly identifying gear that marked them as such. The fact that Carol had tried to jettison this one meant that the creature in question was likely out of uniform, so to speak. So was it a true service animal, or was the owner just trying to pass it off as such because they didn't want to leave their pet in the car?

Her curiosity piqued, Darcy stood and started

walking toward the triage room. It sounded as if Carol might need some backup, and she wanted to see what all the fuss was about. Furthermore, the baby's cries had taken on an increasingly desperate tone, and she knew from experience that pediatric cases could escalate quickly.

The nurse shot her an inquisitive glance as she stepped into the triage exam room. Darcy offered a smile. "Just thought I'd comc see what all the fuss is about..." The words died in her throat as she got her first look at her patient—or rather, her patient's parent.

Ridge Colton.

The sight of him knocked the breath right out of her lungs, leaving her standing there gaping at him like some kind of slack-jawed yokel. On some level, she'd known it was only a matter of time before she would run into him. Granite Gulch was a growing town, but it still had a very local feel to it and everyone seemed to know everyone else's business. Still, she had hoped their inevitable meeting would occur at a time and place of her choosing, not when she was eight hours deep into a twelve-hour shift and looking less than fresh.

"Ridge." His name was barely more than a whisper, but it may as well have been a shout. He glanced over at her and recognition flared in his dark brown eyes, along with another flash of emotion she couldn't decipher. Surprise? Anger?

Disappointment? No matter. It was gone in the next heartbeat, and he'd already turned back to the baby, dismissing her.

The nurse continued her preliminary exam of the infant, rattling off information as she went. Darcy listened with half an ear and forced herself to look away from Ridge and focus on the baby in front of her. There would be time to stare at Ridge later, to look for signs of the boy she'd known in the man's body now before her.

A quick physical exam revealed nothing unusual, nothing to suggest the need for a visit to the emergency room. She shot a questioning glance at Ridge. "What's the problem here?"

Ridge met her eyes, then looked away again. "I'm not sure. I was worried about exposure."

"Exposure?" Darcy frowned at him, certain she had misheard. "How long has she been outside?"

He shook his head. "I don't know."

"Where's her mother?" A small part of her heart tightened at the realization that her first love had moved on with his life, but she pushed the sting aside. Of course Ridge had married and started a family. Why wouldn't he? It was foolish of her to think she'd be the only woman he would let inside his heart.

"I don't know." A muscle in his jaw twitched. Apparently the baby's mother was a sore spot with him. Were they separated? Had she dropped the baby off and left without telling him? But what kind of mother would do that? The Ridge she had known was a good judge of character—surely he wouldn't have a child with a woman who was so irresponsible?

"Can you call her? I need a little more information, please."

"No."

Darcy raised one eyebrow at his refusal. "No?"

He met her gaze then, his dark brown eyes inscrutable. "I told you, I don't know where she is." He practically spat the words out, as if they tasted bad in his mouth.

Okay, time to try a different tack. Darcy turned to the nurse. "Let's do a full work-up, just to make sure we don't miss anything. In the meantime, do we have a bottle?" The poor little one had been rooting around in vain since she had started the exam, and Darcy suspected most, if not all, of the ruckus was simply the sounds of a hungry baby who was getting angry at being denied dinner.

The nurse nodded and walked to the bank of cabinets on the far wall of the room. It took her only a moment to prepare a bottle, and Darcy scooped the baby up and began to feed her. The little one settled down immediately, her cries subsiding as she focused on eating, taking great, gulping draws from the bottle.

Ridge let out a sigh of relief, and Darcy saw his

shoulders relax. There was an approving "ruff" from the floor, and she glanced down to see a dark brown dog staring up at her with surprisingly intelligent eyes. *That must be the service animal.*

"Nice dog," she said, searching for something to say to get Ridge talking. It was clear her earlier line of questioning wasn't getting her anywhere, and she needed to know more about the baby to better treat her.

Ridge glanced down absently, as if he'd forgotten the dog was there. "Oh. Thanks." He sounded distracted, and no wonder. He clearly wasn't used to handling a baby, and if the baby's mother—his wife? Girlfriend?—had left with little to no warning, he was probably more focused on that than anything else.

"We normally don't let animals back here," she continued, trying to sound conversational.

"She's a service dog," he responded, sounding a little more engaged.

"Oh? Like a Seeing Eye dog?"

He shook his head, the ends of his dark hair brushing the collar of his shirt. "No. Search and rescue." He leaned down and gave the dog a scratch behind the ears. "She's the one that found the baby."

Darcy's head jerked up at that. "Found the baby? You mean she's not yours?"

He gave her a puzzled look. "No, she's not. I thought I made that clear."

A strange sense of relief filled Darcy at the realization that Ridge had not moved on with his life, but she pushed it aside. Now was not the time to let her selfish emotions rule. As she fought to find her professional footing again, another, more sinister thought entered her mind.

"Ridge, where did this baby come from?" The young man she had known wasn't capable of malice, but people could change. It had been years since she had seen him. Could she really say she still knew him? What if he had snapped and taken this baby from its mother, then concocted a story about "finding" her? But why would he do that?

"I didn't steal her, if that's what you're implying," he said coldly.

Darcy felt her face heat and looked away. Ten years ago, her father had accused Ridge of stealing an antique pocket watch from his desk drawer. Darcy hadn't believed it but when Ridge had dumped out his backpack, the watch had spilled out. She'd begged him for an explanation—maybe the watch had fallen in his bag by mistake? Maybe he had taken the watch to look at it and had forgotten to return it? She'd been convinced Ridge had a reasonable story that would restore her faith in him and convince her father that Ridge wasn't a bad guy. So she'd stood there, watching and silently pleading for him to explain it to them.

But Ridge hadn't offered any kind of response.

He'd just sat there, stone-faced and silent in the wake of her father's accusations. He'd completely shut her out—he hadn't even met her eyes or offered any sign of acknowledgment that she was in the room. And so Darcy had had no choice but to break up with him. It had shredded her heart to do it, but she couldn't stay with someone who would steal from her family.

She'd never forgotten that horrible moment, and apparently Ridge hadn't, either.

"I don't think you stole her," she said evenly, resisting the urge to snap back at him. He had no right to still be angry with her—he was the one who had done something wrong! But yelling at him wasn't going to get her any closer to learning about this baby, and right now, that was the priority.

She took a deep breath. "It sounds like you have quite the story to tell," she said, trying to sound pleasant. "Let's just focus on the baby, shall we?"

Ridge pressed his lips together and nodded once.

"Okay," she said, some of the tension leaving her muscles now that they were back on track. "So who does this baby belong to?"

Ridge clenched his jaw, biting back a sarcastic response. It had been a long day, and snapping at Darcy wasn't going to solve any of his problems.

Still, the way she was looking at him now, as if she thought he had done something horrible…it hurt. Once upon a time, they had meant something to each other. She'd been the only person who hadn't held his paternity against him, who had actually tried to get to know him, the real him. They had had a few good years together, and he'd foolishly thought their young love would be enough to see them through any and everything life threw at them.

How wrong he'd been. In the end, she'd turned out to be just like everyone else—judging him for something he hadn't done.

It had been years since he'd seen her. He'd known she was back in Granite Gulch, but he hadn't thought to seek her out. She had made her choice, and he wasn't the type to chase after a failed dream.

But seeing her now… She looked amazing. Her auburn hair was longer than he remembered, pulled back into a ponytail that served only to accentuate her slanted cheekbones. Her eyes were the same, though. Dark brown pools that pulled him in, made him feel as though he was drowning. But what a way to go!

Shaking his head, he returned his focus to the baby who was quickly emptying her bottle. A dull throb started in his chest as he stared at the woman he had once loved hold a baby in her arms. It was the very picture of an old dream come true, but it wasn't real and never would be.

"I'll tell you what happened," he began. "But first, I need to call a few people."

"Who?" The word was innocent enough, but he heard the subtle challenge in her voice.

"My brother and sister. Sam and Annabel are both cops. I've had a hell of a day, and I only want to tell this story once."

Darcy pressed her lips together, and he recognized the expression—she had something to say, but she was holding her tongue. For now. She settled for a nod, and he pulled his phone out and dialed.

It took only a few minutes to reach Sam and Annabel, and fortunately his siblings didn't press for details. Ridge hung up with a sigh and dropped into the chair by the hospital bed. Penny stepped over and sat at his feet, then laid her head on his lap in a gesture of support. He stroked her head absently, replaying the moments leading up to her finding the baby. Maybe there was something he'd overlooked in the chaos, some clue that would help identify this child and whoever had dropped her on his porch.

Try as he might, though, there wasn't anything that jumped out in his memories. He hadn't seen any tracks around his cabin, but then again, he hadn't really been looking for any. He hadn't smelled anything unusual, either—no heavy perfumes or colognes had lingered in the air. Of course, Penny would be much better at detecting that kind of thing. Not for the first time, he wished his dog could talk.

"Ridge?" He blinked and looked up to find Darcy staring at him. Her expression made it clear this wasn't the first time she'd said his name, and he muttered an apology.

"Like I said, it's been a long day."

"It's okay," she replied. "But we need to move to an exam room while we wait for your brother and sister to arrive. We have to keep this room free for triage."

"No problem." He stood and stretched, working the aches and kinks out of his back and shoulders. It felt good to move, and now that the baby wasn't crying, his muscles could actually relax and release the tension of the day.

He made a quick gesture with his hand and Penny stood as well, ready to follow him. Then he turned to face Darcy and she quickly looked away, a faint pink staining her cheeks. Interesting. Had she been watching him?

A small, petty part of him hoped she liked what she saw. It was silly, he knew, but just the thought that she might still find him attractive appealed to his ego. She had been the one to walk away all those years ago, leaving him to wonder what he could have said or done differently. It was nice to think he wasn't the only one who harbored secret regrets over the way things had ended between them.

"Where to?" he asked, striving for a casual tone. The last thing he wanted was for her to realize how much he was affected by seeing her again. Her presence brought back too many memories, too many emotions. He didn't have time for this right now—he had to focus on finding this baby's parents and catching the Alphabet Killer before they claimed another victim.

Besides, he wasn't stupid. Darcy had left him before. And even though the only option for them was friendship, he wasn't going to let his guard down again for the sake of nostalgia. It just wasn't worth it.

Darcy led him back into the main bay of the emergency room, then guided him to a room to the left of the main nurses' station. "Why don't you have a seat," she said, indicating the chair with a nod. "I'm going to call in a bassinet for this little one."

"Do you need me to hold her while we wait for it to arrive?"

Her eyebrows shot up. "Really?" She sounded doubtful, as if he was the last person she'd expect to hold a baby. Once again, he pushed back against the sting of her low expectations. Had she always thought so little of him and he'd just never noticed before? They did say love made a man blind…

"I don't mind." Truth be told, he was feeling a little protective. He didn't know who this baby was or where she'd come from, but by some twist of fate she'd been dropped into his life. Now it was up to him to make sure she was safe until they could figure out her story.

Darcy walked over and gently transferred the baby into his arms. He tucked her against his chest, marveling at the warm weight of her small body. How could such a little thing put out so much heat? She let out a sigh and snuggled against him, and his heart did a funny little flip.

"Let me get you a blanket," Darcy murmured. She returned a second later and tucked a swath of flannel over the baby, then stepped back and smiled down at him.

"This is a good look for you," she said softly.

He met her gaze and for a split second, it was as though they were still together, still planning a future and sharing their hopes and dreams. The sense of déjà vu was so intense it made him a little dizzy, and he tightened his grip on the baby to make sure he didn't drop her. Did Darcy feel it, too? Or did the fatigue of the day make him especially susceptible to such a ridiculous notion?

In any event, Penny chose that moment to let out a small, inquisitive noise, breaking the spell of the moment. She walked over to him and the baby and Darcy stepped back to give the dog better access.

It was just as well, he told himself. *No use pining after what might have been.*

Penny nosed the baby, then sniffed his leg. Apparently satisfied that everyone was who they should be, she walked a tight circle twice and settled down to curl up on the floor, closing her eyes with a sigh.

"She's a really good dog," Darcy observed.

"The best," he replied.

"What's her name?"

"Penny."

"Interesting choice," she replied. "She's not really the color of a penny, though."

He chuckled softly. "I named her that because she ate pennies."

Darcy made a face. "Gross."

"In her defense, she was pretty hungry."

"She must have been, to stoop to eating change."

He felt the smile slide off his face as he thought back to the day he'd found the dog. "I was taking a walk in the woods when I came across her. She was a puppy, barely old enough to be away from her mother. She was nothing more than two big eyes and four big paws, and some psychopath had tied her to a tree and left her." He clenched his jaw, feeling his back teeth grind together. Even though it had been several years, just the thought of the cruelty was enough to send his blood pressure into the stratosphere.

Darcy gasped. “That’s horrible!”

He nodded. “It was a good thing I came along when I did. I don’t know how long she’d been out there, but she wasn’t going to last much longer. So I scooped her up, put her in the truck and headed into town to the vet’s office. She was clearly starving, and before I knew what was happening, she’d eaten the change right out of my console.”

“Poor thing. Very resourceful of her, though.” Darcy looked down at Penny, her expression a mixture of sympathy and amusement. “She’s lucky you found her before it was too late.”

“Turned out, we both got lucky that day.” He didn’t bother trying to explain how Penny had helped him as much as he’d helped her. How the dog had healed the cracks in his heart and turned out to be his best friend. It probably said something sad about him that he trusted his dog more than any person, but it was the truth.

Ridge shifted in the chair and glanced down at the baby, relieved to see his movements hadn’t disturbed her sleep. Poor little thing had had quite the day, but she seemed to be a survivor.

As if she could read his thoughts, Darcy spoke up. “She’s going to be okay.” Her words were soft and soothing, and just like that he was taken back to the days when he could tell this woman anything. How many conversations had they had, how many times had he opened his heart to her and shared parts of himself he'd never shown to anyone? He hated to admit it but despite the distance between them, Darcy still held him in her sway.

At least he was able to recognize it before he fell for her again.

His phone buzzed and he glanced at the screen. We're here. Where are you?

"Sam and Annabel are here. What room are we in?"

"I'll go get them," Darcy volunteered. "Will you be okay on your own for a minute?"

He smiled wryly at her concern. "I haven't broken the baby yet."

She nodded. "Fair enough. I'll be right back."

Ridge waited until she had left, then looked down at the baby in his arms. She slept peacefully, curled up like a little shrimp against his chest. She was so small, her cherubic features the very picture of innocence. A range of expressions flitted across her face in rapid succession while she slept, as if she was trying each one on for size. While he watched, her mouth turned up in an impossibly sweet smile, and he felt the weight of responsibility slam down on his shoulders. Even though he wasn't related to this child and had no idea where she had come from, she was his now.

"I don't know who left you on my doorstep,"

he said softly. "But I promise, I will take care of you." It was his calling to take care of the lost—the reason he'd gone into search and rescue in the first place. His brother Trevor, an FBI profiler, had once told Ridge he was drawn to that work because he hadn't been able to help their youngest sister, Josie. Ridge wasn't sure he believed all that psychological mumbo jumbo, but he did know one thing: he took care of his own.

He leaned down and pressed a kiss to the soft hair on the top of the baby's head. "I'll keep you safe," he whispered.

Chapter 3

Darcy stepped out of the exam room and took a deep breath, trying to center her thoughts. Her head was spinning from the events of the past half hour and she had a seemingly endless list of questions demanding to be answered. Where had that baby come from? Why had someone left her with Ridge? What had he been doing over the past decade since she'd seen him last? Had he truly moved on and found someone or was he still alone, as she was?

First things first, she told herself firmly. *Solve the mystery of the baby. Everything else can wait.*

Nerves fluttered in her stomach as she made

her way back into the waiting area of the emergency room. She'd never met any of Ridge's siblings before, since they had all been split up and raised in different foster homes. For reasons she didn't care to examine too closely, she very much wanted to make a good first impression on these people. She knew Ridge was still angry with her for the way things had ended between them, but maybe if his siblings liked her he would soften a bit toward her. Even though there was no chance of them getting back together, it would be nice if they could have some kind of friendship. They'd meant too much to each other to have this bitterness between them persist.

It wasn't hard to find Sam and Annabel, and not just because the waiting room was fairly quiet. She would have recognized them in the middle of a crowd, as they both had the same studious look as Ridge. It must be a common Colton expression, she decided—that sober, thoughtful gaze made it seem as though they were constantly assessing their environment.

Sam turned to face her as she approached. He had the same dark hair and eyes as his brother, but while Ridge was tall with the broad shoulders and muscular arms of a swimmer, Sam had a more rangy build that reminded her of a long-distance runner.

"Sam Colton?"

He nodded, his gaze assessing as he shook her hand.

Darcy turned to the woman standing beside him. "And you must be Annabel."

Ridge's sister offered her a tight smile that didn't quite reach her blue eyes. "Where's Ridge?"

"Right this way," Darcy said, gesturing them forward. "Thanks for coming so quickly."

"Ridge doesn't cry wolf," Sam observed quietly. "He wouldn't call if it wasn't important."

Darcy rapped lightly on the door of the exam room, then opened it and gestured Sam and Annabel inside. The pair took a step into the room and drew up short as they both caught sight of their brother with a baby in his arms.

Sam recovered first. "Well," he drawled. "I leave you alone for a few hours, and you go and get a baby." There was an odd tone to his voice, as if he'd just been kicked in the gut. Was he upset? But why? Something tingled at the back of Darcy's memory, but before she could really hone in on the thought, Sam cleared his throat and smiled, smoothing over the moment.

"Penny found her," Ridge replied, the corner of his mouth curling up. At the mention of her name, Penny lifted her head and snorted in greeting. Annabel leaned down to give her a pat. "Doesn't look like one of your usual strays," she observed.

"Very funny," Ridge said, shooting her a dry look.

"Want to fill us in on the details?" Sam asked.

Ridge glanced at Darcy and nodded at the door. She closed it quietly to give them some privacy.

It didn't take long for him to tell the story of finding the baby, but Darcy had to bite her tongue to keep from interrupting him with questions. To their credit, Sam and Annabel merely listened quietly until he had finished talking. Once he was done, the siblings exchanged a glance.

"Where's the note now?" Sam asked.

"I left it in the car," Ridge responded. "I didn't want more people touching it."

"Good thinking," Annabel said. "Where are your keys? I'll collect it and take it in for fingerprint analysis."

Ridge cocked his hip off the chair and dug into his pocket. "I'm parked in the lot just outside."

Annabel caught the keys midair. "Saw your truck as we pulled in. I'll be right back."

After a moment of silence, Sam let out a sigh. "None of this makes sense," he said, running a hand through his hair.

Ridge huffed out a laugh. "Tell me about it. I'm the last person who needs to be trusted with a baby."

"Oh, I don't know about that," Sam said, a sparkle of humor showing in his eyes. "You've taken pretty good care of that dog. How much harder can it be to take care of a baby?" Once again, his voice sounded forced, as if he was trying to make light of something that bothered him. All at once, Darcy remembered the gossip she'd heard about Sam Colton—how his former fiancée had pretended to be pregnant with his baby so she could con him into marrying her. He'd been about to make things official, but just before the wedding, the woman had been killed—one of the first victims of the Alphabet Killer.

Darcy eyed Sam with newfound respect and a touch of pity. Even though his former fiancée hadn't really been pregnant, Sam had thought she was and had wanted to do right by his child. How sad for him to find out the truth, especially when he couldn't confront the woman who had spun that web of lies in the first place.

Ridge offered him a sympathetic smile, and his brother nodded.

"So we have a baby with dark hair and a mother whose name presumably begins with the letter *F*," Sam said, his tone making it clear he was thinking out loud. "Hell of a coincidence."

"I thought so, too," Ridge remarked.

"The killer has never gone after a woman with kids before."

They must be talking about the Alphabet Killer, Darcy thought. Did they really think the baby's mother was a target?

"There's a first time for everything," Ridge said. "Besides, we don't really know how the victims are chosen. Aside from their physical similarities, that is."

"True."

The men were quiet for a moment, each one clearly lost in thought.

"And you didn't find anyone out there today?" Sam asked.

Ridge shook his head. "No signs of Mr. Johansen's early morning visitor. Or anyone else for that matter."

"Since you didn't find a body, we can assume the mother is still alive. For now, at least."

"Either that, or the killer caught up to her and left her in the woods."

Sam tilted his head in acknowledgment of the point. "That's possible. But Penny stopped after finding the baby, right?"

The dog in question cocked an ear at the mention of her name, but didn't bother to lift her head.

"That's right," Ridge confirmed.

"Wouldn't she have kept going if there was a body around?"

It was a good question, and Darcy found she was curious to know the answer, as well. She'd never been around a search and rescue dog, and had no idea how they worked.

Ridge shrugged. "Presumably she would have indicated if there was another scent around. But she's not trained as a cadaver dog—she goes after the living, not the dead."

"We can send out a team to search the area around your cabin. But I don't think they're going to find anything." Sam paced a few steps in the small room, his hands on his hips. "So where did the woman go after leaving the baby? People don't just disappear."

"Sure they do," Ridge replied easily. "You know that as well as I do."

What does he mean by that? Darcy wondered. Then it dawned on her—his sister, Josie, had vanished a few years ago. Her absence probably weighed heavily on him, since the pair had been close.

Sam frowned at his brother. "Now is not the time to get cute."

"You know I can't control it." Ridge grinned, his dimples prominent even through the dark, heavy stubble on his cheeks. It was the same teasing expression he'd worn so often when they were alone together as teenagers, and it made Darcy's heart tighten to see it now on the face of the man he'd become.

Sam shook his head, but Darcy saw the smile he

tried to hide. "We've got to find this woman—she could be the key to unlocking the whole case." He turned to face Darcy. "Let's start with what we do know. Do you have any idea how old this baby is?"

Darcy tilted her head to the side, considering his question. "I'd say she's about one to two weeks old," she replied. "That range is consistent with her height, weight and reflex responses."

"Okay," Sam said. He gestured to the computer workstation in the exam room. "Can you pull up access to hospital birth records during that time frame?"

"I should be able to," she said. It took a few moments, but she was able to gain access to the records system without much trouble. "It looks like there were nine total births during that period, four of which were female babies."

Annabel slipped inside the room while Darcy searched. "Good thing you put the note in a plastic bag," she commented, pushing wet tendrils of hair off her forehead. "It's really coming down out there."

"Washing away any traces of the person who left this baby on my porch," Ridge commented sourly.

"Can you print off the list of parents?" Sam asked, ignoring his siblings.

Darcy slid him a glance. "I really shouldn't,"

she hedged. "It's a massive patient privacy violation. I could lose my license."

Sam fixed her with a look. "Do you understand what we're trying to do here? This baby's mother is likely the target of a killer. I need that information."

"It might not even help," Darcy hedged. "There's no guarantee this baby was born here. She may have been born at a neighboring hospital, or possibly even at home."

"Maybe," Sam replied. "But I have to start somewhere."

Darcy shook her head. "I'm sorry. I wish I could help, but if I do this and I'm caught it'll wreck my career."

"You're wasting my time here." Sam kept his voice down, but she heard the impatience in his words. He seemed like a man who was used to getting what he wanted and didn't tolerate anything or anyone getting in his way. Darcy appreciated his determination, but she wasn't about to be bullied into doing something she knew to be questionable. She was torn, though—what if her refusal to help cost this woman her life? Could she live with herself knowing a woman had died because she was more concerned about her job than doing the right thing?

"Sam." Ridge's calm tone cut through the growing tension in the room. "You know she's right.

Don't ask her to compromise her professional ethics. How long can it take to get a warrant from a judge?"

"Too long," Sam shot back. He scowled at them both, then shook his head. "But fine, we'll play it your way."

Darcy shot Ridge a grateful glance, but he didn't acknowledge it. "Tell you what," she said, pushing back from the desk. "I need to go find that bassinet for the baby. It'll probably take me a moment to track it down." She deliberately tilted the monitor around so it faced Sam. Recognizing the gesture as the olive branch it was, Sam offered her a tight smile.

"We'll keep Ridge company until you get back."

Darcy slipped out the door, her palms sweating. She'd never done anything like this before. Even though she knew giving Sam access to patient information was the right thing to do in this particular case, it still made her nervous.

"He's a police officer, not some random stranger off the street," she muttered. Besides, she knew a judge would grant him access to the records. She was just cutting through the red tape, she told herself, and hopefully shortening the time it would take to track down the baby's mother. *It's the right thing to do.* And it was. But Darcy had always been one to follow the rules and this departure from the norm made her feel jittery.

"Everything okay in there?" asked George, the other doctor on shift tonight. "I heard there was quite the ruckus earlier."

Darcy tried to smile but it must have come across as more of a grimace, as George frowned slightly at her expression. *Get it together*, she chided herself. *Stop acting strange!* "We're doing okay," she told him. "Someone found an abandoned baby earlier tonight, so we have the police in there now."

"Oh, man." George shook his head. "Is the kid okay?"

"Yeah. We got lucky. I'm trying to track down a bassinet for her now."

"I think I saw one floating around here earlier." He tapped the desk as if he was trying to remember, then he snapped his fingers. "Yep. Give me just a second." He trotted off and returned a moment later pushing a Plexiglas crib. "Here you go."

"Thank you," she said. This time, her smile was genuine.

"No problem. Want me to call CPS for you?"

"Ah, no. I'll let the police handle that."

George nodded. "Let me know if you need any help."

She waved at him and headed back to the exam room, trying to pace herself so as to give Sam the time he needed to look at the patient records. Had she been gone long enough? Hopefully so—she didn't want to have to do this again.

When she opened the door, three faces turned to greet her. Sam was standing next to Ridge, looking down at the baby. The computer monitor had been returned to its original position, and Sam offered her a nod of thanks. Annabel stood in the corner, her phone pressed to her ear. She offered an absent wave and moved to make room for the bassinet.

"How's she doing?" Darcy asked quietly.

"Seems to be fine," Ridge said, his voice low and soothing.

"Are you ready to put her in the crib?"

He glanced down at the baby, his expression softening. "I suppose so."

Ridge stood and moved back and forth for a moment, instinctively falling into the comforting sway deployed by anyone holding a baby. Then, moving slowly and carefully, he deposited the sleeping bundle onto the mattress. He straightened back up but remained standing by the crib, apparently absorbed by the sight of the infant stretching in her sleep.

Once again, Darcy was struck by Ridge's actions. To her knowledge, Ridge had never spent time around babies before. Yet here he was, stepping into the role of caregiver as if he'd been born to it. And for a stranger's baby, no less.

Annabel snapped her phone shut and walked

over to join her siblings by the bassinet. "We have a problem," she said shortly.

Ridge raised one eyebrow. "What's that?"

"CPS can't get here tonight—the storms have washed out several of the roads leading into Granite Gulch."

"Great," Sam groaned. "So what are the options for tonight?"

"She'll have to stay here," Darcy replied. "I can admit her and have her sent to the nursery."

"Will she be alone?" Ridge asked.

"Not really," Darcy said, touched by his apparent concern. "The nursery is staffed 24/7, so she won't be unattended. Just let me put in the order..." She logged back in to the system, but what she saw made her frown.

"What's wrong?" Ridge asked. "Is there a problem?"

"The nursery is full," she replied, peering at the screen as if she could change the information displayed there by staring at it long enough. "I don't believe it."

"How is that possible?" Sam said.

Darcy shook her head. "We're short-staffed, which means we can only take on so many babies in the nursery. They've already got the maximum allowed number there now."

"So what are our options for tonight?" Annabel said.

Ridge stared down at the baby, his expression calculating. "I'll take her."

"What?" The word erupted from Darcy, Sam and Annabel at the same time.

"You can't be serious," Sam said.

"You don't know the first thing about babies," Annabel protested.

Ridge looked from one sibling to the other, a smile playing at the corners of his mouth. "Like you said earlier Sam, how hard can it be?"

Both Sam and Annabel turned to face Darcy, their expressions pleading with her to make their brother see reason. "Can you explain this to him?" Sam said.

"Uh, well," she began, feeling suddenly pressured. "Babies are pretty demanding," she started. "They need to be fed every couple of hours, which means you won't get much sleep."

"Sleep is overrated," Ridge replied.

"You don't have any supplies," Annabel put in. "Formula, diapers, a place for her to sleep. You have none of the things babies need."

"Be reasonable," Sam added. "You're way out of your depth here."

"I can't leave her," Ridge said simply. The words took all the air out of his siblings and they both leaned back on their heels, staring at Ridge as if they'd never seen him before.

"I know it doesn't make much sense," Ridge

went on. "But this baby is my responsibility now. I'm going to take care of her until we find her mother."

Annabel turned to Sam. "Is this even legal?"

He pressed his lips together, considering. "I'm not sure. But given the circumstances, I don't know that we have another choice."

"So it's decided then," Ridge said, sounding determined. "I'll take her home with me tonight. We can regroup in the morning."

Sam and Annabel exchanged a glance, and Annabel shrugged slightly as if to say "There's nothing we can do."

"If you're sure," Sam said slowly.

"I am." Ridge's voice was firm, making it clear he would brook no further arguments.

"All right," Sam said. He turned to Annabel. "I suppose we should get back to the station and get that note to forensics. We've got some work to do tonight."

"Yeah. I think we should bring in Chris, as well—he can start looking for home births."

Sam nodded. "I want Trevor involved, too. He has access to all the evidence the FBI has on our killer. He can go through the letters and hopefully find some clue that will help us identify the mother."

Annabel walked over and gave Ridge a quick

hug. “Good luck tonight,” she said, standing on her toes to press a kiss to his cheek.

“Thanks,” he said softly.

Sam clapped his brother on the back. “Call if you need anything,” he said. “We’ll be at the station.”

“Sounds good,” Ridge replied. “Thanks for your help.”

“Anytime, brother.”

Ridge waited until his siblings had left the room before turning to Darcy. “Well, I guess we should head home.”

“Are you sure about this?”

Ridge’s expression didn’t change, but a coolness entered his eyes and she kicked herself for asking the question. “It’s not that I doubt your capabilities,” she said, trying to smooth things over. “But a baby is a big deal.”

“I’m well aware of that,” he said. “And yes, I’m sure I can handle it.”

Darcy held his gaze for a moment, recognizing the glint of determination she saw in his dark brown eyes. Ridge had the strongest will she’d ever known, and if he’d made up his mind to do something, he would follow through regardless of the consequences.

Knowing she’d lost this battle, Darcy decided to do what she could to help. “At least let me send you home with some supplies.”

Ridge nodded, and she spent the next few moments gathering up all the spare diapers and formula bottles she could find. She returned to the room with her arms full of packages to find Ridge had already moved the baby from the crib to the car seat.

"It's not a lot," she said, setting everything on the exam bed. "But it should last a couple of days at least."

"Thank you," Ridge said. "I appreciate your help."

"You're welcome," Darcy replied. Now that the moment was here, she was strangely reluctant to part from Ridge. Being around him again was unsettling, but a small part of her felt comforted by his presence. *Don't be silly*, she told herself. *You're just tired.*

"Do you need help getting out to your truck?"

Ridge shook his head and she fought off a swell of disappointment. "I've got it," he said, scooping everything up. "Come on, Penny," he said.

The dog got to her feet and stretched then looked up at Ridge expectantly, awaiting his next direction.

Ridge turned to face Darcy. "Thanks again," he said. He took a step toward the door, then stopped and looked back. "It was nice to see you again, Darcy. You take care of yourself."

"You, too," she replied softly. She watched

Ridge walk away, marveling at the way he seemed to take all the oxygen in the room with him. His absence made her feel both relieved and sad in equal parts. "It's for the best," she said to the empty room. "I'm leaving soon, and I don't need a complication like Ridge taking up what little time I have here."

It was the truth, but it didn't help. Even though their relationship had ended years ago, she still felt as if there was unfinished business between them.

Darcy shook her head and pushed a strand of hair behind her ear. Seeing Ridge had been a shock, but she couldn't dwell on the past forever.

Time to get back to work.

"I don't understand what your problem is. The return policy is printed right there on the receipt—thirty days from the time of purchase. I bought this just last week." Francine Gibbons arched a brow at the clerk and stared at her, daring her to argue the point.

"Yes, ma'am, I understand that. But the dress has what looks like a wine stain on the skirt. I'm afraid I can't accept a return of damaged merchandise." The clerk sounded apologetic, but Francine was not appeased. Did she really not know who she was talking to?

"I'm not going to argue with you about this. I want to speak to your manager." It wasn't her fault the dress was ruined—Ted always got a little handsy after a few drinks, and in his eagerness he'd managed to knock over her glass of red wine. The tablecloth at the restaurant had taken most of the damage, but enough of it had gotten on her dress that she wouldn't be able to wear it again. Best to return it and get something new.

"Ma'am, it's store policy," the clerk began, but Francine cut her off.

"I thought I made myself clear. I told you I want to speak to your manager. Why are you still standing here?"

"Is there something I can help you with, Ms. Gibbons?" An older woman glided over, a smile pasted on her face.

Francine shot a triumphant glance at the clerk, who shrank back, looking miserable. "Yes. As I was saying, I want to return this dress. But your employee has been giving me attitude about it."

"I'm sorry to hear that," the woman replied smoothly. "Let me take care of it for you." She shot a warning glance at the clerk who had opened her mouth, presumably to defend herself.

"It's just so hard to get good help these days," Francine remarked, checking her phone for messages while the manager completed the transaction. Then, just for spite she added, "Did you see the new boutique that opened just off Main Street?

They have such lovely clothes, and their service is impeccable."

The manager pressed her lips together in a thin smile. "I haven't had a chance to visit yet."

"You really should," Francine said. "It's just the kind of store we need in Granite Gulch."

"How nice," the other woman murmured. She slid a receipt across the counter, along with a pen. "If you'll just sign there, please. I've credited the dress back to your account."

"Thank you," Francine said archly. She scribbled her signature and pushed the paper back at the other woman.

"My pleasure. May I help you with anything else tonight?"

"No, that will be all." She stuffed her phone back into her purse and tossed her hair over her shoulder.

"Thank you for stopping by. We look forward to seeing you again."

"Hmm. I might be willing to give you one more chance. But you should really educate your employees, especially when it comes to how store policy applies to a repeat customer like myself." She shot a final glare at the clerk before turning and striding out of the store.

The nerve of those people! How dare they try to treat her like one of the masses, rather than the premier customer she was. She'd spent thousands of dollars at that store over the past few months. The least they could do was act as though they wanted her business.

Lightning streaked across the sky as she walked under the awnings that lined the storefronts. She frowned, trying to dodge the worst of the puddles so her suede Louboutins didn't get too wet. She had meant to get home before the storm broke, but people were so incompetent these days and she'd been held up at every store she'd visited. It was almost enough to make her want to hire a personal shopper, but she didn't trust anyone else to get things right.

"I should make them replace my shoes," she muttered, still angry with the clerk for having tried to deny her return. "It's the least they can do to make it up to me."

She reached the end of the awning and paused to fish her umbrella out of her purse. The streetlamps that illuminated the parking lot were burned out, leaving the stretch of asphalt cloaked in darkness. "This place is really going downhill," she grumbled, struggling to open her umbrella. "They can't even be bothered to maintain the parking lot." She would have to mention it to Jill Winthrop during their lunch next week—her husband was on the city council, and they needed to know this area of town required improvement.

She stepped out into the rain and headed in the

direction of her car, peering into the gloom and wishing for a flashlight. A quick press of the unlock button on her key fob caused the lights of her Mercedes to flash, helping guide her through the darkness. The crunch of footsteps on gravel sounded behind her, but Francine was too focused on getting to her car to pay attention.

"Hey."

She ignored the speaker and kept moving forward, intent on getting out of the rain.

"Hey!"

Francine ground her teeth together and rolled her eyes. She did not respond to such casual greetings, especially from a stranger.

"Francine!"

That was odd. She stopped and turned, trying to see who had called out to her.

A dark figure approached, the person's body obscured by a large trench coat and a wide-brimmed hat. "Who are—" Before she could get the rest of the question out, the stranger lifted an arm and a loud *pop* split the air.

Something slammed into Francine's chest, knocking her off her feet and onto her back. She lay there for a moment, stunned, trying to figure out what had happened. Then the pain hit, a white-hot agony radiating from her chest down through her limbs. "What?" she gasped.

The figure walked up and leaned over her, temporarily blocking out the rain. Francine blinked, trying to recognize the stranger. “Why?” she said, struggling to get the word out through lips that had gone numb.

The killer smiled cruelly. “Why not?”

Francine’s vision began to narrow, but she saw the stranger’s arm come up again. There was another earsplitting *pop*, and she surrendered to the darkness.

Chapter 4

Ridge paced in front of the bank of windows that overlooked the woods at the back of his cabin, patting the baby's back with a steady thump.

"It's really coming down out there," he observed quietly to no one in particular. As if to punctuate his observation a flash of lightning split the sky, the brightness illuminating the ground and revealing the raging river his backyard had become. "I hope the barn is still standing," he muttered.

Ridge enjoyed working with his hands, and had taken great pride in building his cabin from the ground up. But after he'd finished construction, he'd felt at loose ends. He was so used to having a job to complete that he'd decided to start working on a barn he could use as part garage, part hobby shed. The project was coming along nicely, but his progress had slowed recently as the hunt for the Alphabet Killer had picked up speed.

He glanced down into the face of the infant he held. "Are you the key to finding the killer?"

She yawned and his jaw ached to mimic her gesture. The day was really catching up to him, and he wanted nothing more than to lay the baby down and sleep for a bit. But every time he tried, she woke up and started crying. The only thing he'd found that calmed her down was for him to pace back and forth, an action that simultaneously kept him awake and made him even more tired.

He glanced over to the dog bed on the floor by the fireplace. Penny had gone to sleep hours ago and she looked totally relaxed, sprawled on her back with her paws in the air. "Lucky girl," he muttered. If only the dog could help him watch the baby!

"We'll find your mother," he said softly. "I just wish she had left your name in the note. What am I supposed to call you?"

The baby in question shifted slightly and emitted a soft squeak, so he increased the frequency of his patting until she sank back into sleep.

"I think you look like a Sara," he said, feeling his heart tighten a little. Saralee had been his mother's name, and it seemed fitting that this lost little one be named after the woman who had been such an important part of his life.

Sara let out a soft sigh, and Ridge decided to try to lay her down again. Moving slowly, he walked over to the makeshift pallet he'd made out of several old quilts and gently set her down. Then he tucked a blanket over her and straightened up, trying to work the kinks out of his lower back. *Please don't wake up*, he pleaded silently, watching the baby as if she were a live bomb about to explode.

She frowned, the expression looking adorably out of place on an infant's face. Ridge held his breath, hoping against hope that this time Sara would remain asleep, now that she was in her bed.

It wasn't to be. The baby wriggled experimentally, as if she was testing the boundaries of her new location. Apparently finding it unsatisfactory, she opened her mouth and let out a wail that woke Penny, who emitted a startled yelp.

Resigned to his fate, Ridge leaned down and picked her up. Once he brought her to his chest she quieted down again, her wails subsiding into small whimpers until she finally fell silent. Penny flopped back down on her bed with a sigh, and Ridge resumed his walk.

Maybe Darcy was right, he thought. Maybe he really had taken on too much. He hated to admit the possibility, especially because he knew she didn't think he could handle this. But he'd be damned before he'd admit it to her face. No way was he going to show any kind of weakness in front of her. He'd made that mistake once. Never again.

A loud clap of thunder split the air, making both him and Sara jump. "That one was close," he said to her, pitching his voice low so as not to fully wake her.

On the heels of the thunder came another pounding, this one at his front door. Ridge frowned. He didn't get many visitors, and the people who did come to his cabin knew to enter through the back door. That meant whoever was out there was a stranger, and given the events of the day, he didn't fancy answering the door with a baby in his arms.

"Who do you think it could be?" he asked softly. The baby's mother, come to claim her child? Maybe she had gotten away from the killer and wanted her baby back. If so, she had a lot of explaining to do. Even though she hadn't been in his life for very long, Ridge had grown attached to little Sara and he wasn't about to just hand her over to the first person who came knocking.

There was another possibility, one that made him frown. What if his visitor wasn't Sara's mother, but the Alphabet Killer, come to tie up loose ends? It was a bold move, but his cabin was on the edge of the woods in a fairly isolated location. And with the weather being so bad it would be days before anyone wondered about him or would be able to check on him. The more he thought about it, the more he realized this was the perfect opportunity for the killer to strike.

He set Sara back down on her bed and tucked a blanket around her, hoping to stave off her cries for at least a few minutes. Then he grabbed the baseball bat propped up in the corner and headed for the door. Maybe he was just being paranoid, but he wasn't going to answer the door unprepared.

The pounding started up again with renewed vigor, as if his visitor was getting impatient. He flipped on the porch light and stopped to peek through the curtains at his front window, trying to identify who might be visiting. Unfortunately, the rain was still coming down hard and it obscured his vision of the porch—he could make out a dark shape, but he couldn't tell if it was a man or a woman.

Only one way to find out. Taking a deep breath and tightening his grip on the bat, Ridge unlocked the door and opened it a crack.

"Ridge?"

"Darcy?" He couldn't keep the shock out of his voice. She was the last person he'd expected to see, especially on a night like this.

"What are you doing here?"

"Can I come in?" She shivered slightly and pushed a wet tendril of hair off her face.

"Oh, of course. Sorry." Ridge propped the bat next to the door frame and stepped back, gesturing Darcy inside. Sara chose that moment to let out a loud wail and Darcy smiled as she stepped across the threshold.

"How's it going here?"

Ridge winced. "She doesn't like it when I set her down." He quickly closed the door, then crossed the room and scooped Sara up again. Just as before, she stopped crying once she was back in his arms. He resumed pacing and eyed Darcy, who was looking around the den with open curiosity.

"This is a great place," she commented, slowly wandering from one side of the room to the other, taking in the pictures on the wall, the books on his shelves and the furniture arranged throughout. "I had no idea it was out here. How did you find it?"

"I built it," he said simply. It felt strange to have her in his home. This was his sanctuary, his safe place. He'd actually never brought a woman here before, and to have Darcy of all people checking out his things made him feel exposed.

"You built this?" She didn't bother to hide the incredulity in her voice. Then she shook her head and bit her lip. "I'm sorry—that's the second time I've implied that you're not capable of something."

He blinked, surprised by her apology. "Uh,

that's okay," he said. "Most people are shocked when they find out I built it."

"How long did it take you?" She seemed genuinely interested and he felt that old familiar tug to engage with her, to share with her.

"Six months," he replied. Darcy whistled softly, apparently impressed, and his cheeks warmed in the face of her approval.

"How did you find me?" Time to get this conversation back on track.

Darcy raised a brow. "You filled out paperwork at the hospital, remember?"

He nodded, kicking himself for having forgotten. "I didn't realize that was an invitation," he said coolly.

If Darcy noticed his tone, she didn't react. "I thought I would stop by and check on you and the baby."

"Because you don't think I can take care of her properly?" The words were out before he could stop them, and he heard the bitterness in his own voice. Too bad. He was tired of people scrutinizing his every move, searching for signs of the father in the son before them. All his life, he'd felt as if he was under a microscope, subject to the judgment of others. Even though he'd dedicated his adult life to helping others, people still gave him a wide berth. They treated him like some kind of half-feral dog, one they wanted to like but didn't fully trust not to attack when their backs were turned.

Darcy held his gaze for a moment, studying him. "No," she said thoughtfully. "Because I thought you might like some company. Taking care of an infant can be isolating."

Her reply took the wind out of his sails and the irritation drained out of him, leaving him feeling oddly empty. "Oh," he said dumbly. How had she known that? Did she have experience caring for a baby, or was it just a lucky guess? Against his better judgment, he found himself wanting to know more about what she'd been up to in the years since they'd parted ways.

She held up a plastic bag. "Also, I come bearing gifts." She set the bag on the coffee table and proceeded to pull out packages of diapers and wipes and several bottles of formula. "I was able to raid the nursery before I left tonight. I know I sent you home with some stuff, but I thought you could use some extra, just in case."

"Thank you," he said, feeling more foolish by the minute. Darcy was just trying to help, and he'd nearly bitten her head off for her troubles. He shook his head, trying to slough off his bad mood.

"I also brought a little something for you, as well," she continued, reaching back into the bag. With a flourish, she withdrew a long candy bar bearing a familiar white wrap and sporting bold orange letters. “Here you go,” she said, extending the treat toward him. “I got you the biggest one I could find.”

Ridge could only stare down at her and the gift she offered, shocked that she had remembered.

Darcy’s expectant expression melted off her face. “You used to love these. Do you not like them anymore?”

He shook his head, not trusting his voice. After all these years, she still remembered his favorite candy bar. It shouldn’t have surprised him—he still remembered her favorite foods and the way she was so particular about the amount of ice in her drinks. But he hadn’t expected the recall to be mutual. Especially not after so much time had passed.

“I’m sorry,” she said, sounding contrite. “I shouldn’t have assumed you would still like the same things after ten years.” She dropped the candy bar back into the bag and set it aside.

“No,” he said, the word coming out a little hoarse. He cleared his throat and spoke again. “No, I mean I do still love them. I’m just surprised you remembered, that’s all.”

“Oh.” Her cheeks went a little pink and she fumbled in the bag for the candy bar, passing it to him with a shy smile. “Here you go then.”

“Thank you.”

She turned away and busied herself with folding

the bag into a small square. "I figured you could use a little treat."

Ridge used his teeth to unwrap the gift, then took a large bite. The combination of sweet caramel and salty peanuts hit his tongue, and he nearly moaned in pleasure. In all the ruckus of the early evening he'd skipped dinner, a fact that his stomach did not appreciate. And while a candy bar was not the most nutritionally sound choice, he could think of no finer meal at the moment. "Man, that's good."

Darcy grinned. "Glad you're enjoying it. Would you like me to hold the baby so you can sit down?"

He started nodding before she could finish asking the question. "Yes, please." His earlier resolve to stand strong and do this on his own crumbled at the thought of being able to sit still for a moment and refuel. Although he thought of himself as an independent man, he wasn't stupid. He'd come to realize taking care of Sara was a marathon, not a sprint, and he'd be wise to take help when and where it was offered.

Darcy walked over to him, stopping when she was mere inches away. Moving carefully, Ridge transferred the little bundle into her arms, trying to ignore the little zings of sensation that arced through him every time they accidentally touched. He told himself to step back once she had a secure hold on Sara, but his feet wouldn't obey his brain's command. This was the closest they'd been to each other in years, and his body wanted to know if she would still feel the same against him.

Warmth radiated off her skin and he took a deep breath, trying to clear his head. It was a mistake. She smelled like the rain, and she'd brought the scent of the woods in with her. It was a comforting, familiar smell that made him want to get closer and he had to force himself to move away before he did something he'd regret.

Darcy looked up at him, her skin damp and shining in the light of the lamp. "She's a beautiful baby," she whispered with a smile.

"Yes, she is."

"And she's very lucky she found you."

His chest warmed at the compliment, and the sensation climbed up his neck and into his earlobes, making them burn. Ridge cleared his throat and took a step back. "I think it was actually the other way around," he said, needing to inject some levity into the moment. "Penny deserves all the credit."

They both turned to look at the dog, who had fallen back asleep and was snoring softly, her paws twitching as she dreamed. A swell of affection filled Ridge's heart, and not for the first time, he wondered what he would do without her.

"Why don't you sit down?" Darcy suggested. "I can walk with her for a while."

"Thanks," Ridge said. He sank into the couch with a sigh, surrendering to the comforting support of the overstuffed cushions. Darcy started humming softly as she walked, a sweet melody that made him want to close his eyes and sleep for the next month. Shaking off the fatigue, he took another bite of dinner and focused on chewing.

"I think it's finally easing up out there," she observed.

She was right. Now that he was paying attention, he noticed the rain did seem to be slowing down. *I should check the barn*, he thought, stuffing the rest of the candy bar into his mouth.

Darcy glanced up when he stood. "Do you mind holding her for a few more minutes? I'm building a barn out back and I want to make sure it's still standing after those storms."

"No problem," she said. "Take your time."

He grabbed a flashlight and paused in the doorway, taking in the sight of Darcy holding Sara close. She was the very picture of maternal comfort and the pair of them seemed to give off a golden glow in the lamplight, lending the scene a dreamlike quality. It would be so easy to stand there and watch them forever, but he couldn't let himself get trapped in this moment. Neither Darcy nor the baby were his, and he'd do well to remember it.

* * *

The rain was cold, and Ridge welcomed the splash of the fat drops against the skin of his face and neck. The shock of it helped to clear his head and refocus his mind. He'd come dangerously close to kissing Darcy, which was a mistake he couldn't afford to make. *We had our chance*, he reminded himself firmly. And things hadn't worked out between them. It was silly to think now would be any different.

He eyed the ground in front of him, trying to pick out the least treacherous path to the barn. His formerly green yard was now a lake of mud interspersed with large puddles of standing water, making the once familiar place look like an alien landscape. There was no help for it—he was just going to have to get dirty.

Resigned to his fate Ridge trudged forward, his boots squelching in the mud. They would be hell to clean, but he had to see if there was any damage that needed to be repaired. The barn was more than halfway complete, so he wasn't worried about the walls falling in. But it would be good to see how the roof had held up under the onslaught.

He ducked inside and passed the beam of the light along the walls, pleased to find there were no damp spots that would indicate a leak between the boards. Then he checked the floor. Not so lucky here. There were several small puddles, which meant he was going to have a lot of patching to do on that roof once the sun came back out.

He glanced around the space one final time, imagining it as a completed barn. The mower would go in the left corner, along with his other yard equipment. There was space for his tools in the far right corner. And then there was some room left over, space he now thought could be used for a bicycle or two. He closed his eyes, picturing it—two large bikes and one small one parked and ready to be used on those lazy summer nights when the fireflies rose up from the grass like living sparks.

The yearning for a family hit him hard, and he leaned against the doorjamb for a moment, his hand to his chest. Where had that come from? Was it being around the baby that made him think this way? Or perhaps seeing Darcy again? *Maybe both*, he admitted to himself. Truth be told, Darcy was the only woman he'd dreamed of having a family with, and after she had dumped him he had given up on the dream ever becoming a reality.

But maybe it was time he took a second look. Holding Sara had rekindled the desire to have his own children. Over the years he had forgotten just how much he wanted a family of his own, one where his children would grow up with both parents and wouldn't be subjected to the whims of the foster care system the way he and his siblings had. He pictured his youngest sister, Josie, and a fresh pang hit him as he recalled the last time he'd seen her, when she'd told him not to visit her again. She'd gone from a sweet girl to a distant, hardened young woman, all thanks to the system. He shook his head. Their lives would have been so much better if they had had someone—*anyone*—else as their father.

But life didn't work that way.

The patter of raindrops began to change, the cadence becoming faster and louder as the rain picked up again. Time to go back inside and check on the girls and get himself dried off. His wet boots were starting to feel tight, and he knew from experience it was only going to get worse if he didn't take them off soon. He cast one last look around the barn before closing things up, then put his head down and took off for the house, trying to dodge the worst of the puddles as he went.

He'd made it about halfway across the yard when a woman's scream pierced the air and froze his blood.

Chapter 5

"No!"

Darcy took a step back, her heart in her throat as she faced down the masked intruder who had forced his way into Ridge's home.

He lunged for her but she sidestepped, narrowly avoiding his grasp. He grunted in frustration and pressed forward, leaving her no choice but to back away.

"Give me the baby," he demanded. His hands were everywhere, grabbing and grasping for any kind of hold. Darcy kicked out but he dodged the blow and kept coming.

Penny barked and growled, darting in to snap

at the man and then pulling away again. She was doing a nice job distracting him, but it wasn't in the dog's nature to be vicious and she seemed reluctant to commit to a bite that might actually hurt him. The intruder seemed to sense her hesitation and lashed out, landing a solid punch to Penny's shoulder. She yelped and skittered away but then darted back in to snap at his hands, trying her best to protect her master's home.

Darcy took advantage of Penny's antics to move farther away from the threat. The man was blocking her access to the door, so she darted to the other side of the room and set the baby on the recliner, freeing up her hands so she could better defend herself and the baby. Then she turned back to face the man, her eyes scanning the room for something, anything she could use as a weapon.

A baseball bat was propped up next to the front door, mocking her. It was too far away to be of any use, but maybe there was something else? She took a step forward, intending to draw the intruder away from the baby. Her foot landed on something hard, and she glanced down to find a large rawhide bone lying next to Penny's bed. Darcy scooped it up and held it high, ready to strike. It wasn't much, but it was solid and the edges had been gnawed down to a fine blade that she might be able to use as a type of knife. He'd have to get close for her to use it, but it was better than nothing.

Penny was trying her best to keep the man occupied, but he had made his way over to the other side of the room, closer to the baby. Darcy had to get him away from the little one, but how? A frontal attack wouldn't work—he was too big for her to stand a chance. She would have to come in from the side and gain the upper hand by attacking from his blind spot. But that meant leaving the baby undefended.

Where is Ridge? She screamed out again, hoping he would hear her this time. She couldn't hold him off forever, and unless Ridge got here soon, the intruder was going to overpower her and take the baby.

It was now or never. Moving as stealthily as she could Darcy crept up alongside the intruder, trying to stay out of his line of sight as she approached. One step, two, and then she was there, within striking distance.

She lifted her makeshift weapon above her head and started to swing, but before she could make contact, the man turned. She saw the glint of satisfaction in his eyes and realized her mistake—he'd known what she was doing all along!

He kicked out, his foot smashing into her left shin bone. Pain exploded at the site, a viscous, black thing composed of tendrils of agony that wrapped around her leg and threatened to take over her whole consciousness. She sucked in a deep breath and pushed back against the darkness. If she fell down, it was all over.

She swung wildly with the dog bone but missed him. To make matters worse, the gesture put her off balance and she listed dangerously to the side. Gravity took hold and she felt herself going down. Desperate to stay on her feet, she scrabbled for some kind of support. Her hand made contact with the back of a chair and she pulled herself up, but her leg wasn't going to hold her weight much longer.

Sensing his advantage, the intruder pushed in close and shoved her down. She hit the floor hard and tried to scramble back to put distance between them, but her body hit the chair and she had nowhere to go.

The man towered over her and raised his arm. Darcy barely had time to flinch before his hand made contact with the side of her head, setting off a cascade of fireworks behind her eyes. She blinked to clear her vision, just in time to see him lift his arm again.

Her muscles tensed, bracing for the blow. But it never came. There was a meaty thud, and she opened her eyes to find Ridge had tackled the intruder. The two men rolled on the floor and crashed into a table, tipping it over and sending picture frames and other knickknacks flying across the floor. They were evenly matched opponents—Ridge was taller, but the other man appeared to be heavier. Darcy didn't wait to see who was going to win the wrestling match. She pulled herself to her feet and limped over to the door, then grabbed the baseball bat. Using it as a cane, she hobbled back to the men and waited for her chance.

It didn't take long. Ridge let out a muffled shout and flipped the intruder over, then pressed his knee into the other man's back, effectively trapping him. Penny stood by her master's side, a low, throaty growl rumbling out of her chest as she stared down at the man who had invaded her home.

"Darcy," Ridge said, his voice strained.

"Yes?"

"Please hold the baby."

She blinked, trying to process his request. Then she heard the crying and realized the little one was screaming her head off, and likely had been for a while. Moving as fast as she could, she made her way over to the chair and picked up the red-faced bundle, crooning softly to her as she pressed the baby to her chest.

The baby stopped crying almost immediately, and the relative quiet made the room feel so much bigger.

"Do you want the bat?" she asked, her eyes never leaving the man on the floor.

"That won't be necessary," Ridge replied. He

took a firm grip on the man. “Now, let’s see who you are.”

Thc man put up no resistance as Ridge rolled him over onto his back. But just as Ridge reached for the ski mask that covered his face, the intruder let out a window-rattling yell and swung his arm up. Too late, Darcy noticed the ceramic bowl in his hand.

“Watch out!” she screamed, trying to warn Ridge.

She watched in horror as events seemed to unfold in slow motion. Ridge turned back to look at the man, his eyes widening as he registered what was happening. He tried to ward off the blow, but the intruder had the element of surprise on his side. The bowl slammed into the side of Ridge’s head with a sickening crack, and Ridge’s body went limp. He toppled off the other man and hit the floor, his features twisting in pain.

The intruder got to his feet and eyed Darcy. She glared at him and lifted the bat in one hand, ready to do battle. He stared at her for a moment, as if he was considering the pros and cons of attacking her again. He leaned forward, but before he could commit to the act Ridge let out a moan and rolled onto his hands and knees.

Apparently deciding it wasn’t worth it, the man shook his head and headed for the door. Darcy maintained her grip on the bat until he was well and truly gone. Then, her heart pounding in her throat, she crossed the room and locked the door behind him. It was a little thing, but flipping the deadbolt gave her a small measure of comfort.

"Ridge." She turned back to him and limped over to the couch, sinking down with a grimace. "Talk to me, Ridge." The blow to his head had sounded painful, and she needed to know if he was injured.

He let out a groan that was part pain, part frustration. "I'm here. How's the baby?"

"She's fine." Darcy couldn't help but smile at his concern for the little one. Whether he realized it or not, Ridge was already starting to act like a father.

He slowly climbed to his feet, his hand pressed to the side of his head. "Come sit by me," she said. "I need to look at your head."

"It's fine," he mumbled, rubbing the affected area gingerly.

"Humor me," she replied.

He plopped down next to her with a sigh. "I should go after that guy," he said.

"No," she replied, her heart tightening at the thought of a groggy Ridge chasing a masked man through the dark woods. "It's not worth it. Call your brother and let the police handle it."

"I will."

She passed him the baby while he dialed, then

turned his head to the side so she could get a better view of his head.

An angry red welt marked the spot where the bowl had hit him. She probed the area with her fingertips, causing him to wince and suck in a hissing breath. "Sorry," she said softly.

"It's okay," he mumbled, wrapping up his conversation with Sam.

"The good news is, nothing seems broken." She moved him through a basic neurological exam to confirm he was indeed fine, then leaned back against the sofa cushion. "Take some ibuprofen and put an ice pack on it. It'll be sore for a few days, but you're basically okay."

"How are you?"

The question made her aware of her body again, and her shin let out a fresh protest as she shifted positions. "I'm okay," she said, trying to keep the pain out of her voice.

Ridge narrowed his eyes as he watched her move. "I don't think so," he said. He placed his fingers on her chin and gently tilted her head, frowning at what he saw.

"He hit you." It wasn't a question.

"It's nothing," she assured him.

"It is to me." His voice was low and lethal, promising retribution for her pain. She shivered at the implied threat. Ridge was normally so calm and even-tempered, and seeing him this way made her realize he was a physically powerful man who could be dangerous if he wanted.

"Where else are you hurt?"

Darcy considered lying for a split second, but dismissed the thought. He would find out soon enough. "My leg," she admitted. "He kicked me pretty good."

Ridge made a low sound in the back of his throat and pressed his lips together. "What can I do?"

"Nothing," she assured him. "Just stay put and I'll get us some ice packs."

Ridge opened his mouth as if to protest, but Darcy pushed herself off the couch before he could stop her. "I'll be right back."

It took her a few minutes to find what she needed in his kitchen, but she managed quickly enough. When she came back out into the den, Ridge was focused on Penny, gently stroking her side and talking to her in a low voice. The dog lifted her head and placed it in his lap, then leaned her body against his legs with a sigh of contentment.

Ridge continued to pet her, and Penny cocked one ear to listen to his words. She heard only snatches of the conversation, but Ridge was clearly praising the dog for her good work. It was well deserved. The dog had been a lifesaver—the only reason the baby was still with them was because

Penny had kept the intruder occupied until Ridge had arrived. If it were up to her, Darcy would buy the dog a whole truckload of chew toys as a reward.

She hung back, watching the pair of them. It was a sweet moment, one she didn't want to interrupt. But her lower leg was beginning to protest and she wanted to get the makeshift ice pack on Ridge's head to keep the swelling down.

"Is she all right?" Darcy nodded at Penny as she handed Ridge the package of frozen corn wrapped in a towel. "She took a hit to the shoulder when she was protecting us."

"Which one?" Ridge asked, casting a concerned glance down.

"Her left side."

Without another word, Ridge took the package from his head and pressed it to Penny's shoulder. Darcy didn't bother to protest, knowing no matter what she said he would put the welfare of his dog above his own.

"I'm sorry." The words were said so softly that at first, Darcy wasn't sure she'd really heard them. But then Ridge turned to look at her, his dark eyes troubled. "I'm sorry it took me so long to get back."

She shook her head. "You couldn't have known."

"I know he was wearing a mask, but did it slip at any point so you could see his face?"

"No. And I didn't recognize his voice, either." But that was no surprise. Darcy hadn't been back in town very long, and the number of people she could identify by voice alone was in the single digits. "You might know him, though," she added, almost as an afterthought.

"Why do you say that?"

"He didn't speak after you came on the scene. He only talked when it was just the two of us."

Ridge lifted one eyebrow, considering. "Did he say anything that could help identify him?" When she shook her head, he frowned. "But who would want to take the baby? More importantly, who knows she's here with me? The only people I told are you, Sam and Annabel. Unless you think it's someone from the hospital?" He let the question trail off suggestively, but Darcy shook her head.

"No. I would recognize someone from the hospital. And I can't imagine anyone working there has a motive to kidnap an abandoned infant."

"I agree," he said. "Which means whoever that guy was, he must somehow be connected to the mother. Or the serial killer," he added, almost as an afterthought.

A chill skittered down Darcy's spine, and goose bumps broke out on her arms. "If the Alphabet Killer really is after this baby, then you can't stay here. You need to take the baby and go someplace safe. Can you stay with one of your siblings? Or maybe a hotel?"

"Maybe," Ridge said thoughtfully. "And the same goes for you—now that he's seen you, he'll know you're connected to us. We need to get you away from here, the sooner the better." He passed the baby to her and stood, then began to gather up the supplies she'd brought earlier.

It took him only a few minutes to pack up the essentials. "Do you have someplace safe to go?" he asked.

"I'm staying with my parents. I should be fine there—they have a pretty extensive alarm system."

Ridge frowned slightly but didn't argue with her. "Sounds good. Make sure you call the police if you notice anything suspicious."

"Where are you going?" She handed the baby back to him, and he buckled the infant into her car seat.

"I think we'll find a motel for the night," he said, straightening up. "If that man decides to follow us, I don't want to put any of my siblings in danger."

"But what about you?" Didn't he understand that going off on his own left him unprotected? "You're injured—you won't be able to fight him off on your own if he does come back."

"Thanks for the vote of confidence," Ridge replied drily.

"This is no time to let your ego get in the way of a good decision," Darcy said.

Ridge shot her a wry half smile. "Don't worry. I'll think of something. Now, let's get you on your way."

He made a gesture with his hand and Penny hopped up, ever alert to her master's signals. "Let's go, ladies."

Darcy had no choice but to follow Ridge over to the door, but she was reluctant to part ways with him. Taking care of a baby was hard enough. Factor in a blow to the head and a crazy intruder and the task became almost impossible. Still, they couldn't stay at his cabin—there was no telling when the man would strike again.

Ridge opened the door just as a flash of lightning lit the sky. He stopped dead in his tracks, then let out a string of curses that turned the air blue.

"What is it?" She strained to see around him, but his broad shoulders completely filled her field of view. "What's wrong?"

"The road is washed out."

Darcy's heart sank and she pushed ahead of him, needing to see for herself. She stared dumbly at the river of mud that filled Ridge's yard, hardly daring to believe it. "We're trapped here."

She felt the breath of his sigh hit the back of her neck. "Looks that way."

"But that means—" She turned to face him, her heart starting to pound in her chest.

Ridge nodded, his expression grim. "The intruder is still around, too."

Ridge handed Darcy a steaming mug of tea and sank down next to her on the couch. "You doing okay?"

She didn't respond right away, and for a second, Ridge wondered if she'd heard him. Then she nodded, the movement a little jerky. "Yeah. I'm just… processing."

"It's been a hell of a night." He glanced over at Sara, who was now sleeping soundly. As far as he was concerned, Darcy was a miracle worker. She had fed the little one and then wrapped her up tight in a blanket—swaddling, she'd called it—and now the baby slept peacefully in the makeshift crib he'd assembled earlier.

"You should try to sleep," he said, noting the lines of fatigue around Darcy's eyes and lips. "I have a guest bedroom where you'll be comfortable."

She made a sound that might have been a laugh. "There's no way I can sleep after what happened tonight."

"He's not coming back," Ridge said, injecting a confidence he didn't feel into his voice. He had called Sam again after refortifying his cabin, but due to the weather the police couldn't get close enough to his cabin to respond. All he could do was stay on guard and hope the intruder had been swept away by the storm's floodwater.

But he didn't want Darcy to know his suspicions. Better for her to think the threat was gone so she could get some rest. In all likelihood, the man wasn't coming back—he'd already failed once, and now that they knew he was out there, they were ready for him to try again. Besides, with the weather being so bad, even if he was able to take little Sara, where could he go? No, he was probably off licking his wounds and planning another attempt.

Darcy took a sip of tea and made a face. "Too strong?" he asked. "I can water it down some if you like."

"No, it's fine," she said. She leaned forward to set the cup on the coffee table and he noticed her hand was shaking. "I'm just not as thirsty as I thought."

Ridge put a hand on her leg and felt the fine tremors running through her muscles. "Hey," he said softly. "You're safe now. I won't let him hurt you or the baby."

She nodded, blinking hard. "I know that. I just can't stop reliving the moment when he came in." She looked up at him, her eyes wide. "He just opened the door and walked in like he owned the place. I couldn't believe it."

"That's my fault," Ridge said. "I forgot to lock the door after I let you inside."

"Yeah, well. It's not like you were expecting him," Darcy replied. "I just hope he doesn't come back." She shivered, and Ridge put his arm around her shoulders and drew her in, tucking her next to his side. She snuggled close and laid her head on his shoulder with a sigh.

His heart tightened as he breathed in Darcy's familiar smell. He couldn't believe that after ten years, she still smelled the same—a potent combination of coconut shampoo and a soft, underlying sweetness that was all Darcy. How many times had he held her like this, while they snuggled together on the couch or went out to a movie? He couldn't put a number to it, and even though it had been so long, his body remembered exactly where to put his hand and how to angle his shoulder so she fit perfectly against him.

"It took years off my life, seeing him looming over you like that," Ridge confessed, his hand automatically running up and down her arm in the casual caress he'd so often enjoyed when they had been together. He clenched his jaw at the memory of Darcy, on the ground and defenseless, while that stranger prepared to hit her again.

In the past, Ridge had heard people talk about

"seeing red" when they got angry. It was something he'd never really understood, but in that moment, seeing Darcy at the mercy of another man, Ridge's vision had gone crimson and a burst of adrenaline had surged through his system. It was a heady, powerful sensation, and he'd felt as if he could have picked up the whole house and thrown it into the woods with no effort.

Instead, he'd settled for tackling the man in a move that would have made a linebacker proud. And while it had been satisfying to feel the give of the man's flesh beneath his fists, it would have been even better to interrogate him and get some answers. Why was he after Sara? What could he want with a helpless infant?

"If it makes you feel any better, I felt the same way when he hit you with the bowl," Darcy said, pulling him out of his thoughts. She reached up to touch the sore spot on the side of his head with gentle fingers. "I'm so glad you weren't seriously hurt."

"Sam's always telling me I have a hard head," he joked.

"Yeah, well. A few inches over and he would have taken out your eye." She shuddered and he gave her shoulder a squeeze.

"But he didn't," he said softly. "So stop thinking about it."

"I want to," she said. "But I just can't. It's playing on repeat in my head, like a bad dream I can't escape." The distress in her voice was plain, and Penny lifted her head and let out a soft, inquisitive whine.

"It's okay," he said, to both girls. Penny laid her head back down on her paws, and he felt Darcy smile against his arm.

"You keep saying that, but it doesn't make it so."

Ridge was quiet for a moment, trying to come up with something comforting to say, something that would ease her mind and distract her from her bad memories. But the magic words wouldn't come.

"I keep saying it because eventually, it will be true," he confessed. "It's the only thing I know to do."

She pulled back to look up at him, her dark brown eyes wide and luminous. "Fake it until you make it?"

He nodded soberly. "Something like that."

The corner of her mouth curved up. "That's not a bad philosophy. It's certainly worked for you so far."

Ridge got a queer feeling in his stomach, a sensation his grandma would have described as a goose walking over his grave. "What do you mean?"

Darcy laid her head back on his shoulder. "You've always been that way, Ridge. Pretending like things were okay even when they weren't. When we first started dating I thought you were just in denial, but after I got to know you better, I realized it's how you cope."

"Oh." He didn't know what else to say. Her comments made him feel naked and exposed, as if she'd stripped him bare and was judging him. Now that she pointed it out, Ridge realized he did always strive to act as though things were normal. It probably stemmed from his family situation—having a dad for a serial killer had marked him, just as if he'd been forced to wear a scarlet *A* on his chest. Growing up had been hell, first with the murder of his mother at the hands of his father and then being put in the foster system, torn away from his siblings. And forget about friends—the other kids had avoided him or taunted him, but no one had ever wanted to be friends with him. Looking back, he couldn't blame them. He was a freak by virtue of his dad, and what parent would want their child associating with the offspring of a madman? Still, it had been a lonely childhood and the only way Ridge had gotten through it relatively unscathed was to pretend as if everything was just as it should be. Even at a young age, Ridge had realized that to acknowledge the unfairness of it all was to surrender to a lifetime of anger and bitterness. Those emotions had ruled his father. He wasn't going to let history repeat itself.

"What's going on in that head of yours?" Darcy asked. "You got quiet on me."

"Sorry. Just…processing," he said, echoing her earlier words.

"There's a lot of that going around tonight."

"Probably because of the weather," Ridge said, trying to keep his tone light. "Rain tends to make people reflective, likely because they're stuck inside with nothing to do."

"Most people watch TV," she said, a teasing note to her voice. "But I notice you don't have one."

He shook his head, the stubble on his chin rasping against her hair. "Never did like it."

"I remember."

They were silent for a moment, the rain hitting the roof and Penny's light snores the only sounds in the cabin.

"Were you scared?" She spoke quietly, giving him the option to pretend he hadn't heard the question.

"I was, afterward," he admitted. "But in the moment, when I rushed in and saw what was going on, I was more angry than anything else. And that scared me."

Darcy leaned back to meet his eyes. "You are not your father," she said firmly, correctly guessing what was really on his mind.

The fact that she could still read him after all these years should have bothered him. But it felt nice to be with someone who seemed to truly get him, someone who understood what he was feeling and didn't make him explain everything.

"That's easy for you to say," he remarked, turning away from her knowing gaze. "But when I had that man pinned under me, I wanted so badly to hurt him. To make him pay for what he'd done, even though at the time I didn't know how badly he'd hurt you." He shook his head. "If that's not my father coming out, I don't know what is."

"Hey." When he didn't look at her, she said it again, this time more forcefully. She waited until he turned back. "I won't pretend to understand what makes your father tick. But I can tell you that your anger and aggression only emerges when you're defending yourself or others. That's normal and healthy. You can't beat yourself up for the way you feel when you're protecting what's yours." He opened his mouth to argue but she pressed on, cutting him off. "And the other reason I know you're not your father is because you didn't go too far. Matthew Colton would have killed that man without another thought. But you didn't. You had every excuse to do real harm, but you held back. That's because it's not in your nature to hurt others, Ridge." She reached up to cup the side of his face, her touch soft and warm against his skin. "You have a good heart. Don't ever doubt that."

Ridge blinked hard, touched by her words. Did

she really see him that way? It was difficult for him to accept she was telling the truth. Especially considering the way things had ended between them. She said he had a good heart, but she had also believed he'd stolen her father's watch. How did she reconcile her lack of trust in him then with her words now?

"I wish I could believe you," he said. He didn't want to dredge up the old argument, so he settled for leaning his head back against the couch cushion and staring up at the ceiling.

"Oh, Ridge," she sighed, sounding disappointed. She shifted against him, and before he realized what was happening, Darcy climbed into his lap and pressed her lips against his.

He sucked in a breath, the contact making his head spin. His body reacted instantly, rejoicing in the feel of her against him, the familiar weight of her in his arms. Her mouth was warm and inviting, and kissing her felt like coming home.

He reached up to thread his hands through her hair, the strands sliding across his skin like silk. She let out a little sigh and shifted closer, pressing against his chest and gripping his shoulders. There was a small sting as her fingernails bit into his flesh, but he didn't mind. The minor pain only highlighted the pleasure of having her back where she belonged.

The kiss started out slow and gentle but quickly

morphed into something hotter as his hands became reacquainted with the lines and planes of Darcy's body. He had the oddest sense of déjà vu as he skimmed his fingertips over her slender frame. It was the same as it had always been, yet different. Her curves had matured into those of a woman—just that little bit softer, more pronounced. He marveled at the changes, wanting to take the time to fully explore and savor them. He needed to get to know this new version of Darcy. Was the inside of her wrist still sensitive? Did that spot on the back of her neck still made her knees go weak? These were the questions he desperately needed to answer.

He moved one hand down to the waistband of her pants, then lifted the hem of her shirt and found her skin. It was like warm satin, impossibly smooth. Had she always felt this way, or had he just forgotten what it was like to touch her?

Her fingers moved down to the buttons of his shirt and she fumbled to work them loose. Goose bumps broke out across his skin when she pulled his shirt open, exposing his chest to the cool air of the cabin. Then she put her hands on him, touching him here, there, running the tip of her nail along his collarbone. She was everywhere at once, setting his nerve endings on fire.

And he was happy to burn.

A small voice in his head warned him that this

wasn't a good idea. They were moving too fast, heading down a dangerous path that would result in another broken heart. But his body didn't care. It had been so long since he'd felt a woman's touch. He had dated others after he and Darcy had split up, but no one had compared to her. No one made his blood race quite like she did. Part of him had wondered if things had really been that good between them or if he'd simply idealized their time together, so that every other relationship paled by comparison. But being with her now made him realize he hadn't exaggerated how good they were together. If anything, he'd forgotten the little details that made their connection so special. His memories had been like a black-and-white film, and he was now living in full color.

Ridge shifted and captured her bottom lip between his teeth, biting gently. She moaned into his mouth and he smiled. It sounded as if he wasn't the only one who had missed this connection. And even though he knew this physical spark wasn't going to result in anything between them, he decided to settle in and enjoy himself. He didn't have a lot of pleasure in his life right now. He wasn't about to turn down a gift like this, especially from Darcy.

As if she'd read his mind, Darcy leaned back and met his gaze. "I know this is sudden," she said, her lips swollen from his kiss. "But I've wanted to do that since you walked in to the ER."

Her words made his ego stand up and cheer, and a sense of smug satisfaction swelled in his chest. It was petty of him, but knowing she had missed him and still wanted him as much as he did her made him feel vindicated.

"I don't mind," he said, the words coming out in a rasp.

Her answering grin made his heart thump hard against his breastbone. "Glad to hear it."

She leaned back in but before she could make contact, a huge clap of thunder shook the house, rattling the windows and waking both Penny and the baby. The dog let out a startled "woof" and shook herself. Then, realizing she wasn't in any danger, she settled back down to sleep. The baby was not so easily soothed. She let out a shout of protest, and both Ridge and Darcy scrambled off the couch and over to her side.

Ridge got there first and gathered her into his arms. He tucked her up against his chest and started the gentle sway that had helped calm her before. It took a few minutes, but she gradually relaxed from a regular wail to the occasional whimper.

He glanced up to find Darcy watching them, an odd expression on her face. If he didn't know better he would have thought it was longing, but that wasn't right. Darcy had never been the type to ooh and ahh over babies, and the one time they had talked about having kids she had been lukewarm on the subject. Her passion had always been medicine. Even when they were younger, she had known she was meant to be a doctor, and she'd worked hard to achieve that goal. She wasn't the type of woman to have second thoughts about her choices.

He'd learned that lesson the hard way.

She noticed him looking at her and the expression vanished, morphing into one of embarrassed regret. It was clear she was rethinking her earlier enthusiasm, now that the moment had passed.

"Ridge—" she began.

"It's late," he said, knowing they wouldn't be picking up where they'd left off. Now that they'd both had a moment to think, it was clear some things were better left unexplored.

"You should get some sleep," he continued. "The guest bedroom is that way—" he indicated the direction with a nod "—and the bathroom is next to it. You should find everything you need inside—towels, soap, a spare toothbrush."

She glanced at the hallway, clearly tempted by the thought of sleep. "What about you? You shouldn't have to stay up all night by yourself."

"I won't," he assured her. "I'm going to give

her a bottle and get her settled again, and then I'll head to bed myself."

She nodded, apparently satisfied with his answer. "I'll take the next feeding?"

"Sure."

She took a few steps toward the guest bedroom, then stopped and turned. "Ridge, about what happened tonight—"

"Good night, Darcy," he said, effectively ending the conversation. He didn't need to hear her say it had been a mistake, that it didn't mean anything and it shouldn't happen again. Those were all things he already knew.

She sighed quietly, then nodded and walked away. Ridge waited until he heard the bedroom door close before letting out his own sigh. Maybe the universe was trying to tell him something. He and Darcy had already had their chance, and they weren't going to get a do-over. The sooner he accepted that, the better.

Sara stirred against him, burrowing her nose into his chest in search of something he didn't have. "Let's get you fed, little one," he said softly. "And then it's off to bed for the both of us."

Too bad he wouldn't be getting any sleep tonight.

Chapter 6

It was close to two in the morning before Darcy finally gave up trying to sleep. It had nothing to do with the unfamiliar bed, the sounds of the storm raging outside or the fact that she was still wearing her scrub top. She'd slept under worse conditions before and as a doctor; she'd learned to take her rest when and where she could find it. No, tonight's insomnia was entirely due to the man down the hall, and her earlier reckless actions.

"What was I thinking?" she muttered, for perhaps the millionth time. Kissing Ridge had been an epic mistake. And to make matters worse, she had done so much more than kiss him. Even now, the thought of how she'd blatantly climbed into his lap and unbuttoned his shirt made her cringe in embarrassment. Talk about throwing herself at the man! "I can't believe I did that."

The problem was, she hadn't been thinking. If her brain had been in charge, she would have stayed on her side of the couch where she belonged. Instead, she'd let her emotions and her body take over.

Hearing him talk about his fears regarding his father had touched her heart, and being pressed up against his side had made her body perk up and take notice. Normally, her self-control would have kept things in check, but the earlier attack had left her feeling vulnerable and out of sorts. Was it any wonder she'd acted irrationally?

But she couldn't deny it had been a wonderful mistake.

She'd spent ten years with the memory of Ridge's kisses keeping her warm at night. And even though she'd dated a little here and there, none of the men she'd seen had come anywhere close to comparing to Ridge. It was unfair, really, the way he had ruined other men for her.

It's not that there was anything wrong with the guys she had dated. They'd been nice, smart, funny—all the qualities she looked for in a partner. But they hadn't been Ridge.

Even now, she still couldn't articulate what

it was about Ridge that made him so special. It wasn't his body. He had a nice one to be sure, and she had definitely enjoyed getting reacquainted with parts of it, but lots of men had broad shoulders, narrow hips and dark hair that was just a little too long. As for his personality, well, he'd always been quiet and reserved. Difficult to get to know. What had made her want to push past his defenses and get to the inner circle? If she could just figure it out, maybe she could find a way to resist the pull she felt whenever he was around.

She sighed and rolled over, punching the pillow back into a comfortable shape. It would be so nice to turn off her brain and pause the merry-go-round of her thoughts, even if only for a few minutes. But that wasn't likely to happen as long as Ridge was so close.

The faint cry of a baby drifted into the room, and she pushed up into a sitting position. It was her turn to feed the little one. She stepped into her scrub pants and headed down the hall, drawing up short at the doorway to the den.

Ridge stood by the back windows wearing nothing but a pair of pajama pants, holding the baby close. The lamp in the corner was on low, casting the room in a warm yellow glow that illuminated his face as he stared down at the baby, totally absorbed by the sight of her eating. His skin looked golden compared to the pale roundness of the infant's head, and the dark hair on his chest further emphasized the differences between the man and the baby he held.

Darcy knew she should offer to relieve him, but he was just so beautiful standing there that she couldn't bear to interrupt. Was this how he would look holding his own child?

A pang hit her as she realized she was looking at the embodiment of a path not taken. If she had made different choices, that could have been her baby Ridge held. Ridge's cabin could have been her home. They would have been celebrating their twelfth anniversary, rather than tiptoeing around each other in the middle of the night.

How different her life would have been!

As she stood there watching the two of them, the first tendrils of doubt began to creep in. Had she made the right decisions? She'd always loved medicine, and she couldn't imagine not being a doctor. But what had she sacrificed to achieve that goal? She loved her patients, but they weren't waiting for her when she came home at night. And while she'd never felt particularly lonely before, being around Ridge and the baby made her painfully aware that something was missing in her life.

But what could she do about it? Even though she still felt an intense connection to Ridge, she was leaving in a few weeks. Her job was waiting in New York and she couldn't walk away from that just because she was feeling a little sad about her single state. Besides, if Ridge's earlier words were any indication, he thought their kiss was a mistake, too. He'd practically pushed her out of the room to stop the conversation. Not that she blamed him. They hadn't parted on good terms all those years ago and he probably still harbored some resentment about it.

She frowned, thinking back to that moment. Ridge hadn't said a word after her father had tipped over his bag and the watch had come tumbling out. She had mistaken his silence for an admission of guilt, but what if that hadn't been the case? What if he'd been so shocked he hadn't known what to say? Her stomach sank as she examined the memory in a new light. Had she made a mistake all those years ago?

Her father's face flashed in her mind, his expression triumphant as Ridge had walked out without looking back. Her parents had never made a secret of their dislike of Ridge. What if her father had planted the watch in his bag and accused Ridge of stealing it so she would have no choice but to break up with him? Her heart hurt at the thought that her parents could be so duplicitous, but she had to admit it was a possibility.

Should she try to find out the truth? Her relationship with her parents was already strained. If she accused them of framing Ridge to get her to dump him it would not improve the situation. Besides, what good could come of it after so many years?

But how could she not ask? If they had lied, she owed it to Ridge and to herself to learn what had really happened. Her stomach twisted at the thought that she had been manipulated into leaving the one she loved simply to satisfy the selfish whims of her parents. And as tempting as it was to bury her suspicions and move on, she had to know for sure.

A soft susurrus broke the stillness of the room, and she realized with a small jolt that Ridge was talking to the baby. Darcy took a step back, suddenly feeling like an intruder. His voice was too low for her to make out what he was saying, but it still felt wrong to stand there and eavesdrop. She took one last look, memorizing the image of his tall, powerful frame cradling that tiny body with impossible gentleness. Then she turned and tiptoed back to the guest room, leaving the two of them in the warm cocoon of the moment.

There was a light on in the house.

He checked his watch. Two thirty. Probably time to feed the baby again. He'd forgotten how often infants had to eat—it had been almost eighteen years since he'd had to deal with one, and he'd hated it the whole time. They were such high-maintenance creatures. But that could work in his favor. If Ridge and his lady friend were exhausted from taking care of the little parasite, they'd be more likely to drop their guard.

And that's when he would strike.

The woman was a complication he hadn't anticipated. Everyone knew Ridge Colton was single. He'd seen the way the women in this town fell over themselves trying to catch the man's eye. But he remained aloof to all their advances, as if he was too good to settle down with someone from Granite Gulch. It was ridiculous, the way a serial killer's son put on airs about being someone special. He shook his head, his hands curling into fists as he felt a renewed urge to punch Ridge Colton in the face. Why should someone like that get all the attention, while decent men like himself were left lonely? It just wasn't fair.

So who was this woman, and what was she doing there? His heart thumped hard as he considered another possibility. Maybe she wasn't a love interest at all, but someone from the state, come to take custody of the baby. Fear drove a cold spike into his chest at the thought of losing the kid. He couldn't let that happen—it would be a disaster. He'd be in big trouble if he couldn't deliver on his promises.

Whoever she was, the woman had been easy enough to handle. And he could take Ridge—almost had, actually. But two versus one stacked the deck against him. He could still come out on top, but it would be harder. He'd have to come up with a better plan. Shouldn't be too hard though, now that he knew what he was up against.

Plus, they were both injured. The thought brought a smile to his face. The woman wasn't much of a threat to begin with—he outweighed her by a good fifty pounds, not to mention he was taller by at least six inches. She'd be easy to overpower, especially now that he'd hurt her leg. Unfortunately, Ridge was another story. He was a big guy, and he moved with the skill of someone who knew how to handle himself in a fight. He had been harder to overcome, but he'd still gone down with a head injury for his troubles.

"I beat him once. I can do it again."

The only problem was that he no longer had the element of surprise in his favor. They knew he was out here, even if they didn't know exactly where. At least he had the weather on his side—the storm had effectively trapped Ridge and his visitor in the house, and since his drive was washed out, they weren't going anywhere soon. Even better, the police couldn't get to them, either. The man grinned, congratulating himself once again on having thought to park about a mile away, his car hidden just inside the tree line. It would be a pain hiking back with the baby in tow, but it could be done.

He propped his elbows on the window ledge and leaned forward, trying to make out the details of the house through the rain. There was a dark shadow moving back and forth in front of the window, but he couldn't tell if it was Ridge or the woman who held the baby. Although he was eager to grab the baby and run, he couldn't risk a second attempt right now. Better to wait until everyone was asleep and vulnerable.

In the meantime, he would do well to get a little rest himself. Once he got the baby, he was going to have to take off. He couldn't afford to let fatigue slow him down, not with so much at stake. He lifted his arms above his head, wincing as the gesture aggravated the sharp ache in his lower back where Ridge had pressed his knee. What he wouldn't give for a stiff drink right now.

He stood, eyeing the floor in search of a dry spot. The damn roof leaked, but the barn's position on Ridge's property made it the perfect place to bunk down and watch the house. And the best part of it was, Ridge didn't even know he was there.

"Night night," he said in a singsong voice. "Sleep well, little one. We'll be together again soon."

It was a promise he intended to keep.

Chapter 7

Someone was watching him.

Ridge jerked out of sleep with a start, feeling as if he'd just been pushed off a cliff. He clenched his fists and glanced around the room, half expecting to find the masked intruder crouching in a corner, ready to pounce. But no one was there. The breath left him in a rush and his muscles relaxed. False alarm.

A steady thump started up at the foot of his bed, and he looked down to find he wasn't alone after all. Penny was stretched out alongside his legs, her eyes glued to his face. When she saw that he was awake her tail started wagging even faster, hitting the mattress with a steady rhythm that would make a drum major proud.

"Good morning," he said, smiling at her hopeful expression. "I suppose you're hungry?"

She let out a soft "ruff" of confirmation and he reached down to pat her head. "I think we can do something about that."

He sat up and took a moment to rub his eyes. Between the baby, the storm and the threat of the intruder returning it had been a long night. His eyelids were heavy, and he wanted so badly to lie back down and surrender to the pull of sleep. But Penny needed her breakfast, and he needed to check on Darcy and the baby.

After a quick pit stop, he shambled down the hall with one thought on his mind: coffee. That's what he needed to feel human again.

He stepped into the den and drew up short at the sight of Darcy on the couch, feeding the baby. How long had she been there? A small stab of guilt pricked through the fog of his fatigue. He hadn't even heard the baby cry—thank goodness Darcy had been here to take care of her.

"Good morning," Darcy said with a smile. She always had been a morning person.

"Uh, hi," he replied, suddenly very aware of the fact that he wore only pajama bottoms. Normally he wouldn't be so shy, but after last night's kiss, he didn't want to send any mixed signals. "I'll be right back."

He returned a moment later fully clothed and feeling more awake. "How long have you two been awake?"

She lifted one shoulder in a shrug. "Maybe an hour? I heard her stir, so I decided to get her a bottle before she started crying. I wanted you to get some sleep."

"Thank you," he said, touched by the thought. He'd lost count of the number of times he'd paced back and forth in front of the window last night. He glanced at the spot now, half-surprised to find there wasn't a clear path on the floor marking his travels. "Is she doing okay?"

"Yeah. She's still eating."

His stomach rumbled, and Penny nudged his hand, reminding him that she was hungry, as well. "Can I get you something to eat? Maybe some coffee?"

"Coffee sounds great, thanks."

He nodded and headed into the kitchen. Ten minutes later, he returned carrying a tray laden with toast, fruit, yogurt and coffee.

Darcy's brows shot up. "Wow. That's quite a spread."

"Breakfast is the most important meal of the day," he said lightly.

"True. I just usually don't have enough time to eat it."

He watched her from the corners of his eyes as he poured the coffee. "I imagine you're very busy."

She tilted her head to the side, watching him arrange the toast and fruit on plates. "It's just all too easy to get caught up in work. I need to be better about taking time for myself to do the important stuff. Like eating and going to the bathroom."

Ridge smiled. "I've learned the work will still be there when you get back."

"I know," she said, using her free hand to snag a triangle of toast. "But it's hard to justify taking a break when my job deals with trying to help people. If I stop working during the day, they have to wait longer for treatment." She chewed for a moment, then spoke again. "It's hard not to feel guilty about it."

Ridge took a sip of his coffee and leaned back. "I get that," he said.

She met his eyes, her expression thoughtful. "You know, I think you might be one of the few people who do. I imagine when you're off on a search, you don't take a lot of time for yourself, either."

It was the truth and he didn't bother to deny it. When he and Penny were working, they were totally focused. Ridge did keep a close eye on his dog, though—it was important Penny not get too tired because she was the most useful part of the team. If she stopped functioning, the search slowed way down.

"Believe it or not, we have mandatory breaks during a search," he informed her.

"Really? I didn't know that."

He nodded. "It's vital Penny keep her energy up. If she gets exhausted, we can't work. So every few hours, we take a rest and do something else."

"Like what?" Darcy sounded genuinely curious, which ignited a small warmth inside his chest.

"Well, it depends. I'll make sure she's fed and that she's had a bathroom break. If she's tired, we'll go somewhere quiet so she can sleep. If she's not interested in napping, we'll go off to the side and play."

"Aren't you worried about losing time?"

Ridge swallowed a spoonful of yogurt. "Yes and no. Like I said, she works better when she's rested. If I were to push her, it could wind up taking even longer to find our target than if we had just stopped for a bit. Besides, there are usually several teams working an area to make sure we have adequate coverage. That means even when we take our break, someone is always searching." He took another bite, then added pointedly, "Just like the hospital has more than one doctor working at a time."

Darcy's cheeks turned a pretty shade of pink.

"Fair point. And normally, I'd agree with you. But the Granite Gulch Regional Medical Center has a real staffing shortage right now. It's why I'm here."

So that explained her presence back in Granite Gulch. It was one of the things Ridge had wondered about, but he hadn't had a chance to ask her yet. Darcy had always been ambitious and she'd made no secret of her desire to practice medicine in a big city. Ridge knew her father worked at the hospital, so he must have pulled some strings to get Darcy back in town.

"Do you like working there?" he asked, trying to keep the conversation away from her family. He heard about their activities through the town grapevine, but since they moved in different social circles he never saw them. It was one of life's small blessings.

"It's not bad. Different from what I'd expected." She popped a grape into her mouth. "I won't be here too much longer, though. I'm starting my job in New York in a few weeks."

"Ah." He wasn't surprised to find her time in Granite Gulch was temporary. Darcy had always been just a little too much for this small Texas town. She would fit in well in New York. He could picture her now, striding confidently down a crowded street, riding the subway with her nose in a book, going out for drinks with friends. It would be good for her to work there—hopefully, she could build a life for herself away from her controlling parents.

Still, the realization she was leaving so soon bothered him on a level he couldn't explain. After all, they weren't going to pick up where they'd left off relationship-wise. But he had hoped to have a little more time with her, to get to know this new Darcy if only for the sake of closure.

Ridge pushed his disappointment aside. "You must be excited," he said, offering a smile.

She nodded. "I am. A little scared, too."

"You'll do great," he said, offering the assurance automatically. He wasn't just saying it to be nice—once she decided to do something, Darcy always succeeded. She had intelligence to spare, worked hard and had enough perseverance to fill Texas Stadium. Once she got started, she was a force to be reckoned with and he had always enjoyed watching her go after her goals.

She gave him a sweet smile. "You were always my biggest cheerleader," she said, her tone a little wistful. "I don't think I ever thanked you for that."

Ridge felt his face grow warm. "No need for thanks," he said, deflecting her gratitude. "I just call it like I see it."

Little Sara finished the bottle and spit out the nipple, emitting a soft belch. Darcy smiled down at her. "Was that a good breakfast?" she asked the baby.

"Here, why don't I take her so you can finish eating?" Ridge gathered the baby and pressed her to his shoulder, then started patting her back to encourage her to burp again.

"Do you know what time the storm let up?" Darcy asked around a mouthful of food.

Ridge shook his head. "No clue. I know it was still going strong when I fed her last, but I have no idea when it left the area."

She frowned. "How long do you think it will take before I can drive?"

"Hopefully, sooner rather than later," Ridge replied. "Now that it's no longer raining, the roads should start to dry out. I'd give it a couple of hours and then you can try to go home."

Darcy nodded. "That sounds reasonable." She took a sip of coffee, then made a face. "Do you think he's still out there?"

He didn't have to ask whom she meant. "I doubt it. He's probably long gone by now." The fact that the man hadn't come back during the night suggested he was no longer around. Maybe they'd gotten lucky and he'd been washed away during the storm…

"I hope so," she said with a small shudder. She stood and gathered the dishes, then picked up the tray and headed for the kitchen. When she walked by the back windows, she drew up short. "Oh man," she said. "Have you looked outside lately?"

Apprehension made Ridge's gut twist. "No. What's wrong?"

Darcy shot him a sympathetic look. "It's really torn up out there. Lots of branches and debris from the storm."

Ridge sighed, the idea of having to clean the yard sapping the little energy he'd gained from breakfast. "That's not surprising. I'll deal with it later."

Darcy eyed him thoughtfully. "You know what? Let's tackle it now, while I'm here to help you. Then you can spend the rest of the day relaxing with the baby."

"Really?" He perked up a bit at her offer. With two people working, it wouldn't take as long to take care of the mess. There was just one problem. "What about the baby?"

"She's got a full tummy. She'll sleep for a while. We can leave her in the crib and check on her often while we work."

"That sounds good." And it did. Even though he didn't relish the thought of dealing with the storm damage, it would be nice to spend a little time outside and get some fresh air. The woods always smelled amazing after it rained—so crisp and clean, as if all the dirt and grime of the world had been washed away.

It didn't take long for them to get Sara settled. Penny watched them, her ear cocked in anticipation. Ridge wanted to let her outside, as she always enjoyed romping in the woods. But he needed her to keep an eye on the baby, at least for the time being. "I'll take you out later, girl," he told her. "I need you to stay and watch the baby now."

Penny huffed out a sigh but walked over and sat in front of the baby's makeshift crib. Darcy watched the whole thing, an amused smile on her face. "It's almost as if she understood exactly what you said to her."

"She did," Ridge said. Darcy chuckled, clearly thinking he was joking, so he didn't press his point. He and Penny had a special relationship, something other search and rescue handlers understood because they shared the same bond with their own canine partners. It was easy to forget that people who didn't spend 24/7 with a dog would see his interactions with Penny as outside the norm.

"After you," he said, opening the back door and gesturing Darcy outside. It took a lot of willpower, but he managed to stop himself from leaning down to take a whiff of her hair as she passed by. *She's leaving soon*, he reminded himself sternly as he followed her outside.

Too bad his body didn't care. He still felt the imprint of her curves against his chest, a phantom sensation that had plagued him all night long. He wanted to haul her up against him so he could feel the real thing again, but he knew it would be a mistake. After all, she clearly regretted their kiss last night. He would look like a clueless idiot if he tried to touch her now.

She bent to pick up a fallen branch and the movement made the fabric of her scrub pants tighten in all the right places. Ridge forced himself to look away, feeling like the worst sort of voyeur. But his eyes kept going back to Darcy, tracing the lines of her body as she moved. His fingers ached to follow suit, so he busied himself with stacking broken branches into a pile. No sense wasting them—he could use them as firewood when the nights got chilly.

Darcy walked over, her arms filled with sticks. She added them to his pile, and as she straightened, he noticed she had some leaves stuck in her hair. Before he could think better of it he reached up and gently tugged them free, then tucked the strands of hair behind her ear.

She smiled at him. "Thanks," she said, her cheeks a healthy shade of pink from the outside air and the exertion.

"My pleasure," he murmured.

She held his gaze and something flared to life in her eyes. An answering warmth started in his chest and spread through his limbs, making him feel as though he was standing in a sunbeam. Slowly, so slowly, they moved toward each other until he was close enough to see the dark gold flecks in her deep brown eyes. He felt trapped in her stare, but he didn't want to look away. She was his past and his present, and he was helpless to resist her.

Her breath ghosted across his lips as she moved up onto her toes to get closer. His body tightened in anticipation of her touch, all too eager to resume where they'd left off last night. She placed her palm against his chest, the contact arcing through him like lightning. Did she feel the sparks, too, or was it all in his head?

He lifted his hand to trace the angle of her jaw with his fingertip and was rewarded with a small shudder. He smiled at her reaction. So she wasn't immune to him. That was good to know.

"Ridge," she murmured, her eyelids drifting down in preparation for his kiss.

I should stop this, he thought. *It's a mistake.* But no matter how many times he thought it, he still found himself leaning down, getting ever closer to Darcy's waiting mouth.

He had just brushed his lips across hers when Penny started to bark, a deep, frantic sound that made his blood run cold.

Darcy drew back, frowning. "What—" she started, but Ridge took off for the house before she could get the rest of the question out.

Penny made that sound only when something was terribly wrong, which meant either she or the baby was in danger. He snagged a branch to use as a club, then ran as fast as he could in the mud, slipping and sliding as he moved. The dog kept barking, but now there was a new note in her voice: fear.

Oh God, he's back. The realization slammed into him and Ridge kicked himself for having left the baby in the house. He'd never forgive himself if something happened to her. He took the porch steps two at a time and lunged for the back door, his heart in his throat.

Please, don't let me be too late.

Darcy stood frozen in place for a moment, still adjusting to the fact that one minute Ridge had been about to kiss her and the next minute he was gone, racing into the house as though it was on fire.

What is going on?

It took her a second to register Penny's bark had changed, going from low and menacing to something more frantic, as if she was being backed into a corner against her will.

The intruder! He must have come back—that was the only explanation for Penny's behavior.

Ridge had already made it to the porch, branch in hand. Darcy grabbed a branch of her own and took off after him, ignoring the ache in her lower leg. No way was she letting him face this guy down alone. He hadn't had a weapon last night, but what if he'd come back with a gun? The thought made her fingers go numb. Ridge could be walking into a trap and not even know it.

She heard a muffled shout from inside the cabin, but couldn't tell if it was Ridge or the intruder. *Please don't be hurt*, she thought, equally scared for both Ridge and the baby. She was so tiny and fragile and the thought of that little baby in the arms of the intruder made her stomach revolt.

Darcy bounded up the stairs and burst into the cabin just in time to see Ridge charge across the room, the broken branch held high above his head. He let out a yell that would have done a banshee proud and swung the branch, aiming for the stranger's head. The man stayed in place and Darcy held her breath, thinking he was going to submit to the blow. But at the last second he dodged, lunging forward and striking out at Ridge with his own baseball bat.

The bat struck Ridge in the stomach and the breath left his body in a sickening wheeze that made Darcy's lungs ache in sympathy. He stumbled back, his face going a deep shade of red as he fought to inhale. The intruder took a step forward, intent on finishing him off, but Darcy darted in to distract him, holding her own branch at her shoulder like a baseball player ready to swing.

The man glanced from her to Ridge, who had now recovered enough to take aim at the man again. Apparently deciding he was outmatched, the stranger backed quickly toward the door and darted out.

Ridge made to follow him, but Darcy grabbed his shirt and pulled hard to keep him in place. He whirled on her, his expression so fierce she took a half step back.

"Let me go! I have to follow him!"

"No," she said evenly, glaring up at him. "I'm not going to let you run off by yourself. Who knows what's out there?"

"This is my best chance of catching him," he said, the words coming out clipped and harsh.

"Oh, please," she snapped back, resisting the urge to roll her eyes. "The whole world is covered in mud right now. Even I could track the guy!"

"Darcy," he said, a note of warning in his voice.

"Don't be an idiot, Ridge," she said. She softened her tone, knowing it was the only way to get through to him. "This is the second time that man has forced his way inside your home in an attempt to get the baby. What if he's not working alone? What if he's acting as bait, to draw you out and away from the baby so someone else can sweep in and take her? It's not worth the risk."

She watched the words sink in and could practically see the adrenaline drain out of his body as he relaxed his muscles. "I suppose that's a possibility," he said grudgingly. He walked over to the baby, his features softening as he looked down at her. Moving gently, he picked her up and walked over to the couch. "Are you okay, sweetheart?" he murmured. "That bad man didn't touch you, did he?"

"Okay," Darcy said softly, exhaling in relief. She knew how stubborn Ridge could be, but the fact that he was now holding the baby meant he wasn't going to chase off after the man. Not right now, anyway.

"Why don't you call your brother?" she suggested. "Now that the storms have passed, he might be able to get some officers out here."

"Let's hope so," Ridge replied. He dug his phone out of his pocket and dialed, updating Sam in a few short sentences. After a moment, he hung up. "He's going to come out himself."

"Good." The knot of tension in Darcy's stomach eased some at the news. She trusted Ridge and had every confidence he would keep her and the baby safe, but the knowledge that the police were on their way made her feel better. When she'd first arrived at his cabin last night, the remoteness of it had seemed appealing. Now, after the two attacks, it made her nervous.

"Would you feed the baby for me, please?"

Darcy turned to look at Ridge, who was sporting a suspiciously innocent expression. "What are you wanting to do?" she asked, lifting a brow to convey her skepticism.

He smiled up at her, looking like a man who didn't have a care in the world. She didn't buy it for a second. "I just want to take a look outside. See if I can tell what direction he's headed in so I can let Sam know."

"Uh-huh. And how do I know you won't take it upon yourself to hold your own personal manhunt?"

He frowned slightly, considering her question. Then his face brightened. "I'll leave Penny here. I can't very well conduct a search without my partner."

Darcy glanced out the window, then back at Ridge. "I don't think it's a good idea—" she began, but he cut her off.

"Please," he said simply. "I promise I won't chase after him. But I have to do something—I can't just sit inside and lick my wounds. This is the second time that man has invaded my home and threatened people I care about. Can't you see I have to respond somehow?"

Sympathy welled up in her chest and she nodded. Ridge was a man of action. It must be killing him to sit inside, knowing the stranger who was hell-bent on taking the baby was moving farther away with each passing minute.

Without another word, Darcy walked over and

held her arms out, silently offering her blessing. The fact that Ridge cared enough to ask her permission was sweet, but then again, he'd always been thoughtful where her emotions were concerned. It was one of the many things she'd loved about him.

"Please be careful," she said softly.

His dark brown eyes met hers. "I will," he replied. He reached out to touch her cheek and she leaned in to the caress, closing her eyes to savor the feel of his skin against her own. Then he was gone, heading for the door with determined, long-legged strides.

Penny made a small whine in the back of her throat when he walked out, but she didn't try to follow.

"It's okay, girl," Darcy offered, trying not to jostle the baby as she sank down onto the couch. "He'll be back soon." She settled in to wait, trying to ignore all the terrifying scenarios her brain was helpfully providing now that she was alone with the baby. Ridge getting attacked and overpowered. The man coming back, this time with a gun. Or with someone else. The stranger ripping the baby from her arms.

The door flew open and hit the wall, making her jump. She instinctively clutched the baby to her chest and curled around her, trying to shield the little one with her own body. Not again!

But it was Ridge who strode into the cabin, not the masked man she was expecting. The lines of his body were drawn tight with barely contained energy, and his expression made it clear that whatever was out there, he wasn't happy about it. She'd never seen him look so angry before, and she shrank back into the couch cushions, trying to look as small and unobtrusive as possible.

He kicked the door shut and shoved a hand through his hair, then paced a few steps, clearly trying to burn off his emotions.

"Ridge?" His reaction was starting to scare her. What had he found outside? Another threat of some kind? Her heart started to pound as she imagined all sorts of horrible possibilities. "What's going on? What did you find out there?"

He shook his head. "Bastard slashed our tires. He's long gone."

"Oh." It was disturbing news, but it hardly accounted for the intensity of Ridge's anger. "Is that all?"

He shifted as if he was uncomfortable and Darcy realized she was right. He was hiding something from her. "Please tell me," she said.

"He left a message," Ridge said, refusing to meet her eyes.

"What did it say?" It couldn't have been very long—the man hadn't had a lot of time on his way out. But it was clearly disturbing, if Ridge's reaction was any indication.

Ridge was quiet for a moment, and Darcy began to think he wasn't going to answer her question. Then he sighed. "He used mud to write on my truck. Covered the windshield with it." He glanced up at her, his expression bleak. "He wrote 'She's mine' and drew a bull's-eye next to it."

A chill trickled down Darcy's back, as if someone had dropped a melting ice cube down her shirt. "Isn't that the trademark sign of..." She trailed off, not wanting to finish the thought.

Ridge nodded, a haunted look in his eyes. "The Alphabet Killer."

Chapter 8

"Took you long enough to get here."

Annabel shot him a warning glance as Sam climbed out of his truck slowly, moving like an old man. "Give me a break," he said mildly. "It's already been a hell of a day."

Ridge frowned at his younger brother, noting the lines of fatigue around Sam's mouth and eyes. "What's going on?"

Sam shot a quick glance at Darcy, who was standing on the porch holding Sara. Sensing his brother didn't want to talk in front of her, Ridge took a step forward.

"We've got another body," Sam said grimly.

Ridge's heart sank. "Damn," he said softly.

Sam nodded. "Found her this morning. We think she was killed last night, but because of the weather, no one was really out and about to discover it until today."

"Were you able to identify her?" And more importantly, was it Sara's mother? He glanced back at the porch involuntarily, his gut tightening at the thought that the little one was now an orphan.

"Francine Gibbons," Annabel said.

The name registered with Ridge, but he couldn't quite place it. "Why do I know that name?" he mused.

"Society debutante," Sam supplied. "Does a lot of charity work and gets her name in the paper for it."

"That's probably it," Ridge agreed. She didn't sound like the kind of person he would encounter on a daily basis. And as far as he knew, she didn't have any children. That meant Sara's mother was still out there, somewhere.

"What's going on?" Darcy asked, picking her way carefully through the mud as she walked over to them. "You all look like someone stole your cookies."

Sam offered her a small smile. "It's been a long morning," he said.

She studied him thoughtfully, then glanced at Annabel and Ridge. "What happened?"

Both Sam and Annabel shifted uncomfortably, but neither offered an explanation. Darcy raised her brow at Ridge and he sighed. "You might as well tell her," he said. "She's part of this now, too."

"The Alphabet Killer has claimed another victim," Sam said, sounding as if he had the weight of the world on his shoulders.

"That's terrible!" she said. "Do you know who it is?"

Sam pressed his lips together, clearly reluctant to say more. Ridge gave him a nod of encouragement and he sighed. "Francine Gibbons."

The color drained out of Darcy's face and Ridge reached for the baby, concerned she might drop her. She handed Sara over without protest, which told him just how upset she was. "Are you sure?" she whispered.

Sam reached out to lay a steadying hand on her arm. "I'm afraid so. Do you know her?"

She nodded, the gesture wobbly. "Let's go inside," Annabel suggested, walking ahead of the group to open the door of the cabin. Once they had all filed inside, his sister went into the kitchen and returned a few minutes later with a steaming cup that she pressed into Darcy's shaking hands. "I'm sorry for your loss," she said softly. "Were you friends with Francine?"

Darcy took a sip and a deep breath. "I knew

her. We were friendly, but I don't know that Francine actually had any friends, if that makes sense."

Sam shot Ridge a questioning look, but Annabel just nodded as if this made perfect sense. "She was standoffish?"

"Snobby, more like," Darcy said. "We went to school together and even then she was very stuck up. I had hoped it was something she'd outgrow, but we met for lunch a few weeks ago since we're both on the organizing committee for an upcoming charity luncheon. She was horribly rude to our waitress, so much so that I suggested we have our next meeting at my parents' home." She shook her head. "We were supposed to meet next Wednesday to finalize the details of the lunch."

Annabel nodded sympathetically. "Did Francine seem normal when you spoke with her last?"

Darcy frowned slightly. "Actually, now that you mention it, she did say she felt like someone was watching her."

Sam perked up at that. "Did she tell you anything specific? Like who was following her or why she felt that way?"

"Not really." Darcy bit her bottom lip, thinking. "I told her she needed to be careful because of the killer on the loose, but she brushed me off. She thought she had a secret admirer and she was actually flattered by the attention."

"Did she receive anything? Any gifts or notes?"

A note of excitement crept into Sam's voice and Ridge found himself leaning forward, wanting to know the answer, as well. Maybe Francine had a token from her "admirer," something they could use to identify the killer. It was just the kind of break they'd been hoping for…

Darcy shook her head, dashing his hopes. "Not that I know of. The way she described it to me made it sound like she had a stalker of some kind—she constantly felt like she was being watched, but she could never really put her finger on who was watching her."

"We should probably search her home, just to be on the safe side," Annabel murmured to Sam, who nodded his agreement. "We might get lucky."

"Are you sure this is the Alphabet Killer?" Darcy asked. "Maybe there's been some mistake."

"I'm afraid not," Sam said. "This has all the hallmarks of the killer." He gave Ridge a telling glance, and Ridge nodded. Best not to go into the details in front of Darcy—she didn't need to know how Francine had died, even if the two of them hadn't been very good friends. There was nothing pretty about being shot in the chest, and she didn't need confirmation that the killer had drawn on Francine's body after her death.

"The bull's-eye?" Darcy guessed. Sam merely nodded while Ridge shook his head. He should have known Darcy would see through the omissions.

"Do you know when she died?"

"Sometime last night," Annabel said. "We're waiting for the medical examiner to give us a more precise time of death."

Darcy turned to Ridge. "Do you think the killer murdered Francine and then came here, after the baby?"

Ridge hesitated, uncertain of how to answer. "No, it's not the same person."

"How can you be so sure?"

He glanced at Sam and Annabel, silently asking permission to share what they knew with Darcy. Annabel nodded and after a few seconds, Sam did, too.

"We're pretty sure the Alphabet Killer is a woman," Ridge said. "We have a…a source who is close to the investigation, and several witnesses who have described a woman arguing with some of the earlier victims."

"But if the man who is trying to steal the baby isn't the killer, then why did he draw a bull's-eye on your truck?"

It was a good question, one he'd been trying to answer since he'd first seen the message. "I'm not sure," he admitted. "It's possible he's an accomplice of the killer."

Annabel frowned. "But none of the evidence we have suggests the killer has a partner."

"I know," Ridge said. "But we have to consider the possibility."

"Or maybe," Sam injected, "we're overthinking this. Maybe whoever broke into your cabin drew the bull's-eye as a red herring to throw us off and make it harder to identify him."

"We just don't know enough to rule anything out yet." Ridge looked down at the baby and was surprised to find Sara's eyes open. Her dark gray gaze was somber, as if she realized the danger she was in. "Who is after you?" he asked. He turned to Sam. "Any leads on her mother yet?"

Sam shook his head. "Not really. The babies born in the hospital are all accounted for."

Darcy let out a quiet sigh of relief. "What about home births?" she asked.

"Still tracking them down. But so far, nothing."

"And I haven't found anything from nearby hospitals, either," Annabel said.

"Did you get any fingerprints off the note?" Ridge asked, holding on to a sliver of hope. If they hadn't had time to process the note yet, they still might have a chance to find the woman.

"We did get prints, but they aren't in the system," Sam told him.

"Which means she doesn't have a file," Ridge finished. "Great." Dejection pressed down on his shoulders. It had been a long shot, but it was still disappointing to know they had zero leads.

"It's like she came out of nowhere," Darcy remarked. "How does that happen in this day and age?"

"You'd be surprised," Sam said drily.

"So, to sum up," Ridge said. "We have a baby of unknown origin and a mystery man who is determined to take her. In unrelated news, the Alphabet Killer has struck again, and there are no new leads on that front, either."

"Well, maybe not," Annabel said thoughtfully.

"What are you thinking?" Sam asked.

She glanced at Darcy. "You said the last time you met with Francine she was rude to the waitress?"

Darcy nodded. "Yes. I was embarrassed to be seen with her, and I left a note of apology when I signed my half of the check."

Annabel's gaze sharpened. "Did she pay with a credit card, as well?"

"I think so," Darcy said slowly. "I'm almost certain she did. Francine didn't like to carry cash. She said it made her feel low-class."

Sam huffed. "What does that even mean?" he said under his breath.

Ridge shook his head. "Who knows?" he muttered. He'd never understood women like Francine, and had no desire to learn.

"Anyway," Annabel said meaningfully, interrupting their side conversation. "Do you remember what the waitress looked like?"

"Not really." Darcy tilted her head to the side, clearly trying to recall the woman. "Brown hair, maybe in her forties? But I really couldn't say." She sounded apologetic. "I'm sorry. I didn't think to really look at her, you know?"

"Don't stress about it," Annabel assured her.

"You think the waitress is our killer?" Sam asked.

"Maybe," Annabel replied. "Or maybe she works at a restaurant and keeps a record of customers who are rude to her or who otherwise push her buttons." Annabel sounded thoughtful, as if she was thinking out loud. "She could get their names from the credit cards, which would explain how she can target them in alphabetical order."

"Hang on," Sam said, holding up a hand. "Let me get Trevor on the phone—I want to hear his take on it."

Darcy shot him a questioning look. "Trevor is a profiler with the FBI," Ridge clarified.

It took only a moment to get Trevor on the line. Annabel put him on speaker phone and relayed her theory regarding the killer.

"I like it," Trevor said. "It's something we haven't considered before, but it makes sense. She has to be coming into contact with the victims somehow—we know they're not just random. It's possible rude customers with long dark hair trigger something for her. Maybe she had a horrible relationship with her mother or a sister who has long dark hair, and that's why she fixates on that particular feature."

"Do you think it's possible she was betrayed by a friend?" Ridge asked. What if the killer was seeking to enact revenge for a slight, real or otherwise? That might drive her to kill again and again.

"Could be," Trevor replied. "I'll mark that down as another potential explanation. Let me get the team working on it and I'll get back to you soon. In the meantime, can you get your people to canvass area restaurants? I'll send over the suspect description we have to make sure it matches yours."

"Roger that," Sam said. "We'll get right on it."

Annabel ended the call and Ridge glanced at his siblings. "Sounds like you guys have some work to do," he said. Part of him wanted to jump in and help, to join the hunt now that they had a good theory to explore. But the other part of him was happy to take care of Sara and work on finding out who was after her. In the end, practicality won out. Sam, Annabel and the rest of his siblings in law enforcement could handle the search for the Alphabet Killer. And since they were all otherwise occupied, he was the only one who could make sure Sara stayed safe.

He glanced down and was rewarded by the sight of those big gray eyes staring up at him with absolute trust. His heart turned over as the enormity of his task sank in. He'd been able to keep her safe so far, but the stranger who wanted her was determined. How much longer could he protect her, especially with the police distracted by their search for the killer?

Sara yawned, her body going limp in his arms as she relaxed into sleep. In that instant, Ridge realized he didn't need to worry about backup. He would take on the world for this little girl.

"What are you going to do?" Annabel asked, smiling at the baby and then at him.

"I'm going to keep her safe," Ridge said simply. Then he glanced at Sam. "But first, I need you to take me into town. I have to buy some tires."

"Where have you been?"

Darcy froze halfway up the stairs, her muscles tensing automatically at the sound of her mother's voice. She turned around slowly, willing herself to relax. She was a grown woman—she didn't owe anyone an explanation of her whereabouts.

But she was staying with her parents while she was in town, and she did want to try to smooth things over with them. Snapping at her mother wasn't going to help her do that.

So she pasted on a smile and met her mother's

icy gaze. "I got tied up with a case," she said, trying to keep the annoyance out of her voice. "So I bunked at the hospital."

Cindy Marrow narrowed her eyes. "Is that so?" Suspicion dripped from every word.

Darcy nodded, refusing to cower in the face of her mother's reaction. "The storm messed up a lot of the roads. I didn't want to risk driving in that weather."

"I see." When her mother didn't respond, Darcy turned back to continue up the stairs. After everything that had happened at Ridge's cabin, she desperately wanted a shower and a nap.

"You know, it's funny you say that," Cindy remarked, walking forward until she hit the base of the stairs. She stared up at Darcy, her blue eyes cold. "Your father had to stop by the hospital last night. He didn't mention seeing you there."

"I didn't realize he was my babysitter," Darcy said evenly.

Her mother opened her mouth to respond, but at that moment, her father walked into the foyer. "Darcy? Is that you?" He moved to stand next to her mother. "I thought I heard your voice."

Darcy nodded. "Hello." *Great. Now it's two against one.*

"Your mother and I have been worried about you," he said, his tone scolding. "Where have you been?"

Darcy closed her eyes and sighed silently, digging deep for patience. "As I was explaining, I got tied up at the hospital and didn't want to drive in the storm."

Clint Marrow shook his head as if he was disappointed in her. "I know you weren't there last night. Why don't you tell us where you really were?"

Ignoring her mother's triumphant glance, Darcy leaned against the banister. They weren't going to drop the subject, so she might as well tell them something. "I stayed with a friend last night," she said, hoping they would accept her answer and leave it at that.

She should have known better. "Who?" her mother asked. "You don't have any friends here."

Ouch. The truth hurt, but Darcy refused to let it show on her face. She wasn't about to give her mother the satisfaction of knowing one of her barbs had sunk in. "I didn't realize you kept such close tabs on my social life," she said.

Cindy narrowed her eyes. "I don't think I like your tone."

"There's a shock," Darcy muttered.

"That's enough," her father said sharply. "Young lady, you are a guest in this home and we have a right to know where you were last night. Now, stop dancing around the question and give us a straight answer."

For a moment, Darcy considered sticking to a half-truth for the sake of convenience. The sooner this conversation was over, the better. But part of her wanted to see how they would react when she mentioned Ridge. She'd been thinking about how things had ended between them for most of last night, and she couldn't shake the suspicion that Cindy and Clint had something to do with their breakup.

"To be honest, I stayed with Ridge last night."

There was a moment of silence as her parents digested her words. Then her mother's eyes widened comically. "You *what*?"

Her father closed his jaw and shook his head. "You slept at Ridge Colton's house? I thought we'd raised you better than that."

Darcy bristled, offended on Ridge's behalf. "What's that supposed to mean? What's wrong with Ridge?"

"Well, for starters—" her father began. Her mother cut him off, her composure sufficiently recovered to allow her to jump in.

"You know very well how we feel about that boy," she said, venom dripping from every word.

"He's not a boy any longer," Darcy replied, feeling her face heat. What was wrong with her family? It had been years since her parents had seen Ridge, and yet their hatred of him was as potent as ever.

"That's not the point and you know it," Cindy shot back. "Do you not remember the kind of people he comes from? What his father did?"

"He's not his father," Darcy said. She knew her protests fell on deaf ears, but she couldn't help but try to defend Ridge. She had thought over the years the prejudices of the town would fade, especially in light of the fact that Ridge and most of his siblings had gone into law enforcement. How could anyone judge them for dedicating their lives to helping others? But it seemed old habits die hard, and if her parents were representative of how the rest of the town treated Ridge and his siblings, she could see why he chose to live in such a relatively remote spot.

"How do you know?" Cindy asked. "His father didn't start killing people until he was older than Ridge. He carries that trait within him—it's only a matter of time until something sets him off and he snaps."

Darcy shook her head, at a loss for words. "I can't believe you think that," she said finally.

"Be reasonable, darling," her father said, his tone conciliatory. "Your mother is just worried about you."

"No, she isn't," Darcy said. "She's worried about how my behavior reflects on her social standing. Just like she always has." She turned back to face her mother. “Isn’t that right, Cindy?” she asked coldly.

Her mother’s face turned an ugly shade of red. “How dare you,” she sputtered. “Everything I have done has been in service to this family.”

Darcy couldn’t hold back her scoff. “Is that really what you think?”

“You have no idea of the sacrifices I’ve made for you! I worked hard to make sure this family had a good social standing in the community, and it wasn’t always easy. *You* certainly weren’t any help.”

“I will not apologize for dating Ridge Colton,” Darcy said, clenching her teeth. Even after all these years, it was the same argument. Were they doomed to fight about this issue for the rest of their lives? Why couldn’t her parents just let it go?

“No, of course not. You never apologize for anything,” Cindy said snidely.

Darcy frowned. “What’s that supposed to mean?”

“Ladies, can we just—” her father said, trying to make peace. But it was too late for that. Cindy was too angry to stop now, and Darcy was too tired to fake a smile and pretend as if everything was okay.

“You have no idea how difficult it was for us when you started stepping out with that boy. Our friends turned away from us. Your father lost some of his patients. It was a very trying time, but you didn't care. We asked you to stop, but you refused to listen. Then you started flaunting it to us—going out in public with him, making sure people saw you two together." Cindy shook her head, her mouth set in a thin line. "It was disgraceful. I just thank God you didn't get pregnant by him."

Her mother's words were like a slap to the face. Darcy could only stare down at her, too stunned by the depths of her mother's hatred to think of anything to say. Cindy Marrow had never tried to hide her dislike of Ridge Colton, but Darcy had never realized how all-consuming her malice and bitterness actually were. To hear her spew such poison now was disturbing, to say the least. After all, she and Ridge weren't together anymore. Why, then, did her mother still despise him so intently?

"Your father and I worked so hard to make you see reason," she went on, warming to her subject. "It took forever, but we finally figured out how to fix things."

"You fixed it?" Darcy interrupted. "What does that mean?" The fine hairs on the back of Darcy's neck stood on end as the implications of her mother's words sank in. Had they somehow orchestrated her breakup with Ridge? Had he been framed after all?

Cindy seemed to realize she'd said too much.

She clamped her mouth shut and glanced at Darcy's father, her expression panicked.

"What did you do?" Darcy descended a step and her mother backed up, confirming Darcy's suspicions that something was off. "Did you frame Ridge?"

Cindy didn't respond, but her pale face and guilty look said it all.

"I can't believe it." Darcy's throat tightened and she struggled to get the words out. "Even for you, that's low."

"That's enough," her father said, his voice harsh. "Both of you. Stop arguing—the housekeeper can hear you."

Darcy rolled her eyes. Of course he was worried only about how their fight would appear to someone outside the family. Heaven forbid they have an actual conversation that included a display of emotions. The Marrow family did not believe in emotions—they were such messy, inconvenient things.

"Forget I said anything," Darcy muttered.

Her parents merely glared at her. "Don't you have something you'd like to say to your mother?" Clint asked. It was clear he expected her to apologize, but Darcy wasn't having any of it.

"No, I don't." She turned and marched up the stairs without a second look. She knew she was being petty, but she was too upset to care.

Ten years, she thought. *I lost ten years with*

Ridge. Even though her parents hadn't actually confirmed their involvement in her breakup, her mother's guilty reaction was enough to convince Darcy of the truth. It broke her heart all over again to think of how much time she'd missed with Ridge. What kind of life would they have had, if she hadn't fallen into her parents' trap? Would they have had their own family by now? She could picture it clearly—two little ones with Ridge's dark hair and eyes, playing with Penny on the floor of the cabin. And her, opening up her own practice on Main Street, welcoming the people of Granite Gulch into her little clinic. That could have been her life…

It was a beautiful dream, one she couldn't shake. A sense of longing for what might have been hit her so hard it made her heart skip a beat, and she realized with a sharp shock that her imagined future with Ridge was the one she had really wanted all along. She'd spent the past few years convincing herself that she needed to practice in a big city, some place far away from here. When the offer from New York had come along, she'd jumped at the chance to get away from her parents. But it was clear to her now she'd taken a job halfway across the country to get away from Granite Gulch and the constant reminders of Ridge and what they could have had together.

Darcy walked into the bathroom, her vision

blurring with tears as her emotions spilled over. Damn her parents for interfering! And damn her for not trusting Ridge! A wave of guilt slammed into her and she leaned against the bathroom counter to steady herself. She could blame Cindy and Clint all day long, but really, this was her fault. If she had truly trusted Ridge she would have never believed their lies in the first place.

"I never should have doubted you," she whispered, the memory of his face haunting her. How could he even stand to look at her now? "I've got to make this right," she said, stepping into the shower and dunking her head under the hot spray. The heat felt good against her sore muscles, and she rested her head against the cool shower tiles with a sigh. Obviously, she'd start with an apology. But what could she even say to make Ridge realize how very sorry she was? More importantly, would he even listen? Maybe he just wanted to leave the past behind and move on. After all, he hadn't brought it up and they'd spent plenty of time together. If he was still bothered by how things had ended between them, surely he would have said something?

I have to try, she thought. Maybe Ridge would listen to her and maybe he wouldn't. But either way, Darcy couldn't live with herself if she didn't at least attempt to repair the damage she'd done.

If only her parents felt the same way. Her mood darkened as she thought of them. It would be a cold day in hell before Cindy and Clint Marrow apologized to Ridge Colton. Or herself, for that matter. Even if she could somehow make them understand how wrong they had been to interfere, they would still never acknowledge their mistake. Marrows didn't apologize, and certainly not to anyone they thought was beneath them socially.

Disgust and shame mingled in her chest, making her feel dirty even as she washed the soap suds off her body. For the life of her, she would never understand why her parents were such snobs. Neither one of them came from money or had grown up with the finer things in life. And it was not as if Granite Gulch had a high society to speak of. But Darcy wasn't going to waste any more time thinking about it—people didn't change, and her parents certainly weren't going to wake up with a sudden change of heart. Now Darcy had a choice to make: cut them out of her life as punishment for what they'd done, or find a way to forgive them and move on.

She turned off the water and stood in the shower, staring at the faucet until she began to shiver. On the face of it, the choice should be an easy one. But no matter what her parents had done, they were still her parents. Could she live with herself if she walked away from them completely?

Fatigue pulled at her as she stepped out of the shower and dried off. Her arms felt heavy and it took almost all her energy to brush out her hair. The logical part of her realized she was too exhausted to think straight and she should forget about everything until she'd had some sleep. But her emotions wouldn't let go—they demanded she do something, anything, to repair the damage that had been done.

Her phone sat on the table, tempting her. She could call Ridge and tell him what she'd learned today. Obviously she needed to apologize in person, but it would be a start. She picked up the phone and started to dial, but stopped herself before she completed the call. He had his hands full with the baby—the last thing he needed was a distraction, especially one concerning a matter that had been settled long ago.

She climbed into bed, her heart heavy and her eyes burning. Part of her understood she needed to gather her composure and move forward. But she wasn't ready to do that yet. The argument with her parents had left her feeling robbed, as if they had stolen a part of her life from her. But she was a Marrow, well schooled in the art of suppressing her emotions and putting on a brave face. And she would. Eventually.

For now, she was going to take the time to mourn what might have been.

Chapter 9

The phone rang just as Ridge set Sara down for a nap. He crossed the room to put some distance between himself and the crib and dug the cell out of his pocket.

"Hello," he said, keeping his voice down so as not to disturb the baby.

"It's Trevor," his brother replied.

"What's up?" Had the FBI already made progress on their investigation of the killer? That was fast. But then again, Annabel's theory had been a good one—maybe it was just what they'd needed to crack the case wide open…

"It's about dad," Trevor said, dispensing with any pleasantries.

Ridge's stomach tightened into knots. "What about him?"

"He's received another letter from the Alphabet Killer."

"Oh?" That sounded like good news. Why, then, did his brother not seem more excited?

"Yeah. And you're not going to believe this—the return address on the envelope is a PO box here in Granite Gulch."

"Do you think it's legitimate?"

"I'm not sure," Trevor admitted.

"Kind of tough to believe the killer would use their actual address. She's been pretty savvy so far," Ridge commented.

"I agree," Trevor said. "But we have to check it out. I'm at the post office with Annabel and Sam now. We're canvassing the workers. So far, we know the woman renting the box matches our suspect description, but she used a phony ID to set things up."

"That's not a surprise," Ridge said. "Are you going to assign someone to watch the place, in case she shows up?"

"Already arranged," Trevor said. "In the meantime…" He trailed off and Ridge realized two things; his brother was going to ask him for a favor, and he wasn't going to like it.

"What?" Ridge said, feeling suddenly reluctant to continue this conversation. Maybe he could fake bad cell service, or claim the baby needed him.

"I may need you to visit him early."

Him meant only one person—Matthew Colton. The dying man had manipulated his kids into monthly visits—one person per month. But it wasn't a sense of nostalgia or paternal tenderness that made him want to see his children. A con man to the end, Matthew had hit upon the one thing they wanted: closure for their mother's death. Matthew used these visits to provide clues as to where he'd buried their mother's body.

He hadn't given them much to go on so far. Sam and Ethan had already been to see him, and Matthew's clues had been maddeningly vague. It was Ridge's turn, and he was dreading it. He hadn't seen his father since the trial, and had no desire to now.

"Why?"

Trevor sighed, and Ridge realized his brother hated having to bring up the possibility. "The letter he got was pretty similar to ones the killer has sent him before. On the face of it, we haven't really found any new information, aside from the return address. Makes me wonder why the killer keeps sending variations of the same message."

"Unless she's not," Ridge said, seeing where

Trevor was going. "Maybe she's sending him some kind of code."

"Exactly," Trevor finished. "And if our leads start to dry up here, I may have to ask you to go in and chat him up about it. See if you can shake anything out of him that could help."

"I see." And he did. If there was a possibility he could help catch a killer by visiting his monster of a father, he'd do it. He would hate every minute of it, but he couldn't live with himself if he didn't do everything in his power to help.

"You know I hate to even ask." Trevor sounded truly remorseful. "But it's your turn, and you know he won't cooperate if we don't play by his twisted rules."

"I know." Ridge sighed. "Let's just hope it doesn't come to that. I was already dreading my visit. I really don't want to have to move it up in the schedule."

"I understand," Trevor said. "I'll do everything I can to make sure you won't have to."

"Thanks." He knew his brother wasn't just trying to be nice. Trevor was one of the smartest guys he knew. If he needed Ridge to gather more information, it was because he was well and truly stuck.

"Good luck at the post office. I hope she turns up," Ridge said.

"You and me both," Trevor replied. "But I have my doubts. She's got to know we'd find that letter. I have a feeling she's not being careless but is trying to taunt us."

"A killer with a sense of humor?"

"If you want to call it that," Trevor said. "She probably sees this as a game—her on one side, us on the other. The victims are caught in the middle."

"What about Matthew?" Ridge asked. "How does he fit in with all of this?"

"She sees him as a mentor of sorts," Trevor replied. Ridge shuddered at the thought that anyone would look up to his father. What kind of sick mind saw Matthew Colton as someone to admire?

"I thought he couldn't write back," Ridge said. "How can he act as a mentor for her when the communication is all one-sided?"

"We think she sees him as more of a teacher. She's writing to report on her activities, let him know how he inspired her. She's basically bragging to him and hoping he'll acknowledge her as his star pupil."

"That's twisted," Ridge said.

"Takes all kinds," Trevor agreed. "Got to go—Sam needs me."

Ridge signed off and shoved the phone back into his pocket. Then he walked over to the back windows and stared outside, his gaze landing on the familiar, comforting sight of the tree line. Thoughts jumbled together in his mind—Darcy, the Alphabet Killer, Sara, the intruder. And now the threat of an early visit to Matthew Colton.

He needed to move, needed to get away. But he couldn't very well leave Sara behind. After a moment's thought, he walked over to the hall closet where he kept his search and rescue gear. It took a little digging, but he soon found what he needed. Then he headed back over to the crib and gathered up the baby.

Ten minutes later, he locked the back door and stepped off the porch, Penny at his side and the baby strapped to his chest. It felt good to be out in the fresh air, and as they headed into the cool stillness of the woods, he felt a calm descend over him.

Hiking like this always helped him organize his thoughts. It was practically second nature for him to seek the solace of the woods whenever he had to think. On several occasions, Annabel had accused him of running away but that couldn't be further from the truth. He just needed that combination of solitude and activity to figure things out.

Like the identity of the mysterious intruder. Whoever was after Sara knew she was here, which meant he knew her mother. That didn't help him narrow the field of possible candidates, but a small part of him wished the man would come back so he could ask about the woman who had left her baby behind. A baby needed her mother, especially one as young as Sara. Thank God Darcy had been there.

His heart did a funny little flip at the thought of Darcy. What was it about that woman that affected him so, even after ten years apart? He'd tried to keep his distance, but being around her again had circumvented his defenses in record time. His heart was all set to take the plunge for a second time, but his brain refused to sign off on that plan. Her parents had made their distaste for him very clear, and even though he couldn't prove it, he knew deep down they had somehow planted that watch in his bag to force Darcy to break up with him.

At first, her lack of trust had hurt—a bone-deep ache that had made him question everything about their relationship. But over time, he'd come to realize Darcy had been played the same as he had. The question was, did she even realize it?

Part of him was tempted to ask her about it, but it wasn't his place to stir up trouble. Darcy had always had a distant relationship with her parents, and he doubted things had improved in the intervening years. The petty, selfish part of him wanted to tell her his suspicions so she would know just how wrong she'd been. And if that information caused her to confront her parents, so much the better. After all, they had caused him a lot of pain. They deserved some of the same in return.

But no matter how satisfying it was to imagine that scenario, he wasn't going to act on those impulses. The Marrows certainly weren't an ideal family, but he had no desire to contribute to their dysfunction. He knew all too well what it was like to lose the people you loved, and even though Darcy had hurt him, he didn't want that kind of pain for her.

His thoughts drifted to his siblings, and how their lives had changed forever on that fateful night twenty years ago when Matthew Colton had murdered their mother. In a matter of hours they'd been thrown into the system, torn from each other and the only family they'd ever known.

They'd all found ways to cope with the new reality—there had been no other choice. But his youngest sister, Josie, had been especially hurt by the situation.

He'd visited her as often as he could, and his heart broke every time he saw how his once vibrant, bright-eyed and curious little sister had been transformed into a sad, lonely girl. She had put on a brave face, but no amount of acting had been able to fool him.

He hadn't been the only one to notice the changes. One by one, he and his siblings had turned eighteen and tried to adopt Josie, to get her out of the foster system in the hopes of bringing back the happy girl they'd known and loved. But she'd turned them down every time.

And then she'd disappeared.

It killed him to think of his baby sister, alone and scared in the world. She'd left six years ago with no warning, and she hadn't tried to contact anyone. Not even a postcard to let them know she was okay. It was as if she had fallen off the face of the earth, as if her very existence had been erased. But the worst part of all? It was possible she was the Alphabet Killer.

He hated to even think his sister was capable of such crimes, but he had to admit, the circumstantial evidence was suggestive. Josie had taken off after her fiancé had dumped her in favor of a young woman with long dark hair. The same kind of hair displayed by all the killer's victims. Had his betrayal been the trigger that set Josie off? He didn't want to believe it, but until Ridge and the rest of his siblings could prove otherwise, the police and the FBI kept her on their list of suspects.

They rounded a bend in the path, and Penny's tail started wagging. They were getting close to the stream that ran through this section of the woods. Normally, when he and Penny hiked this path they stopped at the water so she could play. But since he was carrying the baby today he didn't want to linger too long. She was still sleeping peacefully, but that could change at any moment and he didn't fancy being out in the woods when she woke up and decided to fuss.

"Heel," he said, hating the fact that he was disappointing his dog. Penny fell into place without issue, but she understood there would be no frolicking in the water today. Her tail drooped slightly and she emitted a soft whine, her subtle way of complaining about this unhappy turn of events.

"I know," he said, feeling only a little foolish about explaining himself to a dog. "But we can't stay long today. We need to get back in case the baby needs something."

Penny huffed, as if she found his excuse wanting. But she stayed by his side even when the stream came into view.

As they got closer to the water, Ridge noticed a figure standing on the bank of the stream. He almost didn't notice her—her indigo jeans and dark green T-shirt allowed her to blend in well with the surrounding trees. But now that he saw her, there was something familiar about her…

The hairs on his arms stood on end as he studied the young woman, trying to place her. Then it hit him like a bolt of lightning to the chest.

"Josie?" Her name came out as a rasp, barely audible above the birdsong and the sound of the running water. Ridge stopped dead in his tracks, unable to believe it.

"Josie?" This time he practically shouted her name.

She lifted her head and for a split second he saw her face. Her expression was one of pain, as if the name brought up bad memories. She turned to glance at him and then was gone, moving quickly through the trees and out of sight.

Ridge started after her, but couldn't move very fast without jostling the baby. He cursed the situation and half considered sending Penny after her to track the girl down. But that would be irresponsible. She hadn't done anything wrong, and she didn't deserve to be chased by his dog.

He stopped when he reached the bank of the stream and sat on a fallen log, trying to process what he'd just seen. Had she been real, or a hallucination brought on by his emotions? He'd just been thinking about Josie. Perhaps it was only his imagination that the young woman looked like his lost sister. Her hair had been completely different for one thing—Josie's hair had always been long, whereas this woman's was styled in a short bob.

She could have cut her hair, though, he thought. It was the quickest way to change your appearance, and if Josie really was on the run from someone or something that would be the first thing she'd do.

Be reasonable, he told himself. What were the

odds he'd happen upon his youngest sister while out hiking in the woods? There was no way she was in Granite Gulch—if that was the case, he or one of his siblings would have run into her by now. The town simply wasn't that big. No, Josie was long gone. He was just projecting his memories of her face onto another woman. It was the most reasonable explanation, but he still couldn't shakc the fact she had seemed familiar to him.

More importantly, though, why had the woman run from him? He wasn't exactly a threatening presence, what with a baby strapped to his chest.

"I did yell, though," he muttered. He'd been so convinced it was his sister he hadn't been able to stop himself from calling out. Maybe the stranger had been spooked by the sight of a strange man yelling someone else's name. Now that he thought about it, he had probably looked very much like a crazy person trudging out of the woods. The woman probably hadn't stopped to really look at him before taking off, and he couldn't blame her. With the Alphabet Killer still at large, it wasn't smart for women to be alone right now.

Logically, that explanation made the most sense. But as Ridge watched a leaf float by on the ripples of the stream, he couldn't shake the feeling he somehow knew that woman.

Was she Sara's mother? He glanced down at the little one, trying to impose the young woman's features onto the baby's face. It was possible. The woman had disappeared after leaving Sara on his porch, which meant she had to know these woods fairly well. And given the speed with which the lady had vanished today, she might very well be the one they'd been looking for.

But if that was the case, why had she run? The note left on the baby indicated her mother was coming back. Wouldn't she want to see her child, after having been apart from her for the past few days? Ridge hugged her close, an empty feeling opening up in his stomach at the thought of being away from the baby. He was attached to her already, even though he wasn't related to her and had only known her for a couple of days. He could only imagine the ache of loss her mother must feel over their separation.

A rustle of leaves behind him made him jump. It was probably just the wind, but he was suddenly very aware he was alone with the baby out in the middle of the woods. What had seemed like a good idea before now struck him as profoundly stupid. Who brought a baby to a remote location with a killer at large and a mysterious man hell-bent on kidnapping her still loose in the area?

He stood, one hand on the baby to steady her. "Heel," he said. Penny responded instantly, sticking to his side like furry glue as they made their way back home. Frustration welled in his chest as they approached the cabin. He was no closer to figuring things out, and if anything, the mysterious young woman in the woods had only made him feel more unsettled.

Sara opened her eyes as he climbed the steps of the back porch. She turned her head to face his chest and opened her mouth, clearly expecting him to put something in it. He smiled, marveling at the instinctive display. She was so young, and yet she knew exactly how to communicate her needs. He'd never been around babies before, and he was humbled by the way this little life trusted him completely and without reservation. It was almost like the bond he had with Penny, which surprised him. After Darcy had broken his heart, he'd thought he could never get close to someone again. But this baby had shattered that assumption. He was forced to admit that perhaps he'd stopped trying to connect with people out of fear, rather than because he was broken.

Sara let out a little cry and he picked up the pace, pushing his thoughts to the side. Time to get her a bottle before she became too upset.

At least he could handle that task.

"I need more time."

"That's not the way this works." The woman on the other end of the line sounded annoyed, but he was too desperate to care. It was taking longer to take the baby than he'd anticipated, and he needed an extension. Better to be honest with them about it now. Otherwise, the delay might cause the people who'd hired him to think he was trying to double-cross them. And if that happened, there would be hell to pay.

"Please—I know where she is, but I'm having trouble getting her."

"Why is that?" Her voice sharpened and he realized his mistake—if they thought he wasn't capable, they'd cut ties and walk away. And he was under no illusions they would leave a loose end like him dangling in the wind…

"It's not what you think," he said hastily. "The mother is backpedaling a bit. I just need a little more time to convince her she's doing the right thing."

"I see." There was a pause as the woman considered his words. He held his breath, hoping the excuse had sounded plausible. *Please, please, please...*

"All right," she said finally. "You have an additional twenty-four hours to get the job done. Will that be enough?" Her tone made it clear that if it wasn't, he was in for a world of hurt.

"That's wonderful," he said, trying to strike the appropriate balance between grateful and relieved. Too much in either direction would only further arouse her suspicions. "I'll call you when it's done."

"One more thing," she said, catching him just before he hung up. "Since you are changing the terms of our agreement, I am changing the terms of your payment. Twenty-four hours will cost you ten percent."

He bit back a reflexive protest and silently cursed her. But there was nothing he could do. If he argued with her, she would only lower his payment more out of spite.

"Fair enough," he gritted out. She laughed and he gripped the phone hard to keep from throwing it across the room.

"I look forward to your call," she said, ending the conversation.

He forced himself to gently set the phone down, then gripped the edge of the table to stop his hands from shaking. He needed a drink, just a little something to take the edge off.

There was a half-empty bottle of whisky on the counter and he grabbed it, his fingers fumbling as he worked to unscrew the cap. It seemed to take forever, but he was finally able to get the bottle open. The pungent, eye-watering smell hit him and his muscles began to relax. He forced himself to wait a moment before taking a drink—he had self-control, after all. Then he took a healthy swig, not bothering with a glass. The burning liquid hit his stomach, sending tendrils of comforting warmth through his system.

He should have known better than to ask for a favor. Ten percent wasn't a huge amount of money, but he needed every cent he could get. He wasn't stupid—people didn't exactly leave babies just lying around, so he was only going to be able to pull this off once. It was only fair he receive the maximum financial compensation for his efforts.

For a moment, he considered calling her back and arguing the point. But there was no use. She'd say something about 90 percent being better than 0 percent, and then she'd dock his pay even more. He was better off figuring out how to get the baby—perhaps if he was able to deliver her at the original agreed-upon time, he'd still get the full payment. No sense in making him pay for extra time he hadn't used.

The alcohol was beginning to work its magic, clearing some of the cobwebs from his brain so he could think. If he was going to take the baby, he'd have to find a way to take Ridge Colton out of the picture. The man had obviously grown attached to the little one, and he wasn't going to let her go without a fight. A frontal assault on the cabin hadn't been successful, so he was going to have to come up with a different approach…

Most important, though, he had to make sure the baby didn't get hurt. He wouldn't get paid if he delivered damaged merchandise. That meant no guns. He couldn't take a chance on a bullet missing Ridge and hitting her. The idea of a knife was appealing, but ultimately unpractical. Knives were a personal weapon—you had to get close to your victim to use them. He would prefer to keep Ridge at a distance. The man was strong, and he'd made the mistake of underestimating his fighting skills before.

What he needed was the element of surprise. But now that Ridge knew he was after the baby, it would be a lot harder for him to catch them unawares. Still, there had to be a way…

He tilted the bottle up for another sip, surprised to find it was almost empty. When had that happened? No matter. There was another one lying around here somewhere. One more drink, and then he'd head out again.

And this time, he wasn't coming back without the baby.

Chapter 10

"You do know it's not her, right?" Sam said.

Ridge nodded, forgetting Sam was on the other end of the phone and couldn't see him.

"It's not possible," his brother continued, impatience creeping into his voice at what he thought was Ridge's denial. "I know you miss Josie—we all do. But there is no way she's running around in the woods on her own."

"I know." Ridge was beginning to regret having brought it up.

"Maybe you're just sleep deprived from taking care of the baby. It's got you seeing things."

"That's not it," Ridge said, unable to keep the

annoyance out of his tone. Bad enough he'd been second-guessing himself ever since they made it back to the cabin. The last thing he needed was for his brother to think he was going crazy, too.

"Well, whoever she was, she's probably long gone by now."

"Sure, but don't you think it's suspicious she was there in the first place?"

"How so?" Sam fired back. "People go hiking in the woods all the time. You know that better than anyone."

"Fair enough. But I don't run away when I encounter someone on the trail. That's just strange."

Sam snorted. "Have you seen yourself? You're bigger and stronger than most people. You don't know what it's like to be on the receiving end of physical intimidation."

Ridge was forced to admit his brother was right. He was usually the biggest guy in a room, a fact he normally took for granted. It had never occurred to him to consider how his size made people feel when they first met him. Perhaps he was a little scary, especially to people who didn't know him.

"Maybe," he said grudgingly. "But I can't shake the feeling I know her somehow."

Sam sighed. "Look, I appreciate what you're saying. But the department is stretched pretty thin as it is. I can't very well ask my captain to divert manpower from the Alphabet Killer case in order to track down a young woman in the woods who gives my brother the willies."

"I know," Ridge said. "I just thought it was strange, in light of everything that's been going on around here lately."

"Tell you what," Sam said. "I'll type up a description and pass it around. If I hear anything, I'll let you know."

"Thanks," Ridge said, appreciating the gesture. "That's good of you."

"I'm a saint," Sam quipped.

"Any news on your end?"

"No. The post office was a bust. We've still got people sitting there watching, but she hasn't shown yet and isn't going to."

"You sound pretty confident about that," Ridge observed.

"Call it a solid hunch. In the meantime, Annabel and I are checking out local restaurants, looking for any waitresses or staff matching our suspect description."

"Good luck," Ridge said. "Let me know if there's anything I can do to help."

"Will do. Talk to you later."

Ridge hung up and paced in front of the couch, feeling useless. He should be out there with his siblings, lending a hand in the investigation. Even though he wasn't in law enforcement, there were still things he could do to help them search for the killer. Instead, he was stuck inside, practically sitting on his hands and doing nothing to contribute. It was enough to drive him nuts.

He glanced over at the crib and his impatience softened. It wasn't Sara's fault she'd wound up in his life. And it certainly wasn't her fault she required round-the-clock care. Furthermore, he couldn't very well be frustrated over his circumstances—he had volunteered for the job. Although truth be told, he hadn't realized just how much work babies actually were. While he didn't regret taking her home, he did wish there was a way to balance taking care of her needs with helping his siblings.

Maybe there was, he mused. He might be sitting at home, but that didn't mean he couldn't use his brain. He dug his phone out of his pocket and dialed Trevor.

"What's up?"

"Give me something I can do to help the investigation," Ridge said, forgoing the usual conversational niceties.

"Hello to you, too," his brother joked.

"Come on, man. I'm dying here."

"Okay." Trevor was quiet for a moment, thinking. "I've got something. But it's not going to be fun," he warned.

At this point, Ridge didn't care if he was alphabetizing a spice rack—he just needed to do something productive. "Don't care," he said. "I want to help."

"We've still got stacks of letters here that need to be examined."

"What kind of letters?" he asked, but he already knew the answer.

"Matthew's fan mail," Trevor confirmed, his tone making it clear he found the existence of said correspondence just as distasteful as Ridge did. "Someone needs to comb through the mail and check for any connections to our killer."

It was a job that sounded equal parts boring and disturbing. But it could be done anywhere, which meant Ridge could work from the cabin while taking care of Sara. "I'll do it," he said, his enthusiasm somewhat dimmed at the prospect of reading his father's messages. "Can you drop them off at my place today?"

"Sure thing," Trevor said. "Thanks for taking it on—it'll be a huge help."

That made Ridge feel a little bit better about the situation. "Glad I can be of service."

"Will you be there in a few hours? I can gather everything up and drop it by on my way home."

"Sounds good. See you then."

He hung up to find Penny watching him, her dark brown eyes patient. A pang of guilt speared him as he realized he hadn't been able to spend as much quality time with her as he usually did.

She hadn't complained, but he could tell she was feeling a little neglected.

"Who's a good girl?" he asked. She lifted her head and cocked an ear forward, and a steady thump sounded as her tail hit the floorboards. "Want a treat?" He took a step in the direction of the kitchen and a brown streak shot past his legs as she darted into the room ahead of him.

He found her sitting at the pantry door, excitement making her body quiver slightly while she waited for him to catch up. "Scooch over," he told her, needing her to move so he could open the door. She complied, letting out a little whine of impatience at his slow pace. "I know," he said. "I'm getting it."

Just as he reached inside the pantry, a soft cry came from the living room. Sara was waking up, which meant he should get another bottle ready while he was in the kitchen. He tossed Penny a biscuit and she gobbled it up so fast an outside observer might think she was starving. She looked up at him, licking her mouth, hope burning bright in her eyes. "You know the rules," he told her.

Sara cried out again as he pulled a bottle from the pantry shelf, but there was something different about this sound. There was a note in her voice he'd never heard before, and it made goose bumps pop out on his arms. Forgetting the bottle, he rushed back into the living room.

The baby let out a wail as he reached the crib. But unlike her normal cries, which grew in intensity the longer he made her wait, this cry seemed to grow weaker, as if Sara was too tired to carry on. He reached down to gather her up, and the moment he touched her skin he realized the problem.

She was burning up.

His heart pounded hard against his breastbone as he frantically unwrapped the blanket, trying to cool her off. How high was her fever? He didn't have a thermometer he could use on her, wouldn't even know how to take her temperature if he had. More importantly though, how long had she been this way?

She'd felt normal to him on their hike, so she must have developed the fever sometime after that. Had he done something to put her at risk? His stomach dropped at the thought this was somehow his fault. He'd never forgive himself if he had exposed her to some sinister germ.

He managed to get the blanket off her, but she still felt dangerously warm. Claws of panic raked the inside of his chest as he considered what to do next. Could he give her medication to bring her temperature down? He dismissed the option almost immediately. He had no idea what drug or dose was appropriate for an infant, and he wasn't going to put her at further risk of harm.

A bath then. Maybe a cool bath would help. He

carried her into the kitchen and plugged the sink, then started the water to fill up the basin. Sara continued to fuss, flailing her arms and legs in a weak protest that broke his heart. "Hold on, little one," he said. "I'll make it better."

He prayed he was right.

Darcy came awake with a start, the transition out of sleep so sudden it took her mind a moment to catch up to her body. *What—*

Her phone rang again, the shrill electronic noise piercing the silence of her room. She reached for it automatically and blinked at the display.

Ridge.

The argument with her parents came flooding back, stirring up her emotions again. She still needed to apologize to him, and now that she'd had some sleep, she might be able to think straight and figure out exactly what to say. Taking a deep breath, she took the call.

"Hello?"

"The baby has a fever."

"What?" His words were so unexpected it took her a second to fully register what he was saying.

"The baby has a fever," he repeated, his worry clear in his voice.

Darcy switched to doctor mode immediately. "How high is it?"

"I'm not sure," he said. "The only thermometer

I have is the one I use for Penny. Should I wash it and try to use it on the baby?"

"No," she replied, making a face. She knew of only one way to take a dog's temperature, and no amount of washing would render that thermometer clean enough to use on an infant. She'd just have to take his word for it that the baby had a fever.

"How long has she been like this?" she asked, climbing out of bed and stepping into a fresh pair of scrub pants. It was clear Ridge was worried, and since he was normally so unflappable, hearing him like this told her just how serious the situation was.

"I don't know," he replied, a note of despair creeping into his voice. "I fed her and put her down for a nap after we took a walk in the woods. When she woke up a couple of hours later, she was like this."

"Okay," Darcy said, trying to sound soothing. "If she's as hot as you say, you'll want to take her blankets off."

"I've done that already. I also gave her a bath. Nothing seems to help."

"Does she have any other symptoms? Diaper issues? Vomiting?"

"No. That's good, right?" She heard the glimmer of hope in his question and rushed to reassure him.

"Yes, that's a good sign. I'm on my way," she

said, scooping up her wallet and keys before she walked out of her bedroom.

"Please hurry," Ridge said. "This can't be good for her."

"Just hang in there." She descended the stairs in record time, grateful her parents were nowhere to be found as she walked out of the house. The last thing she needed was to get delayed by one of them. If they found out she was going back to Ridge's cabin, they'd likely bar the doors and try to chain her to her bed.

A dull, throbbing ache in her temples plagued her as she drove, a souvenir from her earlier tears. How was she going to untangle this mess? And more importantly, was it even worth it? What if it was better to leave things as they were, broken but buried in the past?

The question stayed with her as she drove, but she still didn't have an answer by the time she pulled up next to his cabin. The front door flew open and Ridge quickly descended the steps with the baby in his arms. His expression was a combination of panic and relief, and Darcy felt her heart soften even further toward him. It was clear he cared deeply about the little one, and she briefly wondered how he was going to cope once her mother turned up.

"She's not feeling any cooler," he said, his

brows drawn together in a frown as he thrust the baby into her arms. “I don’t know what else to do.”

“Let me take a look at her,” Darcy said, employing the calm, measured tones she used in the emergency room. The baby did feel warm against her, but she needed to examine her before deciding what to do.

She walked back into the cabin, Ridge hovering over the pair of them like a solicitous fly. Darcy had never seen him so distraught before, and she wondered if his emotions were solely due to the baby’s condition, or if something else was bothering him.

It took only a few moments for her to complete a basic exam. The baby’s temperature was high, but not dangerously so. Not yet, anyway. Given her general lack of other symptoms, Darcy figured she was fighting off some kind of virus.

“I think we should take her to the hospital,” she said, pulling out the earpieces of her stethoscope as she straightened up.

All the color drained from Ridge’s face and he put a hand out, grabbing hold of the back of the couch to steady himself. “She’s that bad?” he asked hoarsely.

“No,” Darcy replied, wondering whether she was about to have two patients on her hands. If Ridge fainted on her, she wasn’t going to be able to catch him before he went down. “No, she seems to be okay, aside from the temperature. But it can be dangerous for babies this young to have a fever. I want to bring her in so I can give her the best treatment, and to make sure if something goes wrong she's got immediate access to care."

"That sounds good." Ridge nodded, the movement jerky. Some of the color returned to his cheeks. "You scared me for a minute."

"I could tell." Darcy studied him. "Are you okay to drive?"

"Yes." He sounded more confident now, as if he was back to normal.

"Let's head out then. I'll follow you in my car."

He frowned, his expression indicating he wasn't a fan of that plan. "I can assure you she'll be fine until we get there," Darcy said, assuming he was worried about the baby being in the car.

"It's not that," he said. "I'm just wondering if we can use this to our advantage."

"What on earth are you talking about?" Darcy shook her head, flabbergasted at the thought of an infant's illness being a good thing.

"The intruder," Ridge said flatly. "I'd be shocked if he wasn't still out there, watching and waiting for another chance to strike. I haven't been able to go after him because I had the baby, but if you're going to admit her to the hospital…" He trailed off, and Darcy immediately understood what he was thinking.

"You want to trick him," she finished. "Make him think you've brought the baby home to draw him out again."

"Exactly." Ridge rewarded her with a fleeting smile that made her stomach quiver. "Think we can do it?"

"It's worth a shot."

Ridge placed the baby in the carrier and gestured for Penny to accompany them. They walked down the steps of the porch and Darcy helped him get the baby into his truck.

"I'm sure she's fine," she said loudly, hoping if the stranger was indeed around, he could hear her. "It should only take an hour, and then you can bring her back home."

Ridge shot her an amused glance. "Very natural," he whispered. "I can tell you do a lot of undercover work."

Darcy felt her face heat. "I never claimed to be an actress," she whispered back hotly.

He winked at her and a zing of awareness shot down her spine. "Ready?" he asked.

She nodded, not trusting her voice. There were so many things she wanted to say to him right now, but it wasn't the time. Besides, she needed to put some distance between them before she brought up the subject of her parents. Any time she got near him, her body perked up and started overruling her mind. While it made for some nice sensations,

Darcy needed a clear head for their upcoming conversation.

If she could just figure out what to say! She spent the drive back to Granite Gulch arguing with herself over the best way to bring up the subject. Should she ease into it, or just come right out with it? Things would be less awkward if she could find a way to subtly work their breakup into a conversation, but the thought of the verbal gymnastics required for that approach exhausted her. Better to say it outright then. It would likely be a shock to him, but at least she wouldn't have to dance around the topic, waiting for the right opening.

But should she also confess her feelings for him? That was a stickier subject. It was one thing to apologize for the way things had ended between them. It was quite another for her to reveal that her feelings for him had never really gone away. She imagined telling him she still loved him, but try as she might, she couldn't picture his response. Would he be happy and confess his own feelings in return? Or would he turn away, rejecting her like she had once rejected him?

Darcy parked next to Ridge and helped him get the baby out of the car. She glanced up at him as they walked toward the hospital entrance. He moved quickly but calmly, and his earlier panic seemed to have faded into a controlled worry. Penny trotted next to him, her devotion plain to see.

Why don't my parents understand? Darcy wondered as they entered the ER. A blind man could see how much love Ridge Colton carried inside him. From his dog to this little foster baby, Ridge didn't hesitate to step up and take care of the less fortunate. It was one of his best qualities and Darcy ached to be on the receiving end of his care again.

It didn't take long to get a room for the baby, and Darcy ordered the standard set of tests to rule out more serious conditions. Shortly after a dose of medication, the fever broke and the little one settled down again. Ridge shot Darcy a grateful glance, his relief obvious. "Thank you," he said, packing a lot of gratitude into those two little words. "It's a real load off my mind to see her feeling better."

"Something bothering you?" she asked. She felt a small spurt of satisfaction at the fact that her earlier supposition had been correct. It seemed she could still read Ridge after all. "Besides the baby's illness, I mean."

He lifted one shoulder in a shrug. "I thought I saw my sister today, but it's not possible. It just threw me for a loop."

Since he saw Annabel on a regular basis, there was only one sister he could mean. "Josie?"

He nodded. "I took the baby for a walk in the woods, and came across a woman who looked like

Josie. But when I called out her name, she ran away."

"I'm sorry." She placed her hand on his shoulder and squeezed gently. Ridge had always been close to his youngest sister—he'd visited her regularly in her foster home, and Darcy knew he had tried to adopt her when he'd reached the legal age. She still remembered the day he'd set out to ask Josie, brimming with an excitement that was almost palpable. Hours later he'd returned, a changed man. He never did tell Darcy what Josie had said to him, but her rejection of his offer had hurt him deeply and taken some of the sparkle out of his eyes.

And then a few weeks later, Darcy had dumped him…

She shook her head, fighting off a new wave of guilt. The past was the past—she couldn't change it. The only thing to do now was move on.

"Are you okay?" Darcy came back to the conversation to find Ridge was staring at her, his expression concerned.

This was her chance to tell him how she felt—she couldn't ask for a better moment. Her heart started to pound, and a flock of butterflies took flight in her stomach. She took a deep breath. *Here I go...*

The baby stirred and let out a soft cry. Ridge's focus shifted immediately, and he laid his hand gently on her stomach. “She’s hungry,” he announced. He glanced up. “Can I feed her?”

“Of course,” Darcy said. There was no medical reason why the baby shouldn’t eat, and it would likely help her feel better.

Ridge pulled a bottle from his backpack, then scooped up the little one and sat, murmuring to her while she nursed. After a moment, he lifted his head and met Darcy’s gaze. “You never did answer my question. Are you all right?”

Darcy nodded, knowing the moment was gone. “I was just thinking about the intruder coming back. I’d hate for you to try to face him alone.” It was the truth—the man had already managed to hurt Ridge twice. What if he came back with a gun and shot Ridge when he discovered the baby wasn’t there? A shiver ran down her spine as she pictured Ridge lying on the floor of his cabin in a spreading pool of blood.

“It’ll be okay,” he said, but Darcy shook her head, cutting off his assurances.

“Why don’t you call your brother Sam? He can stay there with you.”

Ridge dismissed the idea. “No. If the stranger sees Sam’s truck there, he won’t try anything. It has to look like I’m there alone with the baby. Besides,” he added, almost as an afterthought. “Sam and the rest of the force are busy chasing down leads in the Alphabet Killer case. I’m not going to pull someone off that investigation when there's no guarantee the man will even come back."

He was right, but it didn't make her feel any better. "I don't like it." Ridge's plan had seemed like a good idea at first, but now when she really thought about everything that could go wrong she wanted him to stay far away from the stranger.

"What if he has a gun?" Surely Ridge could see he was putting himself in real danger. The intruder was unpredictable and Ridge's cabin was on the outskirts of town, too far away from help in an emergency.

"I think if he had a gun he would have brought it by now," Ridge replied, sounding too casual about the possibility for her liking.

"But—"

"Darcy," Ridge said, cutting her off. "I know you're worried. And I appreciate it. But this has to end. I can't stand living under the threat that some stranger is going to break into my home. I'm tired of looking over my shoulder." He glanced down at the baby, who was almost done nursing. "I promised I'd keep her safe," he said, his voice softening as he watched her. "It's time for me to keep my word."

"And what's going to happen to her if you get hurt? Who will take care of her then?"

Ridge looked up, wearing an expression of equal parts sadness and acceptance. "She can't stay with me forever. I had hoped to keep her out of the system for as long as possible, but the state will eventually take her from me. Unless by some miracle we find her mother first."

"Do you think we can?" Darcy asked softly. "The police seem pretty focused on the killer, and they don't have any leads on her mom. I got the impression their investigation was stalled."

"It is," he confirmed. "But I'm hopeful the intruder can help in that respect. He has to be connected to the mother—I just need to find out how." He placed the empty bottle on the hospital bed and carefully moved the baby to his shoulder, then started in with a rhythmic pat on her back.

"If it makes you feel any better, I wish there was some other way," he said. "I'm not crazy about taking this guy on again, but someone has to."

"I know," Darcy admitted, resigned to the fact that Ridge was right. The man did need to be stopped, and given Ridge's overdeveloped sense of responsibility, he saw it as his duty to take care of the situation.

She wanted to be mad at him for taking such risks, but it was hard to muster up anger when she knew he wasn't doing it for the adrenaline rush. No, he was stepping up because he thought it was the right thing to do.

And unfortunately, he was right.

The baby stiffened against Ridge, then let out a

soft belch. Her body went limp against him as she sank back into slumber, and he gradually stopped patting her back. Moving carefully, he placed the little one in the hospital crib and tucked a blanket around her.

"Will you stay with her until I get back?" he asked, his voice pitched low so as not to disturb her sleep. "I don't want her left alone, especially sincc this is a strange place for her."

"Of course," Darcy said. She wasn't working today, so it would be no trouble to remain with the baby until Ridge got back. *And he will return*, she told herself firmly, pushing down the fear that made her insides quiver.

He nodded, then motioned for Penny to stand. They headed for the door and Darcy followed, reluctant to part with him.

"Ridge," she said softly.

He stopped and turned, one brow lifted in a silent question.

"Please be careful." Before she could overthink it, she rose to her tiptoes and pressed a kiss to his lips.

He blinked down at her, apparently shocked by the gesture. She held her breath, waiting to gauge his reaction. Would he welcome her kiss? Or had she made a mistake and offended him?

After what seemed like an eternity, he smiled and his dark brown gaze warmed. "I'll be back soon," he promised, running his hand down her arm in a gentle caress that sent zings of sensation through her limbs.

Darcy nodded, and he turned and walked out the door. "You'd better," she said softly as she watched him walk down the hall. "I already lost ten years. I don't want to waste any more time."

Chapter 11

Ridge drove back to the cabin on autopilot, his mind still on Darcy and the kiss she'd given him as he'd walked out the door. Did it mean anything? Or was it simply an automatic gesture with no special significance?

More importantly, which option did he prefer?

He liked the idea that she still had feelings for him. It made him feel less pathetic about pining over her since their breakup. But the more he thought about it, he was forced to admit it would be better if the kiss had no meaning. After all, it wasn't like they had a future together. Darcy was only in town temporarily—she'd be leaving for her new job before long, and he wasn't interested in a short-term fling. He'd prefer to remain alone rather than have her walk away from him again. It had been bad enough the first time—his heart couldn't take another hit like that.

He turned down the long gravel road that led to his cabin, the truck rattling as he drove over new potholes the storm had left behind. The rough ride helped him shift focus from Darcy and his unanswered questions to the stranger who was hopefully still watching the cabin.

Ridge didn't relish the thought of confronting the man, but he would rather risk getting hurt than spend another minute waiting for the stranger to make his move. It had been a long time since Ridge had lived at the mercy of another person's whims, and he didn't enjoy the feeling. It had to end, today.

He pulled up next to the house and cut the engine. Penny jumped out when he opened the door, and he walked around the hood of the truck to the passenger side.

"Let's get you inside, little one," he said, making a show of adjusting the blankets in the baby carrier. Darcy had rolled up a spare sheet to approximate a body, and he'd put her blanket on top to complete the deception. It wouldn't fool anyone up close, but from a distance it made a convincing baby.

He climbed the porch steps with his keys in his

free hand, and paused for only a moment when he noticed the faint scratches on the lock. “So that’s your strategy,” he murmured to himself. Apparently the intruder had grown tired of the direct approach and had opted to break into his cabin while he was gone. But where was he now? Just inside the door, ready to pounce the moment Ridge walked in? Or hiding in a closet, waiting for the opportune moment to sneak out and strike?

Adrenaline flooded Ridge’s system and his muscles tensed in anticipation. He gestured for Penny to stay put on the porch—she’d already been hit once by this man, and he didn’t want to risk her getting hurt a second time. She gave him a quizzical look but plopped down on the worn wooden boards as instructed. Good. One less thing for him to worry about.

He took a deep breath, willing his heartbeat to slow down. Then he pushed open the door, waiting on the threshold for a second to dodge any immediate blows from the intruder. But none came.

Moving cautiously, Ridge pushed the car seat through the door first, hoping to use it to keep some distance between himself and any attack. He glanced around as he walked farther into the house, but nothing seemed out of place. Even so, Ridge could sense the stranger in his home. The air was thick with anticipation, as if the very walls were watching him with bated breath. It was a troubling sensation that kindled a spark of anger in Ridge's chest. This home was his safe place, his sanctuary. But knowing a stranger lurked within ruined the comfort he normally found here.

Just act naturally, he told himself. But that was easier said than done. He moved into the den and placed the baby carrier on the recliner in the corner. "Time for a bottle," he announced, then turned and walked into the kitchen, his senses hyperattuned to every bump and creak in the house. He was providing the intruder the perfect opportunity to make his move. Would he take advantage of it?

It didn't take long for Ridge to get his answer. After a moment, Ridge heard the telltale creak of the floorboards as the stranger moved into the room. He stayed in the kitchen, pretending to be busy so he could draw the man farther into the den.

The intruder grew increasingly bold, his steps sounding louder as he abandoned efforts to conceal his presence. He was either overly confident of his abilities to evade detection, or the excitement of seeing the unguarded baby carrier was making him careless.

Ridge grabbed the frying pan and entered the den, moving lightly so as not to make a sound. He stepped over the creaky board just in front of the kitchen and slowly crept forward, following in the stranger's footsteps as he approached the baby carrier. Hopefully the man would be fooled a little bit longer…

The intruder suddenly stopped short a few feet away from the chair. Ridge could practically feel the man's confusion, which morphed quickly into disbelief and then anger as he recognized the deception.

"Looking for something?" Ridge said, taking a swing with the frying pan. He landed a solid blow on the man's shoulder, knocking him to the ground. The stranger grunted and rolled over, trying to stand. Ridge dropped the pan and tackled him, pinning him to the floor before he could gain his feet.

The intruder went limp underneath him, apparently sensing he was beaten. Ridge kept one hand pressed to the man's shoulder and reached up with the other to grab a fistful of the guy's ski mask. It came free with one quick tug, exposing the mystery man's face.

"Dennis Hubbard?" Of all the men in town, he was the last one Ridge had expected to see. "What the hell?"

Dennis glared up at him, his features twisted with rage. "Let me go!" he yelled, the words flying out in a cloud of alcoholic fumes so pungent it made Ridge's eyes water.

"I don't think so," Ridge replied, tightening his grip. "Why are you here?" Dennis was a well-known figure in town. After losing his wife to cancer a few years ago Dennis had turned to drink, hitting the bottle hard in an attempt to handle his grief. His habit had earned him frequent flyer status at the local jail, where he regularly slept off the effects of overindulgence. Most people felt sorry for him, but didn't see him as anything more than a nuisance to be avoided. He'd certainly never seemed capable of violence before. And what on earth could he want with a baby?

"You know what I'm after," Dennis grunted, his jaw tight.

"But what I don't know is why," Ridge countered. "And that's what most interests me at the moment."

Dennis remained stubbornly silent, his eyes shooting daggers up at Ridge. After a moment of this impromptu staring contest, Ridge let out a sigh. It was clear Dennis wasn't going to tell him anything and he didn't care to stay sprawled on the floor, pinning him down.

He leaned back, still keeping some weight on Dennis to discourage any movement on his part. Then he fished his phone out of his pocket and dialed Sam—his brother should have been here by now.

The next thing he knew, Ridge hit the ground hard. He reacted instantly, his body scrambling to avoid further injury while his brain worked to process exactly what had happened.

He saw the frying pan on the floor nearby and stretched to grab the handle, brushing it with his fingertips. But Dennis was faster. He snatched it away and squared off to face Ridge, a cruel smile on his face.

Dennis swung just as Ridge gained his feet, the heavy metal pan making contact with his right knee. The joint exploded in pain and Ridge cried out, unable to remain quiet in the face of such agony. His leg gave out and he sank back to the floor, gritting his teeth to stop another groan from escaping.

"Where's the baby?" Dennis advanced on him, still holding the pan. Ridge pushed himself across the floor out of striking distance until his back hit the recliner. Keeping his gaze on Dennis, he managed to scoot himself up to a standing position.

"She's someplace safe," he said, taking a small measure of satisfaction at the frustration flaring in Dennis's eyes.

"Where is she?" he asked again, raising the pan threateningly.

Ridge shook his head. "Go ahead," he taunted. "Beat me all you want with that. But I'm not going to tell you. She's safe from you and that's all that matters."

Dennis made an inarticulate sound of rage and

took a step forward, clearly intending to pound Ridge into a bloody pulp. Ridge straightened, ignoring the fiery spikes of pain emanating from his knee. Moving quickly, he took out his pocketknife and flicked open the blade. It wasn't a very long blade but it was sharp and it would do some damage. Ridge had hoped to avoid using it, but he wasn't going to let Dennis take him down without a fight. A bitter, metallic taste flooded his mouth and he swallowed hard, trying to clear away the distraction as he prepared to defend himself.

Dennis paused when he saw the flash of metal in Ridge's hand, indecision flickering across his face. Sensing his advantage, Ridge pressed forward. "I don't want to hurt you," he said, making sure Dennis got a good look at the shiny, sharp blade he held. "But if you don't leave right now, I will be forced to defend myself." His stomach twisted at the thought of drawing blood with the knife, but he pushed aside the instinctive revulsion. If using the blade was the only way to keep Dennis from beating him, then that's what he'd do.

To his surprise, Dennis lowered the pan. "You don't understand," he said, desperation entering his voice. "I need that baby."

Ridge frowned, not trusting this sudden change in demeanor. "Why?" he asked shortly.

"I'm not going to hurt her," Dennis said, dodging the question. "Just tell me where she is." He sounded pleading, and there was something else in his tone—a note of fear.

It dawned on Ridge that Dennis didn't want the baby for himself. It sounded as if he was on a mission to deliver her to someone else. But who would hire him to do such a thing? And why?

He opened his mouth to ask that very question but before he could get the words out, his front door flew open and Trevor barreled inside, Penny close on his heels. His brother skidded to a stop and straightened, then walked over to stand next to him.

"The door was unlocked," Ridge said mildly. "No need to break it down like that."

"I like to make an entrance," Trevor replied, his eyes never leaving Dennis. "Who's your friend?"

Dennis inched closer to the door, clearly planning on making his escape. "Stop right there!" Ridge yelled.

It was no use. Dennis dropped the pan and ran, moving surprisingly fast for a man his size and age. Ridge lunged forward, intent on chasing after him. But his injured knee couldn't support his weight and he fell, hitting the wood floorboards with a bone-jarring crash.

"Ridge!" Trevor was by his side in an instant, a look of horrified concern on his face.

"Don't worry about me," Ridge told him, ignoring the throbbing pain in his knee. "Go after Dennis!"

Trevor glanced at the door then back at him, clearly torn about what to do. "Go!" Ridge urged. This might be their only chance to get some answers. Now that Dennis knew they were after him he was likely to skip town, leaving them no closer to solving the mystery of Sara's origins.

After a few seconds of indecision, Trevor shook his head. "No. You're hurt. I'm not going to leave you like this."

"I'm fine," Ridge said, trying to hide a grimace as he shifted on the floor. "Just go!"

Trevor took a step toward the door, but stopped when Penny let out a whine. He turned back and lifted one brow when he saw the dog nose Ridge in concern. Ridge scratched her ear and told her to go lie down in her bed, but she refused to leave his side.

"That settles it," Trevor said. "If the dog won't leave you, I'm not going to."

Ridge let out a groan of frustration. "It's too late now," he said, shaking his head. "Dennis is probably long gone." He let out a string of curses and slapped the floor so hard it made the dog jump.

Trevor held his hand out and Ridge gripped it hard, using it as leverage to pull himself up. "Care to tell me what happened here?" Trevor asked.

Ridge hobbled over to the couch and sank down

with a sigh. Then he filled his brother in, telling him about the attacks and the near abductions of the baby.

"I still can't figure out what he wants with her," Ridge finished.

Trevor pressed a knuckle to his lips. "You said he sounded afraid?"

Ridge nodded. "A little."

"Do you think he's the baby's father?"

"I hope not," Ridge said, shuddering a little at the thought. Dennis would be a terrible father in his current alcoholic state. And Ridge couldn't imagine any woman getting involved with the man, especially given his recent troubles with the law. But stranger things had happened...

"What's he got to fear, though?" Ridge asked. "That's the part that doesn't make sense."

"He might be trying to sell the baby," Trevor mused.

"What?" Ridge shook his head, certain he had misunderstood. "Sell her?"

Trevor nodded, his expression sober. "Human trafficking is a huge black market, and babies fetch some of the highest prices."

Ridge's stomach cramped as a wave of nausea hit him, threatening to drag him under. "That's horrible. How do you know that?"

His brother pressed his lips together in a pale line. "Don't ask," he said tightly.

"My God," Ridge said softly. "Does that really happen here in Granite Gulch?"

Trevor lifted one shoulder. "It happens everywhere."

"I've got to call Darcy." He had to warn her that Dennis was still at large. He might head to the hospital for a last-ditch attempt at taking Sara. Maybe he could get Sam to post a guard on the room until they managed to arrest the man.

"Darcy?" Trevor asked. "Is this the same Darcy you dated?"

Ridge nodded. "She's a doctor now, and she's looking after the baby at the hospital."

"Is everything okay?"

"The baby spiked a fever today. We brought her in just to be safe." Ridge glanced around, searching for his phone. Trevor followed his gaze and bent down, then handed him the phone.

"Thanks," Ridge said.

"Don't mention it," Trevor replied. "But I wouldn't worry about calling her. If she's at the hospital, you'll see her soon enough."

"What are you talking about?"

Trevor gestured to his knee. "You need to get checked out."

"I'm fine," Ridge said dismissively, but his brother shook his head.

"A knee injury is nothing to mess around with. If it doesn't heal properly, you'll never be able to walk without pain." He glanced at Penny, then back at Ridge. "I'm going to assume, given the nature of your work, that you need to be able to move around easily?" His tone was all innocence, but Ridge wasn't fooled.

He glared up at his brother, hating that he was right. "Fine. You win."

Trevor nodded. "A wise decision," he said sagely.

"Do you always have to act like a big brother?" Ridge grumbled.

A wide grin split Trevor's face. "I am what I am."

"What are you doing here, anyway? That was some pretty good timing on your part."

"The letters, remember? I was stopping by to drop them off."

Oh, yeah. Ridge had forgotten about that project in all the excitement. Truth be told, he was even less enthused about it now. He wasn't going to be able to focus on anything other than keeping Sara safe, at least until Dennis Hubbard was behind bars.

Trevor seemed to sense his change of heart. "I can ask someone else to do it," he offered. "You look a little distracted."

Ridge shot his brother a grateful glance. "Thanks," he said. "I just need to make sure the baby is taken care of. Once I know she'll be safe from Dennis, I can turn my attention to the letters."

"Understood," Trevor said. "Now, let's get you loaded into my truck. I've got a lot of updates for you."

"It sounds like things are moving along," Ridge commented, trying to ignore the pain in his knee as Trevor managed to run over every pothole in the road. He clenched his jaw, determined not to say anything, and made a mental note to write a letter to the mayor. Who knew the city's infrastructure was in such dire need of repairs?

"We got lucky," Trevor replied. "Annabel's theory regarding local restaurants was solid."

"And you got a hit?"

"The Blackthorn Diner in Rosewood," Trevor confirmed.

"Sounds like the kind of place that has a lot of employee turnover."

"It is," Trevor said. "But fortunately, the manager recognized our suspect description and gave us a few names. We were able to eliminate some of the women right away, but you want to know the best part?" Excitement crept into his voice and Ridge couldn't help but smile.

"I'm on pins and needles here."

"One of the waitresses is using a false identity. She's pretending to be Michelle Parker, a housewife who died over a year ago. We think the woman working in the diner is really Ida Wanto, the same one who rented a room at a boarding house in Rosewood."

"Wasn't that the site of one of the murders?" Ridge asked, trying to recall the exact details.

"It was," Trevor said. "The manager of the house confirmed our suspect description, and we watched the place for a while. But the woman never came back."

"What kind of a name is Ida Wanto?" Ridge mused.

"It's clearly a play on 'I don't want to,'" Trevor replied, slowing down for a speed bump.

Ridge scoffed. "Not very subtle."

"It's not," Trevor said. "But that tells us something about her."

"Oh?" Ridge had to admit he was fascinated by the way his brother could take a simple fact about a person and use it to paint a vivid picture of their personality. More than once, Trevor had cracked a case wide open by focusing on a clue other investigators had overlooked.

"She didn't put a lot of time or effort into coming up with a false name. That tells me she's impulsive. She probably has self-control problems, which suggests she may also have some addictions. Alcohol or smoking or maybe even something heavier. That also means she likely doesn't spend a lot of time scouting out victims—she picks people she comes across, but doesn't go out hunting like most serial killers."

"She probably has the most encounters with people while she's at work. Do you know if all the victims ate at the diner?" Ridge asked.

Trevor let out a small sigh. "Unfortunately, no. The manager looked through the receipts, and it turns out the second, fourth and fifth victims did eat there and paid with a credit card. But there doesn't seem to be a connection between the diner and the other victims."

"Maybe they paid in cash," Ridge suggested.

"It's possible. But I've been doing a little digging into victim number six, Francine Gibbons. She doesn't strike me as the type of woman to eat at the Blackthorn Diner."

"That's true," Ridge said. Trevor's assessment certainly fit what Darcy had said earlier regarding Francine's habits. That meant the killer must have come across her in another context. But where?

"I need to find out if Francine frequented the bar in Granite Gulch," Trevor said, as if he was adding the task to a mental checklist of things to do.

"Wasn't one of the victims found in the parking lot?" Ridge said.

Trevor nodded. "Victim number five, Erica Morgan. Witnesses said she'd gotten into an argument with a woman matching our suspect description prior to her murder."

"We can ask Darcy," Ridge said. "She knew Francine."

"Were they good friends?" Trevor sounded hopeful.

"I don't think so," Ridge said, hating to burst his brother's bubble. "But they did know each other and Darcy could probably give you an idea of the places Francine frequented on a regular basis. It might help you narrow down the locations shared by the other victims."

"That would be nice. I feel like we're chasing smoke here. We get close, but she somehow manages to slip through our fingers right before we can grab her."

"We'll get her," Ridge said firmly.

Trevor gave him a sidelong glance. "I wish I shared your confidence."

"She'll slip up. Maybe not today, but she will eventually make a mistake. And we'll be waiting to catch her."

"Yeah, well I just hope that happens before any more people get killed."

A terrible thought popped into Ridge's head. "So far, she's only killed one person for each letter of the alphabet, correct?"

"As far as we know, yes," Trevor said. "Why?"

"The baby's mom left a note signed with the

letter *F*. We know Francine was not the baby's mother, but since the woman still hasn't turned up yet, I thought maybe the killer had done something to her, as well."

Trevor frowned. "It's not likely the killer would change her pattern so suddenly. Serial killers generally stick with what works for them."

"But what if the baby's mother interrupted the killer or somehow got in her way? She might not have been the primary target, but if she saw something she shouldn't..." Ridge trailed off, letting his brother fill in the blanks. That was why their mother had died—she'd seen their father's bloody clothes and the red marker he'd used to mark each victim. She'd made the mistake of insisting Matthew turn himself in and he'd killed her for her efforts. Was it possible the Alphabet Killer, so eager to follow in Matthew Colton's footsteps, had done something similar?

"We haven't found any other bodies," Trevor pointed out, but his tone lacked conviction. They hadn't found their mother's body, either.

"I hope we don't," Ridge said. "But we've got no leads on the baby's mother. It's as if she doesn't exist."

"Chris hasn't been able to dig up anything with his PI connections?"

Ridge shook his head. "Like I said, the woman's a ghost."

Trevor whistled softly. "That's tough."

"It breaks my heart to think about putting that little baby in the foster care system," Ridge said, his stomach dropping as he imagined it. "It was bad enough when it happened to us, and we were older."

Trevor was quiet for a moment, likely lost in his own memories of that time. Finally, he cleared his throat. "If it's any consolation, she'll probably be adopted quickly," he said. "Everyone wants the babies."

It was true. As older kids in the foster care system, it was one of the first lessons he and his siblings had learned. People wanted to adopt babies because they viewed them as blank slates full of possibility, with no bad habits or emotional baggage requiring attention. No one wanted to take a chance on older kids—it was too messy, too much work to forge a relationship with children who had already erected protective walls around their hearts.

It hadn't taken long for Ridge to give up the hope of being adopted. Rather than brood over it, he'd focused on counting down the days until his eighteenth birthday when he'd be free of the system. But some of his younger siblings hadn't been so quick to adjust. Especially Josie. She'd been only three years old when Matthew had killed their mother, which meant she'd spent the longest amount of time in the system. Was it any wonder she'd changed? Fifteen years of rejection was bound to affect a person.

He could still remember every detail of their last visit. Ridge had picked Josie up from school and taken her out for a milk shake. Strawberry-vanilla for her, chocolate for him. He'd waited until they were both enjoying the frozen treats before asking the question that had been weighing on his mind.

"Will you let me become your guardian?"

Josie froze, the spoon halfway to her mouth. She stared at him as if she didn't understand the question, and he wondered if he should repeat it. He opened his mouth to do just that when she shoved the spoon back into her shake and pushed the glass away.

"No." The word was quiet but firm and it was the exact opposite of what Ridge had expected her to say.

"No?" he repeated. "What do you mean, no?"

She tilted her head to the side and pinned him with a haughty glare. "You're eighteen years old and you don't know what the word no *means?" She was baiting him, trying to start an argument about her attitude so he'd change the subject. It was a classic defensive move, one she'd employed time and again.*

He wasn't falling for it.

"I thought you wanted out of the system," he

said, forcing himself to take another sip of his shake. It tasted like chalk to him now, but he swallowed it, determined to pretend everything was normal. Disappointment was a crushing weight that made it hard to breathe, but he didn't want Josie to know.

She shrugged. "It's not that bad. The Carltons are nice people."

"But they're not your family." The words were out before he could stop them, and he immediately wished them back. Josie's gaze grew hard, making her look much older than her twelve years.

"They're the closest thing I have to parents," she said shortly. She pulled her glass back and attacked the shake with her spoon. "Why would I want to walk away from that?"

"I can take care of you," he tried, hoping a different approach might work. The waitress approached to check on them and he waved her away, keeping his focus on Josie. He had to make her see how important this was. Matthew Colton had torn their family apart—it was time for them to put the pieces back together.

"Really? How are you going to do that?" she challenged. "You're starting college in a few months. Where are we going to live—your dorm room?" She scoffed. "I don't think so."

Ridge took a deep breath. "I'm sharing a place with Christopher and Trevor. You'd live with us."

"That sounds great," she said sarcastically. "I've always wanted to share a bathroom with three guys."

"We'll make it work," he said, ignoring her snarkiness. "Will you please at least consider it?"

Josie shook her head. "I don't need to. My answer is no."

"Why?"

She blinked at him, as if she hadn't expected him to ask that question. "Because."

"That's not an answer," he pointed out.

Her expression shifted, became closed off. "It's the only one you're going to get," she replied.

Ridge waited for a moment, hoping the silence would drive her to elaborate. But it didn't. She was too stubborn for that.

She went back to eating her milk shake, acting as though she didn't have a care in the world. Ridge put his spoon down, unable to stomach another bite. This hadn't gone at all the way he'd planned.

He'd spent hours picturing this moment. Josie was supposed to be thrilled with his offer. She was supposed to jump at the chance to leave the foster care system and live with her brothers. Never in his wildest dreams had Ridge imagined her inflexible, knee-jerk refusal. Had she even considered the question before shooting him down?

"Your shake is melting," she pointed out, as if

she hadn't just wrecked his carefully crafted plans for putting the family back together.

"I'm not hungry anymore," he said dully.

She shrugged and pulled his glass across the table, digging in to the half-melted shake in a businesslike manner.

"What?" she asked, catching his stare. "It's bad luck to waste chocolate."

"Josie—" he began, but she cut him off.

"No. And don't ask me again."

He hadn't, and not long after, Josie had cut off all communication with him. He had tried to call, had written letters. Hell, he would have used smoke signals if it had meant getting through to her. But she'd never responded to any of his attempts to reach out.

And then one day she was gone.

"Ridge?" Something touched his leg and he jumped, driving a fresh spike of pain into his knee.

Trevor was watching him, his brows drawn together in concern. "Are you okay?"

"Yeah." Ridge shook the memories off. There was no sense in reliving the past—nothing was going to change. He glanced around, recognizing the parking lot of the hospital. "We're here."

"That's right," Trevor said, employing the kind of encouraging, helpful tone one used when potty training a small child. Ridge glared at him. "Is that really necessary?"

"Are you sure you're okay?" Trevor asked. "You checked out on me there for a while. Did you get hit in the head and not tell me?"

"No. I was just thinking."

"Hmm." Trevor pulled the keys out of the ignition and opened the door. "Try not to do that until we get inside. Don't want you to hurt yourself. You're too big for me to carry."

Ridge made a crude gesture in his brother's direction, but Trevor only laughed. "Come on," he said, rounding the hood and opening the passenger door. He offered the support of his arm, but Ridge ignored him. Each step was torture, but he'd be damned before he leaned on Trevor. His brother would never let him hear the end of it if he used him as a crutch.

Penny walked beside him, slowing her gait to match his labored strides. She would have been happier at home, but he didn't want to risk leaving her there alone. Dennis was still out there and was probably very angry at the way things had turned out. There was no telling what he'd do to get back at Ridge for ruining his plans—he had a reputation as a mean drunk.

Ridge stopped as a new thought struck him. What if the Alphabet Killer had nothing to do with Sara's mother? What if she had disappeared because she'd refused to give Dennis what he wanted, and he'd taken out his anger on her?

"Do you need a wheelchair?" Trevor's question broke into his thoughts and Ridge realized they were still in the parking lot.

"No. I'm good. Say, do you think Dennis Hubbard may have something to do with the disappearance of the baby's mother?"

Trevor tilted his head to the side, considering the question. "It's possible. You think he approached her for the baby first and when she didn't hand her over he lost his temper?"

"Something like that," Ridge said. "It makes sense. How else would he know where to look for the baby? The mother had to tell him where she'd stashed the little one." He had a sudden vision of a young woman, her eyes red-rimmed and her cheeks streaked with tears as she begged Dennis not to hurt her.

"And if Dennis went too far..." He let the suggestion trail off. "Well, it's no wonder she hasn't come back to claim her child."

Trevor nodded. "It's a solid theory," he said. "Now we just need to figure out where Dennis might have stashed her body, if he did in fact kill her."

Ridge shook his head. "I'll let you and your team work on that. I have no desire to learn more about him and his habits." Especially if Trevor's suggestion was correct—was Dennis really trying to sell Sara on the black market? If so, was this his first time, or was he an old pro at stealing children from vulnerable women and turning a profit on the misery of other people? The thought made his stomach heave, and he swallowed hard to clear the foul burn of bile from the back of his throat. Just how extensive was this shadow network?

He picked up his pace, ignoring the protests of his knee. The possibilities of human trafficking, the foster system and the death of Sara's mother swirled together in his head, creating a black storm of thoughts that made him anxious to see the baby. He needed to hold her, to feel her little body against his chest and know on a visceral level that she was truly okay. The world had turned into a very scary place, and he wanted to wrap her up tight and shield her from the evils of life for as long as he could.

He hadn't been able to protect Josie, and the knowledge that he had failed her haunted him to this day. He was determined not to make the same mistake again.

Chapter 12

Darcy thumped softly on the baby's back, swaying back and forth as she stood in the middle of the exam room.

"I know you've got a burp in there," she said quietly. "Give it up, little one."

The baby let out a sigh and started to squirm against Darcy's shoulder. Darcy kept patting, knowing if she didn't get the baby to burp after feeding she would spit up once Darcy laid her down. Having just tackled a soiled diaper, Darcy didn't fancy cleaning up another mess so soon.

There was a soft knock at the door and a nurse entered. "Test results," she said, passing them over.

Darcy scanned the information, relieved to see everything was normal. The baby was probably just fighting off a virus, and since her temperature was now under control, there wasn't much more to be done.

"Thank you," she said.

The nurse smiled back at her. "I'm glad everything looks good," she said.

"Me, too," Darcy replied.

The baby chose that moment to let out a belch, as if to add her two cents to the conversation. "Good job," Darcy said, surprised to find she was genuinely pleased. Since when had she gotten so excited over a baby burping? A week ago she probably wouldn't have cared all that much, but being around Ridge and this baby had changed her perspective on a lot of things.

The thought of Ridge made her heartbeat pick up. He'd been gone awhile, certainly long enough for him to make it home. Had the masked intruder taken the bait and tried to attack again? Had Ridge been able to get the information he needed out of the man? Most importantly, was Ridge okay?

The baby wriggled and let out a soft whimper, and Darcy realized she was squeezing her little body too tightly. She relaxed her grip and laid the baby back in the hospital crib, tucking a blanket over her to ward off the chill of the room. Then she started pacing, trying hard not to imagine Ridge unconscious on the floor of his cabin.

Or worse.

"He's fine," she told herself firmly. Ridge Colton was a large, strong man. The chances of someone overpowering him were very small.

But he was a little banged up from the earlier attacks, her nerves helpfully pointed out. What if the blow to his head or the jab to his ribs had hurt him more than he'd let on? It would be so like him to pretend he was fine when he was in pain. Had she been fooled by his act and missed the true extent of his injuries?

"Doctor of the year, that's me," she muttered, working to keep her fears from taking over. Ridge had trusted her to keep the baby safe, and she couldn't do that if she let her emotions rule. Besides, he was probably going to stroll through that door any minute now, flush with the triumph of his victory over the mystery intruder.

Yep. Any minute now.

She stared at the door, willing it to open. *Come on, Ridge*, she pleaded silently. *Where are you?*

The door offered no response, so she went back to pacing. *I could call him*, she thought. Then she shook her head, dismissing the idea almost as quickly as it had come. If Ridge was in the middle of an encounter with the intruder, she didn't want to distract him. But she could call Sam and fish for an update. After all, Ridge had only asked her to take care of the baby. He hadn't said anything about leaving his brother alone…

She dug her phone out of her purse and started to dial, but was distracted by the sound of raised voices outside.

"Sir, you can't bring a dog in here!"

Darcy rushed to the door and threw it open, just in time to see a tall, dark-haired man help Ridge onto a gurney. Penny sat at the foot of the bed, alert and watchful, totally oblivious to the protests of one of the nurses.

"It's okay, Linda," she called out. "Penny is a service dog."

The woman clamped her mouth shut and nodded, but didn't look happy about the presence of a dog in the ER. A few days ago Darcy would have felt the same way. But after seeing Penny work to protect Ridge and the baby, Darcy was willing to throw the dog a ticker tape parade if it would make her happy.

"What happened?" She took a step out of the room but then remembered the baby and stopped, feeling torn in both directions. She wanted nothing more than to rush over to Ridge and make sure he was okay, but she couldn't leave the baby alone. Things could change in an instant, and even though she'd only be a few feet away, she wasn't willing to risk it.

Ridge glanced up at her and gave her a wry smile. "The usual. How's she doing?"

"Better." Darcy held up a finger and retreated back into the room. She grabbed the edge of the hospital crib and pushed, rolling it out of the room and over to Ridge. Problem solved.

He glanced into the crib, the lines of pain around his eyes softening when he saw the sleeping baby. "Hi there, little one," he said quietly.

The baby stirred, turning toward him in unconscious acknowledgment of his voice. Darcy felt her heart swell. "She loves you," she told him softly.

He blinked hard at her words and the corners of his mouth curled up in a small, shy smile. "Feeling's mutual," he said gruffly.

The man next to him cleared his throat unobtrusively. She turned toward him, noting the strong resemblance between the two of them. This must be another one of Ridge's brothers.

"Darcy, right?" he said in a friendly tone.

She nodded. "That's me. And you are?" She offered her hand and his grip was warm and solid.

"Trevor Colton."

"The FBI profiler," she said, the pieces clicking into place.

"That's right." If he was surprised she knew his profession, he didn't show it.

"Nice to meet you." She'd known about Trevor's existence while she and Ridge were dating, but this was the first time she'd met him. The Colton siblings had been scattered across the foster system, which meant for all practical purposes, Ridge had been an only child.

Trevor opened his mouth to say more, but Darcy turned back to Ridge. It was rude of her, but she wanted to know what had happened at the cabin, and why Ridge had needed help walking in to the ER.

"Where are you hurt?" she asked him, effectively ending her conversation with Trevor.

"I'm fine." Ridge dodged the question, refusing to meet her eyes.

"I've never known you to need help walking before," she pointed out. Ridge kept his attention on the baby, his jaw set in a stubborn line.

Darcy appealed to Trevor with a look. "His knee," he said helpfully. "But I don't know if that's the only spot."

"Thank you," she said, turning back to Ridge. "Let me take a look. Please," she added, hoping if she acted as if he was doing her a favor he'd cooperate more readily.

He leaned back reluctantly, stretching out his leg with a grimace that told her just how much pain he was in.

"Can you take your pants off, or do I need to cut the fabric?"

Despite his discomfort, Ridge still managed to

flash her a heart-stopping grin. "I bet you say that to all the guys," he teased.

Darcy felt her face heat. If he only knew the truth! "Just you, honey," she said, trying to keep her tone light. Now was definitely not the time to share her feelings, especially while his brother stood there watching them, a speculative gleam in his eyes.

"I'll help you," Trevor offered. "It would be a shame to ruin a good pair of jeans. Besides," he added, a playful note entering his tone. "I have absolutely no desire to watch a woman take your pants off."

Darcy couldn't help but laugh as the tips of Ridge's ears turned red. "You don't have to vocalize every thought that pops into your head," he muttered. Trevor merely winked at Darcy, ignoring his brother's griping.

It took only a few minutes to get Ridge back on the bed. He had remained quiet through all the maneuverings, but his face was now the color of old milk and there was a fine sheen of sweat on his forehead. It was no wonder he was in such pain—his knee was a swollen, purple mess that was hot to the touch.

"This doesn't look good," she said grimly.

"You should see the other guy," Ridge replied.

"I'm serious, Ridge. You're going to need an orthopedic consult."

"Sounds like something that will take a while," Ridge said. "I don't have that kind of time. Can you just wrap it up and send me on my way with some ibuprofen or something?"

"Are you out of your mind?" Darcy said. "Look at your knee—this isn't the kind of injury you can just shake off. Besides, where do you need to go? What's so important that you can't take the time to heal properly?"

Ridge looked away again, which triggered alarm bells in her head. "You want to go after the intruder again, don't you?" He didn't reply, which only confirmed her suspicion.

Darcy stared at his knee, feeling her temper build like a summer storm. "You always were a little reckless," she said, her throat tight with the need to scream. "But I never thought you were stupid. I guess I was wrong."

Ridge jerked his head up, a spark of temper in his eyes. "What the hell is that supposed to mean?"

"You heard me," she said evenly, crossing her arms.

Apparently, the baby sensed the growing tension in the room. She let out a squeak of distress, but neither Ridge nor Darcy softened.

"I think we'll just step outside," Trevor said. He took hold of the crib and pushed it out of the room, shutting the door quietly behind him.

"I know who the intruder is," Ridge said

through gritted teeth. "I need to go after him and finish this."

"No," Darcy replied. "He's already hurt you three times—is that not bad enough?"

"He got lucky."

"He seems to have no shortage of luck when he's attacking you," Darcy said. She saw Ridge clench his hand and knew she had landed a blow to his ego, but she didn't care. Better to hurt his feelings than have him run off again and wind up dead.

"Darcy—" he began, a note of warning in his voice.

"No, Ridge," she said, cutting him off. "You're being ridiculous. Just call your brother and tell him who the attacker is. Let the police deal with him."

"I'm going to," he said with exaggerated patience. "But they'll need my help."

"Oh, so you're a cop now, too?"

"I'm a tracker." His voice was lethally quiet, and Darcy realized she'd pushed too hard. He was about to shut her out completely, if he hadn't already done so. "The man's been in my house several times. Penny can get his scent, and we can find him. It's what we do."

She swallowed hard, then tried a different approach. "Your knee is too fragile right now. If you go hiking after the intruder, you will probably do permanent damage to the joint, which means you'll be dealing with chronic pain in the future. Is he really worth it?"

Ridge studied her for a moment, his dark brown eyes inscrutable. "What's this really about?" he asked finally.

It was Darcy's turn to look away. "I don't know what you mean."

"You're awfully worked up about this. Why do you care so much what I do?"

"Your knee—" she began, but he interrupted her.

"To hell with my knee. It's more than that, and I want to know what's going on. Why are you suddenly so worried about what my future holds? You're not going to be around to see it."

She flinched, but she couldn't deny the truth of his words. "We're friends," she said, the excuse sounding lame even to her own ears. "Friends care about each other."

"Yes, they do," he agreed. "But are we friends? Because that's not how I remember things ending between us." He sounded curious now, all traces of his earlier anger gone.

Darcy took a deep breath. She might as well tell him. If she passed on this opportunity, it would only put more distance between them. "I was wrong," she blurted out. Nothing subtle about that.

Ridge didn't react to her declaration. She lifted her head to find him watching her, his expression patient. "Breaking up with you was a mistake. I know now, my parents framed you to make me think you had stolen the watch. I believed their lies, and I'm sorry. I should have trusted you, not them."

His face went blank. "I see."

"I hate that we missed out on ten years together." Might as well tell him everything, before she lost her courage. "But now that I'm back, I was hoping maybe..." She trailed off, watching his face for signs of what he was thinking.

"Maybe what?" he asked, sounding a little wary.

Her stomach sank. "Well, I thought we might be able to try again."

She held her breath, waiting for his response. He stared at her for a moment, clearly trying to process what she'd said. Then he shook his head slowly. "You want to pick up where we left off, ten years ago?"

Darcy frowned. "No, not exactly. I know we've both changed. But I thought we could give things another shot, see where they lead."

"I already know where they lead," he said. "Your future is in New York. Mine is here. There's really no point in discussing this further."

"Is that the only reason you think it's a bad idea?" A spark of hope kindled to life in her chest. If Ridge still had feelings for her they could find a way to make everything else work.

He frowned at her. "Isn't that enough? I'm not interested in a long-distance relationship or a temporary fling. That doesn't leave us with any other options."

"You didn't answer my question," she pressed.

"What do you mean?"

She took a deep breath and spoke before she could change her mind. "I want to know if you still have feelings for me the way I do for you."

He turned away and Darcy's heart sank. "I don't see how that's relevant," he said stiffly.

Tears sprang to her eyes and she blinked hard, determined not to cry in front of him. "It's relevant to me," she said, struggling to keep the quiver out of her voice. It was masochistic of her, but she needed to hear him say he didn't care about her anymore. It was the only way she'd be able to move on.

"Darcy—" he began, but was interrupted by a short knock at the door.

They both turned in time to see Sam walk in. He glanced from Ridge to Darcy and lifted one brow. "Am I interrupting something?"

"Yes," Ridge said at the same time Darcy said "No."

"No," Darcy repeated, mustering up a smile. "You're not. Please, come in. I was just about to step out—I need to see if we've located an overnight room for the baby."

"You're keeping her?" Ridge asked, a note of alarm in his voice.

"I think it's best she stay for a bit, just to make sure she's really on the mend," Darcy said. She smoothed her hair back with the palm of her hand and headed for the door. "I'll check on that orthopedic consult for you, as well," she said, then slipped out of the room before he could launch another volley of protests.

Once she was safely on the other side of the door, Darcy let her shoulders sag. She leaned against the wall and closed her eyes, wanting nothing more than to retreat to the nearest supply closet and have a good cry in peace. But that wasn't an option. She needed to get the baby sorted—once that was done, she could leave and put some distance between her and Ridge.

His rejection stung. She'd considered the possibility that after ten years, whatever feelings he'd had for her would have faded, especially given the way things had ended between them. But she hadn't expected the reality to hurt so badly. Not that she blamed him. She was asking him to take a giant leap of faith. Once upon a time they'd been close enough that he would have trusted her completely. But she'd betrayed that trust, and to make matters worse, they'd spent too much time apart. They might as well be strangers now.

Soft footsteps sounded to her right, followed

by a quiet cough. Darcy opened her eyes to find Trevor standing nearby with the baby, his mouth turned down sympathetically.

"He's always been stubborn, sometimes to the point of being a fool." He turned and leaned against the wall next to her, mimicking her pose so they both stood facing the hall. She appreciated the gesture—she wasn't up for eye contact with anyone right now.

Darcy nodded. "I won't argue with you on that."

"Did I see Sam walk in there?"

"Yes," she confirmed. "Do you want me to hold her so you can join them?"

"No," he said, surprising her. It must have shown on her face, for he grinned. "I love my brother, but right now he's all twisted up over some local man who wrecked his knee. I've got bigger fish to fry."

"The Alphabet Killer?" Darcy guessed.

Trevor nodded. "I was hoping you could help me."

"Me?" Darcy frowned. "I don't see how."

"Ridge tells me you knew one of the victims. Francine Gibbons."

"Yes, I did. We were coordinating a charity luncheon together."

Trevor nodded, as if she'd just confirmed something he already knew. "Were you good friends with her?"

Darcy shook her head. "No. And not to be rude, but I already told Sam and Annabel all I know about Francine. It's not much," she added, apologetically. "Like I told them, she and I did not have a lot in common and I didn't spend a lot of time with her."

"I understand," Trevor said easily. "Would you just humor me, though? I'd like to hear for myself what you have to say about her. Sam and Annabel are great cops, but I prefer to get my information from the source if I can."

Darcy raised a brow, but nodded. She'd been looking for some kind of distraction. She didn't want to stay at the hospital and she definitely didn't want to go home and face her parents again. Talking to Trevor would be a good way to pass the time.

Even if he did share the same dark eyes as his brother.

"Before we get started, I need to find out if they've come up with a room for the baby." She held out her arms and he handed the infant over. "It'll just take a few minutes. Do you mind waiting?"

"Not at all. Why don't you meet me in the hospital cafeteria? I'll buy you a cup of coffee and we can have our chat."

"That sounds good." And surprisingly, it did. Even though they were going to discuss a murder investigation, it would be nice to talk to someone without emotions getting in the way. After the argument with her parents and then the conversation with Ridge, she was feeling raw and exposed. Talking to Trevor would help her calm down again.

And maybe, said a small voice inside her head, *Trevor can shed some light on what Ridge has been up to the past ten years.* As much as she wanted to run away and lick her wounds, she was going to have to talk to Ridge again.

And the next time she did, she wanted to be emotionally prepared.

"Dennis Hubbard?" Sam's features twisted in disbelief and he stared down at Ridge with doubt in his eyes.

Ridge shifted on the bed with a grimace. "Yes. For the millionth time, it was Dennis Hubbard." He didn't bother to keep his annoyance out of his voice. The sooner Sam believed him, the sooner he could start looking for the man. Ridge wasn't going to be able to rest easy until he knew Dennis was securely behind bars.

Sam shook his head. "But he's never been violent before."

Ridge lifted one brow. "Oh, really? Then why does he spend every other Friday night in a holding cell?"

Sam dismissed the point with a wave of his

hand. "You know what I mean. He gets into bar fights, but he doesn't have a history of breaking and entering or attempted kidnapping."

"Maybe he's just never been caught before," Ridge said darkly.

Sam was silent a moment as he considered the implications of that point. Then he shrugged. "Not likely. We haven't had any unsolved burglaries lately."

"I don't think he's interested in stealing things," Ridge said. He quickly filled his brother in on Trevor's suspicion that Dennis was involved in human trafficking. Sam rocked back on his heels, clearly shocked.

"I hope nothing like that is moving into Granite Gulch," he said. "We're already seeing gang and drug activity creep in from Dallas and Fort Worth. That's bad enough."

"You're telling me," Ridge said grimly. "We haven't had to step up the number of missing persons searches, but it's possible the people getting caught up in this thing are on the fringes of society, anyway. Hard to know someone's gone missing if there isn't a report."

Sam conceded the point with a nod.

"I just wish I knew why he's so obsessed with this baby. How did he even come across her in the first place?"

Sam's brows drew together in a frown.

"Doesn't—" he began. Then he rocked back on his heels as if he'd been punched. "My God," he whispered.

"What?" Ridge pushed himself up on the bed, his heart pumping hard at his brother's reaction. What did Sam know?

"Dennis has a daughter."

Ridge could only stare at Sam as the implications of his words sank in. "A daughter?" he repeated. He cleared his throat, feeling the first tingles of adrenaline enter his system. "How old is she?"

Sam shook his head. "I'm not exactly sure. Sixteen, maybe seventeen? Old enough to have a baby."

"Has anyone seen her lately?" Could she be Sara's mother? But if so, where was she now? Had Dennis hurt his daughter when she'd refused to hand over her baby?

"I don't know," Sam replied. "Give me a minute." He pulled out his phone and started to dial.

Ridge watched his brother's face as he placed his call, trying to gauge the information he was getting based on his expression. Someone had to know where the girl was, or if she'd recently been pregnant. He just hoped they weren't too late…

Sam shoved the phone back in his pocket with a muttered curse. "She's not in school. Dennis pulled her out several months ago, said he was going to homeschool her."

"That's allowed?"

"In a word? Yes." Sam paced a few steps in front of the bed. "She's underage, he's her parent. Legally, he can pretty much do whatever he wants."

Ridge's stomach sank. "So no one has seen the girl in months. And if he yanked her out of school because she was pregnant, I doubt he took her to a doctor for prenatal care."

Sam huffed. "I think that's a safe assumption. He's not exactly father of the year material."

"Do you think he kept her locked in the house until she gave birth?" He could picture it all too easily—a young woman, pregnant, alone and afraid, locked in her room while Dennis raged at her from the other side of the door.

"Probably." A muscle in Sam's jaw tensed. "I'll call it in and have some officers stop by his house. They'll be able to determine if he's been keeping anyone locked up. If she gave birth in the home, there should be evidence of that, too."

Ridge shuddered at the thought of the girl laboring with only Dennis for help. Poor thing. "Maybe we'll get lucky and she'll still be there." It was a long shot, but where else could she go?

"Don't get your hopes up," Sam cautioned.

"I know. In the meantime, we should get started on the search for Dennis."

"We?" Sam raised a brow and nodded meaningfully at Ridge's knee. "I don't think there's going to be a 'we' on this search."

"I'm fine."

"Don't be an idiot," Sam said.

Ridge felt his face heat. "That's the second time today someone has implied I'm stupid. I'm getting a little tired of it."

"Then quit acting like it," Sam said, his exasperation clear. "What were you thinking, trying to take this guy on alone? Do you have any idea how badly things could have turned out? You're lucky a busted knee is your only souvenir."

"You guys were busy. I figured I could handle it."

Sam shook his head. "If this is you handling it, I don't want to see the alternative."

"I want to do my job."

"So do I." Sam crossed his arms over his chest. "Let me break it down for you. If you go off half-cocked and join the search for Dennis Hubbard, you're a liability. That means instead of focusing all our efforts and attention on finding him, we have to babysit you, as well. You'll slow us down. Is that what you want?"

Ridge hated to admit it, but Sam was right. Much as he wanted to pretend otherwise, his knee was on fire and it was only getting worse. Still, he had to do *something.* "I can't just sit here. I need to help out in some way." He thought of the letters to his father, but dismissed the idea. The aftermath of his earlier adrenaline rush had left him too keyed up to sit patiently and read through all the crazy. That was a task better suited for when he was more relaxed and less likely to miss any subtle clues that might be found.

Sam nodded slowly and scratched the side of his jaw. "As it turns out, I do have a job for you."

"I'm all ears."

"I want you to stay here." He lifted a hand to stave off Ridge's objection. "Let me finish. I want you to stay here and keep tabs on the baby. We don't know where Dennis is now, and if there are other players involved in his scheme then the baby is still a target. We're stretched pretty thin between the Alphabet Killer investigation and now this, so you'd be doing me a favor by standing guard yourself. Keeps me from having to lose a man."

Ridge nodded, knowing he didn't really have another choice. He'd rather be out there on the trail, but until his knee healed he would have to get used to staying on the bench.

"Good. I'll check in with Darcy on my way out. Maybe she can get you a bed in the room with the baby—that way you can keep your leg up."

"Too bad I left my stash of bonbons at home," Ridge said darkly.

"That is a pity," Sam replied, ignoring the sarcasm. "Maybe you could get Darcy to peel you some grapes instead. Although given the temperature of the room when I walked in, I don't think she'd take kindly to that request."

Darcy's scowl flashed in his mind and he squirmed involuntarily. "Probably not."

"I couldn't help but notice you two were pretty cozy-looking the other morning. What changed?"

Ridge considered staying quiet, but it would be nice to get his brother's take on things. Darcy's apology had stunned him, and he still wasn't sure what to make of her suggestion they try again. He sighed, then broke it down for Sam.

To his credit, Sam didn't interrupt. He remained quiet while Ridge told him the whole sad story, starting with the way Darcy had dumped him ten years ago and ending with her earlier apology.

"Wow." Sam ran a hand through his hair. "I got the impression things had ended badly between you two, but you never wanted to talk about it."

"Can you blame me?"

"No. What are you going to do now?"

Ridge shrugged. "I told her no. What else could I say?"

Sam's gaze sharpened. "Do you still care about her?"

His heart screamed yes but he settled for a nod. "But what does that matter?"

The corner of Sam's mouth tilted up. "If you ask me, that's the only thing that matters."

"She's moving to New York. Did you miss that part?"

"No, I heard all of it. But it seems to me if you both still care for each other, you'll find a way to make it work."

"I don't see how," Ridge grumbled.

"Get creative," Sam suggested. "It's worth it."

"When did you turn into such a romantic?"

Sam's expression softened, and Ridge knew he was thinking of Zoe. "I've learned some things over the past couple of months. Sounds like you could stand to learn them, too."

It was the truth, and Ridge felt an inner pang of jealousy. He didn't begrudge Sam his happiness with Zoe—if anyone deserved love, it was his brother. But Ridge wanted to experience that for himself. He'd been lonely for so long. What would it be like to have a woman who loved him despite his flaws? He wasn't an easy man to get to know—he recognized that about himself. But he still held out hope he would someday find a woman who would make him feel whole.

Once upon a time he'd thought Darcy was that woman. Maybe she still was.

"You deserve to be happy again," Sam said.

"But you have to take a chance to find that happiness."

And that was the problem, wasn't it? His fears were getting in the way. What if he and Darcy did try to reconnect and then a few months down the line she decided she didn't want him after all? Could he really withstand her rejection again, knowing this time it would be so much worse? Ten years ago they'd still been kids. Sure, they had loved each other, but it had been the passionate, all-consuming kind of love that burned hot and bright and flared out just as easily as it had sparked to life. They were older now, more mature. If they came together again, it would be as adults who wanted to build a life together. Darcy was asking him to give her his heart and soul, and he just wasn't sure he could afford to take that risk.

But if he refused, was he destined to spend his life alone?

"I'm heading out now," Sam announced, interrupting his musings. "Let me know if anything happens here."

"Same to you," Ridge said. "Keep me posted, please."

The door closed with a soft *click*, leaving Ridge alone again with his thoughts. He had to decide what to do about Darcy. The idea of being with her again was powerfully appealing, but she was moving to New York soon and his life was in Granite Gulch.

He tried to imagine living in the big city, but he just couldn't picture it. And what about Penny? He glanced down and gave her a scratch behind the ear. She would hate living in a concrete jungle. She was used to the freedom of the woods, and it would be cruel to take her away from that. Moving away would also mean separating from his siblings, a thought that sent a chill through him. They'd been isolated from each other for so long already—could he really walk away from them now that they had started to rebuild their family?

I could ask her to stay here. It was a wild thought, and for a second he indulged in the fantasy. He'd come home from work to find her in the cabin, warm and pink from the fire. Their kids would play with Penny, looking like miniature versions of Darcy. They'd go hiking on the weekend and he'd teach the kids how to fish and how to track. His chest warmed as he pictured it. It would be so perfect.

But he knew right away it wouldn't work. The dream faded away, leaving him cold inside. Darcy wasn't meant to stay locked up in Granite Gulch. She was a bright star, and she deserved a chance to shine. Even though it would kill him to watch her walk away, it was for the best. If by some miracle he did convince her to stay, she'd grow to resent him for it later. Better to have her leave now than to see the love slowly fade from her eyes as she came to realize she'd made a mistake.

In the end, his choice was clear. Much as he wanted to be with Darcy, he couldn't uproot his life and sacrifice his family and his dog for a relationship that might not work out. His heart tightened as disappointment flowed over him, but he pushed it aside. He had made his choice, and he would have to live with it.

Alone.

Chapter 13

"I don't like leaving her alone."

Darcy held back a sigh, knowing Ridge was just being overly cautious. He'd been on edge about the baby's safety since confronting Dennis earlier today, and she really couldn't blame him. It was unsettling to know he was still out there.

The name Dennis Hubbard hadn't meant anything to Darcy, but Ridge's description of the man made her hope the police would find him soon. He sounded like a loose cannon, which meant he was a danger to the baby. *And others*, she thought, glancing at Ridge's knee.

"There's a hospital security guard right outside her door," she said calmly. "Only nurses and doctors are allowed to enter the room. She's safe, Ridge."

He frowned but didn't protest. She pulled the wheelchair to a halt and locked the wheels. "Can you stand?"

"Yes." He took a deep breath and pushed himself up, and she helped him pivot so he landed on the bed. He didn't make a sound but she could tell by the set of his mouth he was in pain.

"We'll get you something to take the edge off as soon as we're done here."

He nodded, relief entering his eyes. "Do you think it will take long?"

"It shouldn't. I had a peek at the schedule—it's not full today."

"Thank you," he said.

"No problem." Her reply was automatic. She moved to leave, but Ridge's hand flashed out and grabbed hers in a surprisingly tight grip. "I mean it," he said, holding her in place. "You've helped me so much over the past few days. I haven't really thanked you for it, but I do appreciate everything you've done."

"You're welcome," she said, her breath catching at the intensity of his gaze. Emotions swirled in the dark depths of his eyes, one shifting into another before she could fully identify them.

His thumb slid across her skin in a small, gentle caress that she felt all the way to her toes. Did he know what he was doing to her? Or was it just a casual gesture for him? He knew how she felt about him. Was he teasing her now, seeking to get some of his own payback for the way she'd treated him long ago?

She dismissed the thought almost immediately. Ridge was many things, but he wasn't vindictive. It wasn't like him to deliberately hurt someone just for fun.

He wasn't his father.

"About what you said earlier—" he began. Her heart picked up speed, thumping against her breastbone like a bird trying to break free from a cage. This was it—he was going to tell her how he felt.

Her conversation with Trevor had been illuminating. According to him, Ridge hadn't really dated anyone in the years they'd been apart. It was something they both had in common. The news had made her feel even closer to him, and had reignited the hope that he might still care for her.

She tried to keep the hope off her face as he opened his mouth to continue. But before he could speak again, the door opened and a nurse walked in.

"Mr. Colton? I'm here to help with your MRI."

Darcy bit back a scream of frustration. Why did this woman have to interrupt now, of all times? She took a deep breath and moved away, pushing down her disappointment. The MRI scan itself wouldn't take very long, and then she and Ridge could finish their conversation.

But it was not to be. The procedure was quick, but the nurse insisted on wheeling Ridge back to the room herself, effectively eliminating any chance of a private conversation. Darcy marched alongside the wheelchair, a smile pasted on her face. The nurse was just doing her job, she reminded herself. She could wait a few more minutes to talk to Ridge.

As they approached the baby's room, Darcy slowed. Something felt off, but she couldn't put her finger on what it was.

"Where's the guard?" Ridge asked. "I thought you said there was hospital security standing outside her door."

"There's supposed to be," Darcy replied, scanning the hall. But there was no sign of the guard. Where was he?

Just then, a high-pitched, thin cry started in the baby's room. Ridge shot to his feet but fell back into the chair with a groan of pain. "Darcy!" he shouted.

She responded immediately, knowing what he wanted her to do. Brushing past the befuddled nurse and the chair, she hit the door hard and burst into the baby's room.

It took a few seconds for her eyes to adjust to the dim light of the room. But then she saw him—a shadowy figure standing by the bed, frantically trying to shush the baby's cries.

"Put her down," Darcy ordered. Her voice was steady but her nerves were anything but. What was she going to do if the man refused? She couldn't physically tackle him without hurting the baby.

The figure turned to her and backed up a step, taking the baby with him. Darcy scanned the room, searching for something she could use as a weapon. She wouldn't attack him while he held the little one, but she wasn't going to let him get past her, either.

There was a commotion in the hall and a moment later, Ridge hobbled into the room. "Let her go," he said, his voice booming in the small room.

The baby stilled for a moment, hearing him close. But the calm didn't last long. When she realized Ridge wasn't going to hold her she increased the volume of her cries, sharing her unhappiness with the world.

The figure backed up another step, but there was nowhere to go. Darcy and Ridge blocked the only exit.

"What is going on in here?" It was the nurse from the MRI. She stepped into the room and flipped on the light. Darcy blinked as the sudden brightness rendered her temporarily blind. Then she blinked again, certain she was seeing things.

She had expected to find the hulking intruder from the cabin, come to steal the baby away. Instead, a young woman in a set of baggy scrubs stood clutching the baby to her chest, her tear-stained face a mask of fear.

"Please don't hurt me."

"Who are you?" Ridge deliberately kept his voice calm but the girl still shrank back, her eyes wide.

"My—my name is Flo," she stuttered, tightening her grip on the baby. Darcy took a step forward, her arm outstretched, but the girl jerked back as if she'd been poked with a cattle prod.

That solved the mystery of the note's author. "You must be Dennis's daughter," Ridge said, glancing meaningfully at Darcy.

Her head snapped back in shock. "How did you know that?" she whispered.

A swell of relief filled him and he leaned against the wall to steady himself. Thank God, the girl was safe! Dennis hadn't harmed her, after all.

"Your father—" he began, then trailed off. What should he tell her? *Your father has spent the past few days attacking me in an attempt to get his hands on the baby? Your father wrecked my knee while trying to steal the baby today?* In the end, he settled for "Your father has made it clear he wants the baby. We've been trying to figure out why." Maybe she could shed some light on the situation.

Flo hid her face in the baby's blanket, making herself look even smaller. "He wasn't bad at first. He said we could make it work."

Ridge cast a confused glance at Darcy, who shrugged. "Why don't we all sit down and you can tell us about it?" she suggested.

"I don't want to let go of my baby." Flo glanced around nervously, clearly intending to bolt at the slightest provocation.

"You don't have to," Darcy soothed. "You can keep holding her while we talk. How does that sound?"

The young woman nodded uncertainly. "Okay." She perched on the bed, the baby still clutched to her chest. Ridge ached to take little Sara from her, but he knew it would only spook the girl if he made a move in her direction. He settled for sinking into the rocking chair and Darcy moved to the foot of the hospital bed.

"Why don't you start from the beginning?" Darcy suggested.

"All right." Flo took a deep breath, bracing herself. "I didn't mean for it to happen."

"What's that?" Darcy's voice was soft and soothing.

"Getting pregnant. Kenny and me..." She

trailed off, color flooding her cheeks. "We tried to be careful."

"Of course you did," Darcy said. "Mistakes happen to everyone."

"Did you go to school with Kenny?" Ridge asked.

She nodded. "Yes. But he moved right before I found out I was pregnant. I didn't know how to get in touch with him, so he still doesn't know about the baby."

Sympathy welled in Ridge's chest. Poor girl. It had to have been difficult for her, losing her mother and then her boyfriend. Finding out she was pregnant must have been terrifying.

"Did anyone else know you were pregnant?"

"My dad. I started to show and I couldn't hide it anymore."

"How did he take it?" said Ridge. "Was he upset with you?" That would certainly fit with his usual behavior, especially if he'd been drinking.

"I think he was more disappointed," she said. "He seemed to get over it after a couple of days, though. He said I could keep the baby and between the two of us we'd figure out how to afford it. I was shocked—I thought for sure he was joking. But he kept telling me it was okay. Even helped me fix up half of my room to make a nursery. And he took me shopping for baby stuff one day. He seemed like he was excited about becoming a grandpa."

Ridge frowned. He didn't know Dennis very well, but from what he'd heard, he wasn't the type to cheerfully shop for baby supplies. Had Flo mistaken the reason for her father's excitement?

"What changed?" Darcy asked.

Flo shrugged. "He had me quit going to school. Said I needed to stay home and rest for the baby. He brought home a stack of old textbooks and told me to read them. At first, I didn't mind. I was so tired all the time, anyway. But then I started to get bored. I don't think he liked me saying that."

"Didn't your friends wonder why you weren't in school?" Darcy sounded incredulous, and Ridge had to agree. It was hard to believe Flo hadn't told anyone else about her pregnancy or her father's homeschool plan.

"I don't have many friends," Flo said, looking down. "I hung out with a couple of girls from school, but that's about it. They came by the house one day looking for me. Daddy met them at the door and told them I was being homeschooled now and for them to leave me alone. They never came back."

Ridge exchanged a horrified look with Darcy.

"Did he ever take you to see a doctor?" she asked.

"No. He said it would be too expensive." She lowered her voice in an attempt to imitate Dennis. "'Doctors are for sick people. You're young and healthy.'"

"But what about your delivery?" Darcy said, her concern clear. "Didn't he get you help when you went into labor?"

Flo shook her head. "It all happened so fast. I woke up in a lot of pain. He said he was going to get his friend to come help and left. By the time they got back, she was already here." She looked down at the baby and smiled faintly. "She cried at lot at first, but I got her to stop by trying to feed her." The young woman sounded proud of this accomplishment, and Ridge felt his heart break. Flo was barely old enough to drive and she'd had to deliver her baby alone, something no woman should ever have to do. He shook his head, his anger at Dennis building anew. What kind of father left his daughter alone and in pain like that?

Darcy's voice interrupted his thoughts. "I'm sure you did great," she said, smiling at the girl. Then she looked over and he saw his own horror reflected in her eyes. It was a wonder Flo and the baby were alive—so many things could have gone wrong during the birth, and since Dennis had left her alone, no one would have been there to help.

Not that Dennis would have been much help anyway.

"What happened after they arrived?" Ridge asked, trying to keep his anger at Dennis out of his voice. Flo's eyes widened briefly, but she didn't shrink away. That was progress.

"They looked at her and told me I'd done a good job. Said she was perfect." Flo dipped her head and pressed a soft kiss to the baby's skull. "I knew that already, but it was still nice to hear. Then Daddy asked his friend when he could take her. It scared me, you know? 'Cause all this time he said I could keep her, and then he was talking about some stranger taking her away." She tightened her arms around the baby, as if to protect her from the memory. "I asked him about it, but he told me to shush."

"What about the friend?" Whoever Dennis had brought was almost certainly part of the trafficking ring. If Flo could provide a description, Sam and Annabel could start looking for them.

"He said it was too early and a few days would be better. Then he asked if I was going to be any trouble." She shivered. "He said something about a two for one, whatever that means. Daddy said no and the man just laughed. Then they left."

"Did you see him again?"

"No. Only Daddy came back the second time."

"What did he say?" Darcy asked, leaning forward. She was hanging on Flo's every word, and Ridge found himself doing the same. It was quite a story, made all the more compelling because it was true.

"He stroked my hair and told me it was all going to be okay. That he'd figured out a way to make it work. I told him I didn't like his friend, and he said not to worry, that I wouldn't have to see that man again. Then he told me to take good care of the baby because she was priceless."

Ridge bit his tongue to keep from cursing the man. Darcy saw his struggle and spoke to distract Flo. "When did you realize he planned to sell the baby?"

"I figured it out the next day. I overheard him on the phone, talking about how much money he was going to get in exchange for my baby. That's when I knew I had to do something."

"How did you get away from him?" Ridge asked. Dennis had been so careful to keep her locked away during her pregnancy—surely his paranoia had only increased after the baby's birth.

Flo bit her lip. "I told him I needed formula to feed the baby. That I couldn't…you know." She gestured vaguely to her chest, her cheeks going pink. "I offered to go get it myself so he wouldn't suspect anything, but he said no. I waited until he left, then I packed her up and took off. I didn't get as far as I wanted to and I knew he was going to come after me. So I left her on your porch and headed in a different direction, hoping to trick him."

"A good plan," Ridge said, letting his admiration show. She was a resourceful young woman, he'd give her that. Not many teenagers would have had the courage to do what she'd done, nor the strength to hike so far just after giving birth. The fact that Flo had put herself in danger like that said loads about her character.

"What made you decide to come back now?" Darcy asked.

Flo's face brightened. "Today is my birthday," she said, as if this fact should clarify everything.

"Uh, happy birthday," said Ridge. "I still don't understand why you picked today of all days."

Her smile slipped. "I'm finally eighteen." When neither he nor Darcy responded, she sighed. "Daddy can't take my baby if I'm legally an adult. Now that I'm eighteen, I don't have to worry about it anymore."

Ridge felt his jaw drop and glanced over to find an identical expression on Darcy's face. "Who told you that?" Darcy asked slowly.

The color drained from Flo's face. "You mean it's not true?" she whispered. "They can still take my baby?"

"No," Ridge said firmly. "She's your baby—no one can force you to give her up, no matter what your age is."

"Really?" She looked simultaneously hopeful and guarded, as if she was afraid to believe him. Ridge couldn't blame her—Dennis had spent the past six months lying to her. Was it any wonder the girl had trust issues?

"He's right," Darcy confirmed. "That baby is yours."

The girl's relief was almost palpable. The tension drained out of her body with a sigh, and her eyes grew bright with tears. "Thank goodness," she breathed. "I don't have anywhere to go, and I don't want to leave her again."

"You never have to leave her again," Ridge promised.

Flo looked up at him and for the first time, there was no fear in her eyes. "Thank you," she said, her heart in the words. "Thank you so much for taking care of her. I hoped that whoever found her would be good to her."

Ridge looked down, unable to meet her gaze. For the first time, it hit him that he was going to have to say goodbye to little Sara. He'd known the time would come, but he hadn't expected it to be so soon.

"Ridge did an amazing job," Darcy said. "You couldn't have picked a better man if you'd tried."

Flo studied him a moment, then nodded thoughtfully. "I think you're right. I noticed how the baby calmed down once you came into the room."

Ridge shrugged, trying to appear nonchalant. "We spent a lot of time together," he said, glossing over the strength of his attachment to the little one.

Flo looked down at the bundle in her arms. "You know, I left her so soon, I didn't even get a chance to name her. I have no idea what I'm going to call her."

"I've been calling her Sara." The words were out before he could stop them and he immediately wished he could take them back. Flo looked thoughtful, as if she was considering it for the baby. But Darcy's eyes grew misty, and he knew she recognized the significance of the name.

He swallowed hard, wishing the floor would open up underneath his feet. He hadn't told anyone about his personal name for the baby. It was private, something the two of them shared that made him feel close to his mom again. Now that his sentimentality had been revealed, he felt exposed and raw.

"I like it," Flo said at last. "She looks like a Sara." She glanced at Ridge, then back at the baby. "Sara Ridge Hubbard. That's your name, little girl. What do you think?"

Ridge sucked in a breath at the honor. "You can't name her after me," he protested weakly. "She needs a pretty name to go with Sara."

Flo shook her head. "Nope. I want her to know who it was that saved her. You've been her guardian angel. I won't ever forget that."

He could only nod, the words he might have said piling up behind the lump in his throat. His nose started to burn and he hastily wiped his eyes before anyone could see his tears fall. If he had to say goodbye, at least the baby would have something to remember him by.

"That's a beautiful name," Darcy said, her voice a little wobbly. "Very fitting."

Flo smiled down at her daughter, her adoration for the infant plain to see. Then she frowned and glanced up again. "I almost forgot to ask—why is she in the hospital? Is she okay?"

Darcy nodded. "She had a slight fever so we brought her in as a precaution."

"But she's fine now?"

"I think so, yes."

Ridge cleared his throat, feeling sufficiently recovered now that he was no longer the focus of attention. "How did you know she was here?"

"I've been checking up on her every so often. Just enough to know she was okay. I saw you load her in the truck, and heard something about a hospital." She lifted one shoulder in a casual shrug. "So I walked up here and stole a pair of scrubs and waited until she was alone."

"You walked here from my cabin?" Ridge was incredulous. It was a wonder she'd made it, with the roads and trails having been damaged by the recent storms.

She shot him a grin. "Took me forever, but I made it."

"Have you had anything to eat today?" Darcy asked.

Flo shook her head. "I was too focused on getting back to my baby."

"I'll have the cafeteria send up some food for you," Darcy said. "You look like you haven't eaten in a while. And I'd also like to examine you, if that's all right."

The girl's expression turned wary and a hint of suspicion crept into her voice. "Why?"

"Because you've just given birth," Darcy explained gently. "I'd like to make sure you're okay, since you didn't receive any medical care."

"Is it going to hurt?"

Darcy shook her head. "It shouldn't, no. Besides," she added, smiling, "you gave birth alone, with no medication. If you can handle that, you can handle pretty much anything else."

Flo nodded. "I guess you're right. But…" She trailed off and glanced furtively at Ridge, the tips of her ears going pink.

Recognizing his cue, he pushed himself out of the chair. "I'll be outside," he said. Before he could think better of it, he limped over and pressed a kiss to Sara's forehead, taking one last whiff of that sweet baby scent.

"Goodbye, little one," he whispered.

Then he turned and walked away, his heart cracking a little with every step.

Chapter 14

She found him in an empty room down the hall, sitting in the chair and staring out the window. Penny sat next to him, and she lifted her head and woofed quietly in acknowledgment when Darcy walked in. Ridge didn't turn to face her, but she could tell he knew she was there by the way his shoulders stiffened slightly.

"How are you doing?" she asked. When he didn't respond, she paused, searching for something else to say. "Flo's exam went well. She doesn't appear to have suffered any lasting physical damage from giving birth alone."

Ridge still didn't reply.

"Sara's looking good. I think whatever was causing her fever is long gone, but we'll keep her a bit longer, just to be on the safe side."

He nodded.

"Flo hasn't set her down once. She's so happy to have her baby back."

"She'll be a good mother." His voice was rough as sandpaper.

"She said you can visit the baby whenever you want."

"That's sweet of her."

"I get the impression she hopes you'll stay a part of Sara's life."

He tilted his head. "It's a nice thought."

"I figured you'd be happy about that. Everyone can see how much you bonded with the baby."

He huffed out a laugh. "It's that obvious?"

She smiled. "Only if you know what to look for."

Silence fell in the room again, and in the stillness she could practically feel his pain. It was clear his heart was breaking over the baby, and she wanted so badly to help him hold the pieces of it together. But what could she say to offer him comfort? Words were a poor salve, and she'd never been very eloquent. But she had to try. It killed her to see him suffering like this.

"Her name," she began tentatively. Ridge tensed, as if bracing himself for a blow. She forged ahead. "You named her after your mother, didn't you?"

For a long moment, she thought he wouldn't respond. Then he nodded, once.

"It's a beautiful tribute," she said. "I'm glad Flo decided to keep the name."

"Me, too." He shifted in the chair but didn't meet her eyes. "It's a name that should live on."

"I always figured you'd have a daughter named Sara one day." *Our daughter*, she thought suddenly, her heart tightening.

He smiled, but it didn't reach his eyes. "I guess that's as close as I'll come."

Her heart dropped at the finality of his tone. "Maybe not," she said, trying to keep her voice light. "Anything is possible."

"I can't give you what you want."

Darcy's gut twisted, and she swallowed hard to keep from throwing up. "What do you mean?"

Ridge turned to face her then, his eyes dark twin pools of sadness. "We can't be together. Your place is in New York. Mine is here. I can't go there with you, and I'm not going to ask you to stay here with me."

"But—" How to explain she was having second thoughts about New York? That she was more interested in staying here and seeing where things led with him?

He shook his head. "Don't make this harder than it already is, Darcy. We had our chance. There's no point in trying to repeat history. Let's just move on."

"Ridge—"

"I'm sorry. I know that's not the answer you wanted to hear. But I think it's for the best."

Her temper spiked and she gave up trying to be polite. "Will you stop interrupting me!"

He leaned back and blinked, clearly surprised by her outburst. "Ah, okay," he said, his tone the verbal equivalent of a man holding a ticking bomb. "I'm sorry."

"There's something you need to know. About that job in New York."

Ridge's brows drew together. "What's that?"

Darcy took a deep breath, feeling as though she was about to step off a cliff. "I'm thinking a lot about quitting."

His face went blank with shock. "What? Why on earth…"

She held up a hand to halt his questions. "I'm starting to realize there's more to life than my career. And if I'm going to have a shot at any kind of personal life, I want it to be with you."

Ridge opened his mouth so she forged ahead, needing to get it all out before he spoke. "You said we didn't have a chance because I was leaving for New York and you were staying here. But what if

I stayed in Granite Gulch? What if there was no distance between us? Would that make a difference to you?"

Ridge couldn't believe his ears.

Was Darcy really offering to stay in Granite Gulch? Did she truly mean to quit her big-city job and stay in this small Texas town?

She certainly looked and sounded sincere about it. Her big brown eyes were clear, with no hint of reservation. But did she really know what she was giving up?

"Are you sure?" The words were no more than a whisper, but she heard them.

"I am." Her tone was final and without reservation. "If you tell me we have a chance, I'll stay here."

Joy flooded him in a rush, making him feel lighter than air. This was it—their second chance at happiness. He wanted to run down the halls of the hospital, shouting the good news for everyone to hear. But something kept him glued in place. It was everything he'd dared to hope for, but a small, scared part of him was gripped by terror. What if this was too good to be true?

He hated to admit it, but deep inside he was still that scared little boy who had been ripped from his family and sent to live with strangers. While the adult, logical side of his brain scoffed at his insecurities, the small, frightened part of him worried the people he cared about were always one step away from leaving him.

"Ridge?" Darcy's expression was gradually shifting from optimistic to concerned. "Will you just say something?"

He shook his head, trying to dislodge some words. But his brain and tongue refused to cooperate and he was left dumbfounded, staring at her in slack-jawed amazement.

After a moment, Darcy's face fell. "Okay," she said softly. "I see." She turned away, and Ridge knew with terrible certainty if he let her walk away now, he'd never see her again. The realization was enough to break his paralysis. "Darcy, wait."

She glanced up, a flicker of hope in her dark brown eyes. "Yes?"

"Please don't go."

A smile played at the corner of her mouth. "Are you saying what I think you're saying?" She took a step closer and he held out his hands, wanting to draw her near.

He nodded, not trusting his voice.

She took another step, then reached up and cupped the side of his face with her palm. He turned into her touch, savoring the contact between them. "Say it," she whispered. "I want to hear the words."

He opened his mouth to do just that, but before he could speak a high-pitched scream split the air.

Chapter 15

Ridge scrambled down the hall, ignoring the pain in his knee as he made his way back to the baby's room. There was no sign of the hospital guard outside the door, but as he got closer, he saw the man lying on the floor just past the bench in the hall.

He hit the door hard with his shoulder, his momentum carrying him into the room several feet. As he skidded to a halt, he saw Flo standing in the corner, clutching the baby to her chest in a mimic of her earlier pose. Dennis advanced on them, his expression murderous.

"You can't take her," Flo yelled. "She's my baby and you can't have her!"

Dennis didn't bother to respond. He took a step forward, clearly intent on taking Sara by force.

"Stop," Ridge commanded.

Dennis paused at the sound of his voice and glanced over, his eyes widening briefly when he saw Ridge. "You're still around?" he asked snidely. "I thought I put you out of commission."

"Just leave them alone," Ridge said, ignoring the other man's taunts. "It's over. The police know what you're trying to do, and they're looking for you now. You can't win here."

Dennis paused, a range of emotions shifting across his face. Then his features set in a mask of determination. "If that's the case, I guess it doesn't matter what I do now." Something glinted in his hand, and Ridge's gut cramped as he realized Dennis had brought a knife.

Ridge cursed silently, knowing his injured knee put him at a disadvantage. Dennis Hubbard was a man with nothing left to lose, which made him dangerous. Ridge had to find a way to get him out of there, but he couldn't do anything that would put the baby at risk.

He circled around until he put himself between Dennis and Flo. It wasn't enough, but at least he could try to block Dennis if he lunged for his daughter and granddaughter.

"You can still run," he suggested, inching forward. If he could keep Dennis distracted, perhaps he could herd him out the door without the other man realizing what was happening. "The police aren't here yet." *Hopefully, Darcy is calling them now.* "You can make a clean getaway and head out before they find you."

"Shut up," Dennis snapped. He craned his neck, trying to catch a glimpse of Flo and Sara, but Ridge moved to block his view at every turn. "Give me the baby, Flo," he ordered. "It's for the best."

"No." Flo's voice was strong despite her obvious terror. "She belongs with me."

"Dammit, girl!" Dennis charged forward, apparently intending to bowl over Ridge so he could get to the baby. But Ridge planted his feet and squared his shoulders, bracing himself for the impact.

Dennis hit him hard and managed to push him back a few inches. Flo screamed, but Ridge couldn't spare a glance for her. Instead, he wrapped his arms around Dennis and shoved, driving his shoulder into Dennis's abdomen.

They slipped and slid across the tile floor, each man vying for purchase. Dennis jabbed wildly with his hand, and Ridge grunted as hot, searing stings told him the knife had made contact with his back.

Ridge kept his head down and pushed as hard as he could, throwing all his weight into it. The flat soles of his boots made it hard to gain traction on the waxed tiles, and he churned his legs to maintain his momentum. His foot hit a slick spot on the floor and he lost his balance, sending both him and Dennis sprawling to the ground. There was a sickening thud as Dennis's head hit the floor, and Ridge felt a spike of pain as his nose made contact with the man's breastbone.

It took a few seconds for Ridge to realize Dennis had stopped moving. He levered himself off the man, felt hands grabbing at him to help him stand. Dennis moaned but didn't try to get up. Ridge stared down at him, hesitant to leave in case Dennis was just playing possum. He didn't seem to be faking, though.

Small red dots appeared on Dennis's shirt, and Ridge belatedly realized his nose was dripping blood. Not knowing what else to do, he used the sleeve of his shirt to try to staunch the flow. It was probably ruined anyway, thanks to Dennis's knife.

"Come, sit down." Darcy put her hand on his arm and gently tugged. "Hospital security is here to take care of Dennis, and the police are on their way. I need to check you out now."

She guided him to the bed where he sat next to Flo, who was shaking so badly he thought she might drop the baby. Moving slowly so as not to scare her, Ridge put his arm around the girl, drawing her into his side so he could support both her and the baby. She leaned against him with a shuddering sigh, her panting breaths slowly subsiding as the adrenaline left her system.

"I think he was going to kill me," she whispered.

Sympathy welled up in Ridge's chest and he gave Flo's shoulder a squeeze. He knew all too well what it was like to be terrified of a parent. It was a horrible sensation, one no child should ever have to experience.

"He can't hurt you now." Ridge leaned back a little so Flo could look past him to see the hospital security officers restrain Dennis. They hauled him into a sitting position and then marched him out the door, supporting him on either side as he stumbled woozily.

"Thank you," she said, her eyes bright with tears.

"No thanks required," he said gruffly, breathing in with a hiss as Darcy probed one of the cuts on his back.

Flo's eyes widened. "You're hurt! Oh my God, is it serious?"

"I'm fine," he said. Darcy huffed behind him, so he said it again, this time with a little more steel in his voice. The last thing he wanted was for Flo to get even more upset. She needed to stay calm for Sara's sake.

"Is it really that hard to stay out of trouble?"

Ridge glanced over his shoulder to see Sam standing in the doorway wearing a bemused expression. Ridge shook his head. "I was just doing the job you gave me," he reminded his brother. "It's not my fault you missed all the action."

"I wouldn't say that." Sam walked around the bed to face Ridge and offered Flo a kind smile. "You must be the baby's mother."

She leaned ever so subtly into Ridge's side and nodded. "Yes. Sara is my daughter."

Sam's face went blank as the name registered. For the barest second, Ridge saw the hint of pain in his brother's eyes. Then he blinked, and the emotion was gone. "That's a lovely name," Sam murmured, glancing at Ridge, who nodded.

"Well." Sam rocked back on his heels and hooked his thumbs into his belt. "While you were busy here, we searched the house."

"Find anything?" Ridge bit his lip as Darcy found an especially sensitive cut.

Sam nodded, then looked at Flo. "It looks like your father was going to sell the baby on the black market. We found a list of names and phone numbers for some of his contacts. Some of the numbers are out of state, so we've brought in the FBI to help in the investigation."

Flo shook her head sadly. "I can't believe my own father wanted to sell my baby."

"People will do almost anything for money,"

Sam replied gently. "But the most important thing is that both you and the baby are safe now. You don't have to worry about anyone trying to steal her from you again."

Darcy tugged the back of Ridge's shirt down, signaling an end to her exam. "You're going to need stitches on some of these," she said. "Let's go into the next room and I'll get a suture kit."

Flo stiffened against his side. "I won't be far," he told her. "And Sam will stay here with you and Sara. You really are safe now." But it was probably going to take a while before she believed it.

She eyed Sam shyly and nodded. Apparently sensing her hesitation, Sam stepped closer and made cooing noises at Sara. The baby focused on him with surprising intensity, her forehead wrinkling as she stared up at him.

Ridge used the distraction to slide off the bed, and Sam effortlessly took his place, keeping his focus on the baby. Satisfied the girls were taken care of, Ridge hobbled out of the room and into the next one, letting out a sigh as he climbed onto the hospital bed.

Darcy shut the door behind them, then walked around the bed until she faced him. Without saying a word, she put her arms around Ridge and pulled him close, stroking his hair in a gentle caress that made him sigh. They stayed that way for several quiet moments, the pain from his injuries receding as he focused on the feel of the woman in his arms.

"You scared me," she whispered. "When I saw Dennis stabbing you, I thought my heart was going to stop."

He smiled into her hair. "If it makes you feel any better, I wasn't enjoying the experience."

"I should think not." She slowly eased back, keeping her hands in his hair. "You really do need sutures," she said ruefully.

"It's a small price to pay," he assured her.

She shook her head, a smile playing at the corners of her mouth. "How do you do it?"

"What?"

"You take care of everyone around you without giving any thought to yourself. You're one of the most selfless people I know."

He squirmed, her praise making him uncomfortable. "It's really not like that—"

She pressed her fingers to his lips. "Don't bother denying it. I know what I see." She removed her hand and replaced it with her mouth, kissing him softly.

Ridge closed his eyes, melting into the kiss. But what she had said bothered him a little. After a moment he pulled back, brushing a strand of hair behind Darcy's ear. "Don't put me up on a pedestal," he warned. "I'll only disappoint you."

Her dark brown eyes searched his. "If you say so."

He nodded. "I don't want to give you any reason to leave me again."

"Believe me, you won't. I'm not going anywhere." She kissed him again, fast and hard. It was a kiss of ownership, as if she was putting her mark on him. Ridge gave as good as he got, happy to return the gesture. After a moment, Darcy pulled away with a smile. "Now, let me see about fixing your back."

Ridge waited until she had moved behind him before asking the question that weighed heavily on his mind. "You're really staying?"

He heard the smile in her voice. "I really am."

Something inside him calmed at her assurance. "I'm glad." And wasn't that the understatement of the year? But he didn't know how to put his feelings into words. How was he supposed to describe the swirl of relief, excitement and anticipation building in his chest? How was he supposed to tell her about his dreams for their future when words alone wouldn't do them justice?

In that moment, Ridge realized his initial fear that Darcy would come to regret her choice was born of the past. He had to let go of the worry or it would plague him for the rest of his life. Darcy had asked him to trust her. If they were to truly build a life together he had to do just that. If he allowed his doubts to continue he would always hold part of himself back in a misguided attempt at self-preservation, and it would kill their relationship.

His mind made up, he resolved to let go of his fears. He and Darcy had a bright future ahead of them, and he couldn't wait to embrace it.

Darcy finished tying off the last suture and leaned back to get a better look at Ridge's injuries. Dennis had sliced his back in several places, but most of the wounds were superficial. They would sting, but as long as Ridge kept them clean they should heal soon with no problems. It was the same for Ridge's nose—thankfully, it wasn't broken. His knee was another matter. His tussle with Dennis may have aggravated the injury, so she made a mental note to order another scan for him.

But first, she wanted to hold him again.

Seeing Ridge fighting with Dennis had terrified her on a level she hadn't known existed. The fear of losing him again had gripped her on a soul-deep level, paralyzing her and rendering her helpless to do anything but watch as the man she cared for risked himself once again to protect another. It was the stuff of nightmares, and something she'd never forget.

She walked around the bed until she faced him again. He smiled at her, but the lines fanning out from the corners of his eyes and the set of his mouth told her he was still in pain. “Promise me something?” She brushed a tuft of hair off his forehead, loving the feel of the thick strands against her fingertips.

“What’s that?” His voice was low and soft and felt like a caress.

“Don’t ever put yourself in danger like that again.”

“I’ll do my best.”

She nodded. “That’s all I can ask of you.”

Darcy leaned forward to kiss him, but before she could make contact with his mouth, the door flew open. She jumped back, startled at the sudden movement. Ridge put his hands on her waist to steady her and turned around to face the door.

“Dr. Marrow.” His voice was cool and steady.

Darcy’s heart kicked into high gear at the sight of her father. He stood in the doorway, surveying the room with a frown. “The officer next door said I’d find you here.” He spoke to Darcy, ignoring Ridge’s greeting.

“Ridge needed some stitches,” she said, moving to collect the debris.

“I see.” Her father eyed Ridge up and down, apparently looking for obvious signs of his injuries. Then he looked back to Darcy.

“Did you need something?” Why was he here? He clearly wasn’t happy to see her with Ridge, but that was just too bad. She was done living her life to suit other people's expectations. Ridge was her past and her future, and her parents were just going to have to accept it.

"Actually, yes." Clint Marrow pursed his lips, as if carefully considering his words. "I've spoken to your coworkers, and they all have very positive things to say about you."

"Oh?" Darcy tried not to let her confusion show. Was this some kind of performance evaluation? If so, why couldn't it wait until later?

"You also have an above average patient satisfaction score," he continued, as if she hadn't spoken. "And a review of your cases indicates you make sound medical decisions."

"That's good to hear." Would he get to the point? She glanced at Ridge, but he looked just as confused as she felt.

"All of this is to say, you would be an asset to the hospital."

Darcy's skin began to tingle as her father's words sank in. "Are you offering me a job?"

He blinked at her directness. "Well, yes. We are terribly short-staffed, and it would be a great help if you agreed to stay on permanently."

She didn't try to contain the grin spreading across her face. "Yes."

"I know you already have job in New York," her father went on, apparently missing her acceptance. "But Granite Gulch is a growing community, and we serve an expanding patient population. You wouldn't see the kind of trauma cases that you'll get in New York, but I think you will find working in our emergency room is a satisfactory challenge to your skills."

"Yes."

"Not to mention, the cost of living in Granite Gulch is significantly less than that of New York. Your quality of life will be better if you stay here."

Darcy shook her head slightly and grinned at Ridge, who smiled back.

"And of course—" he went on.

"Dr. Marrow," Ridge interrupted gently. Her father stopped talking and stared at Ridge, plainly having forgotten he was in the room. "Yes?"

"I already said yes, Dad," Darcy said. "You don't have to keep selling the position. I'd love to stay here."

"Oh." He straightened his tie, then touched the stethoscope around his neck in a nervous gesture. "Well. That's wonderful. Happy to hear it." He nodded, gave her an awkward smile, and nodded again. "Excellent. I'll just go start the paperwork then." He headed for the door and paused on the threshold.

"Your mother," he began, then halted.

Darcy felt her defenses go up. "Yes?"

Her father shot her a pleading look. "She's not

happy about your earlier conversation. She asked me to try to smooth things over with you."

Of all the things she had expected him to say, that was last on the list. "I see," she said, keeping her tone neutral.

Clint looked down a moment and took a deep breath. "We made a mistake, Darcy," he said finally. "We did what we thought was best for you at the time. It wasn't the right thing, but we are only human."

Darcy couldn't believe her ears. She had never heard her father apologize before and she had no idea how to respond now. Part of her wanted to tell him that it was okay, that they should let the past stay in the past. The other part of her wanted to rail at him, to let him know just how much pain he and her mother had caused. She glanced at Ridge, trying to gauge his reaction to this revelation. But his expression was carefully neutral, as if he was trying not to influence how Darcy responded.

"I'm not the only one you and Mom hurt," she said finally. Ridge was just as much a victim of their actions, and he deserved an apology, as well.

"You're right," her father replied. He turned to Ridge. "My wife and I would like to apologize for our actions. We shouldn't have meddled in your relationship with Darcy."

"Thank you," Ridge said simply.

Clint Marrow nodded. "Your mother and I

would like it if you came to dinner tomorrow night. Both of you," he added quickly.

Darcy looked at Ridge, silently asking his opinion. He nodded. "That would be nice," he said.

"Very good." Her father turned to leave again, but Darcy stopped him. "Dad," she called out.

"Yes?"

She should probably let sleeping dogs lie, but Darcy's curiosity got the better of her. "Why are you apologizing now? It's been ten years—why are you and Mom suddenly sorry for what you did?"

Her father sighed and his shoulders slumped a little, making him look his age. "We had a long talk after your argument the other day. Your mother told me some things I hadn't known before, and I realized mistakes had been made. I knew if we didn't try to make things right, we'd lose you forever."

Darcy's shock must have shown on her face because her father smiled sadly. "Do you really believe we don't care about you?"

Her first instinct was to lie, but she decided he deserved the truth. This was the most real conversation she'd ever had with her father, and lying to spare his feelings would only cheapen it. "Sometimes," she admitted.

He blinked hard and hung his head. "It seems your mother and I have made several mistakes," he said softly. Then he looked up and met her eyes. "It's time we started correcting them."

Darcy could only nod, unable to speak past the lump in her throat. Her father left the room, closing the door behind him with a quiet *click*.

She stood motionless for a moment, trying to process what had just happened. It was almost too good to believe. She and her parents had never been close, and their relationship hadn't improved over the years. For so long, she'd assumed she was the only one bothered by the lack of a connection, but it seems she was wrong. Having her father admit he and her mother had made mistakes was a revelation. It gave her hope that she and her parents might actually build a meaningful relationship, especially since she was going to stay in Granite Gulch.

Ridge touched her arm gently, pulling her out of her thoughts. "That was unexpected," he said.

"No kidding." She shook her head, still not sure how to respond. "I want to forgive them—I really do. But I can't forget what they did and the fact that it cost us all that time we could have had together."

Ridge watched her thoughtfully for a moment. "I think it's time to move on," he said with a squeeze. "We have so much to look forward to. But we can't plan our future together if we're always looking behind us at the past."

The truth of his words hit her like an electric shock. He was right, of course. Darcy would need to let go of her anger and disappointment toward her parents, or she would never be able to give her relationship with Ridge the energy and focus it deserved. Besides, if the Alphabet Killer had taught them anything, it was that life was too short to waste it holding a grudge.

She smiled and leaned in to kiss him, holding his face in her hands. "When did you get to be so smart?"

The corner of his mouth twitched up. "Everything I know I learned from my dog," he quipped.

"Is that right?"

The humor faded from his eyes as he stared at her. "I'm not going to ask you to do something that makes you uncomfortable. But I think you'll be happier in the long run if you try to repair your relationship with your parents."

Darcy nodded. "I'm willing to give it a shot. But I'm going to need you to remind me why I'm doing this when my mother gets on my nerves. Which she will," Darcy added, holding up a hand to stave off his objection. "The woman is so status conscious it makes my head hurt."

"Just take it one step at a time," Ridge counseled.

"As long as you're walking with me," Darcy said.

He smiled. "I think I'll be hobbling for a while, but I'll be there."

Chapter 16

It took longer than he expected to get out of the hospital. Darcy had insisted he get his knee examined again, and while he'd grumbled about it, he'd been secretly happy to get another exam. Tussling with Dennis had left him in even more pain than before, and it was a relief to find he hadn't further damaged the joint.

"Looks like some soft tissue damage," the specialist had said. "I'll prescribe some anti-inflammatories and something for the pain. Take it easy for a few weeks, and if you're still in pain, come back and we'll talk about physical therapy."

Ridge had nodded, his muscles relaxing at the news he didn't need surgery. At least not yet.

He'd been all set to leave, but then Sam and Annabel had needed to take his statement. They'd tried to speed the process along, but it had taken a while to answer all of their questions. The only thing that had made it bearable was the fact that his statement meant Dennis was going to stay in jail for a very long time.

Finally, though, he'd been given the green light to leave. And now that he was home, he didn't ever want to leave again.

Penny made a beeline for her bed, walking a circle twice before settling down with a sigh. He smiled at the sight—it had been a long day for both of them, and she'd handled things like a real pro.

"Looks like someone's happy to be home," Darcy said behind him, a smile in her voice.

"We both are," he said. It was true. His little cabin had never felt more welcoming or more peaceful, despite the evidence of his earlier fight with Dennis that was still strewn about the main room.

"Why don't you sit down?" Darcy suggested. "I'll feed Penny and then I'll make you something to eat."

His stomach growled agreement with that plan, and she laughed. "I'll take that as a yes."

Ridge sank into the softness of the couch and closed his eyes, breathing in the familiar scents of home. He desperately wanted a shower, but it felt so good to just sit for a minute…

The next thing he knew, Darcy was gently shaking him awake. “Hi.” She smiled down at him, her head rimmed in golden light from the glow of the lamps. “I would have let you sleep, but you need fuel.”

Ridge shook his head, trying to break free of the grogginess of sleep. “How long was I out?” he asked, rubbing his eyes with the heels of his hands.

“Only about forty minutes.” She sat next to him and rubbed his shoulder. “I let you sleep as long as I could, but your soup is getting cold.”

He smelled it then, a delicious aroma that wrapped around him and made his stomach cramp with the sudden, fierce need to eat. He took several gulping bites, ignoring the slight burn to his tongue as he tried to consume as much as possible.

“Penny?” he asked between slurps. In the foggy depths of his memory, he remembered Darcy mentioning something about feeding the dog, but he needed to make sure.

“Already taken care of,” she assured him. “I fed her while I heated up the soup. She’s already asleep.”

He glanced over and smiled at the sight of his partner, lying on her back with her legs in the air. She snored softly, telling him she was well and truly relaxed.

"Thank you," he said. Darcy nodded her head.

"It was my pleasure."

"What about you?"

Darcy leaned forward and picked up her own bowl of soup from the tray. Ridge slowed his pace, and they sipped in companionable silence together as the sun sank below the tree line.

It felt so good, so right to have her next to him like this. For the first time in years, Ridge felt at peace. It was as if Darcy had filled a hole in his soul, making him a complete person once more. He wished they could stay like this forever—just him, the woman he loved and his dog.

Darcy seemed to enjoy it, too. She let out a contented sigh, then scooted next to him and placed her head on his shoulder. They stayed like that for a while, breathing in rhythm, neither one talking. Just happy to be next to each other, to feel each other's warmth.

He was exquisitely aware of the lines of her body against his own as they watched the sky transition from fiery orange to coral, finally fading into the cool blue of a fresh bruise. Pinpoints of light flickered in the trees as the fireflies came to life, zigging and zagging in complex patterns obvious only to them. Ridge couldn't think of a more perfect view for their first evening together.

Finally, Darcy stirred. "How are you feeling?" she asked quietly.

He shifted a bit, testing out his knee, his back and everything in between. "I'll survive."

"Glad to hear it." She rested her head against him once more, the trust and affection in that simple gesture warming his heart.

He wanted to stay like this forever, but his earlier movement had reawakened his aches and pains and his body cried out for the relief of a hot shower. He moved again, trying to be unobtrusive about it so as not to disturb Darcy. But she felt his motion and sat up.

"Sore?"

He nodded. The fact that he didn't have to explain how he felt—that she just knew—served only to emphasize their connection. "I'm going to take a quick shower."

"A bath would be better," she replied. "You need to keep the stitches on your shoulder dry."

He'd forgotten about that part and felt a momentary pang of disappointment that he would be denied the restorative powers of a shower. But a soak in the bath was almost as appealing, and would definitely help soothe his aches.

He pushed himself off the couch and hesitated, uncertainty tying his tongue. What was Darcy going to do? They hadn't talked about it on the drive over. Was she going to spend the night, or had she come over only to make sure he got inside safely? He didn't want her to go, but he also didn't want to try to rush her into something she wasn't ready for.

Truth be told, he was more interested in her company than in sex. Not that he would turn it down, if she offered. But being near her again was just so amazing he wasn't ready to have her leave, even if they were going to only be apart for a few hours. So much for being an independent adult—he and Darcy had only been around each other for a few days, and he was already a needy mess.

But he wouldn't have it any other way.

Darcy stood and shoved her hands in her pockets, apparently feeling just as awkward as he did. "Um..." She trailed off, clearly at a loss. "Do you need any help?" A blush darkened her cheeks and her eyes widened. "Wow. Talk about being forward." She laughed. "Not trying to put you on the spot or anything. I just figured with your knee..." She gestured to the joint in question.

Ridge didn't try to stop his laugh at her discomfort. "It's okay," he said. He leaned down and kissed her very softly. "I like it when you're bold. And as for needing help... I think I can manage on my own, but I wouldn't turn down any assistance you might care to offer." With that, he turned and hobbled out of the room, giving Darcy space to decide. If he stayed, he'd be tempted to try to convince her to "help" him. And while the idea had merit, he wanted Darcy to come to him because she was ready, not because he'd pressured her into it. They had shared intimacies ten years ago, but given the time that had passed it was foolish to think they would just pick up where they had left off. They were going to have to find their way back to that part of their relationship as they worked to forge their new union, and while he couldn't wait to find out what new mysteries Darcy possessed, he also wanted to savor the journey.

The tub sat at the end of the bathroom under a large window. Since he lived on the outskirts of town, Ridge had never worried about his privacy. But now that Darcy was in his life, he would need to hang curtains to preserve their modesty. It was one of a long list of adjustments, both large and small, he would have to make to accommodate her presence in his life. But the thought of so much change didn't scare him. Rather, it filled him with anticipation as he pictured making those changes with Darcy by his side.

It took several minutes for the tub to fill. While he waited, Ridge shucked his clothes and tossed them into the corner. He'd deal with the laundry later. Right now, the hot water was just too appealing to pass up.

Steam rose off the surface of the water in lazy tendrils and soon the room felt like a sauna. He climbed into the big tub slowly, carefully, wincing only a little as he lowered his punished body into the hot relief. The cuts on his back stung when they first hit the water, but it was a cleansing, almost cathartic burn that receded into numbness. He stretched out his legs with a sigh, suddenly very grateful he had splurged on an oversize bathtub.

After a moment he leaned back, making sure to keep the stitches on his upper shoulder dry. As the heat permeated his muscles his brain emptied, leaving him feeling pleasantly detached. It was a wonderful sensation after the general craziness of the past few days. An image of little Sara floated into his mind, but he pushed it aside. He didn't want to think about the baby right now, or about how much he was going to miss her. There would be time for that, later.

There was a soft stirring outside the bathroom door, and he froze, feeling like a rabbit caught out in the open. Was Darcy going to join him, after all? Or was she merely going to say her goodbye through the door? His heart rate kicked up a notch and his muscles tensed in anticipation, ruining the relaxing effects of the bath.

The doorknob moved slightly and then ever so slowly, it began to turn. Ridge held his breath, hardly daring to believe it. He forced himself to remain still, afraid that if he moved at all, Darcy would change her mind.

But she didn't. The door swung open on silent hinges and she stood at the threshold, backlit from the lights in the hall. It took a second for his eyes to focus, but once they did, his mouth ran dry and he swallowed hard.

She was wearing one of his shirts. It was a red-and-black-plaid flannel number, one he'd donned a thousand times before. But it had never looked quite this good.

The neck hung off one shoulder, leaving it enticingly bare. She had most of the buttons fastened, save for a few at the top and bottom. The shirt fanned over her chest in a deep V, revealing the curves of her breasts. Ridge tracked his gaze down the lines of the fabric to where it ended midthigh, the tails flaring out and hinting at what lay underneath.

Darcy had pulled her hair out of its customary ponytail, and the auburn waves hung free about her shoulders and framed her face, highlighting the angles of her cheekbones. The casual style made her look softer somehow, warmer. His palms tingled to feel the silky-smooth strands, and he clenched his fists to keep from reaching for her then and there.

"Hi," she said quietly. She sounded almost shy, and Ridge was grateful his waist was below the level of the tub. If Darcy could see how much he wanted her right now, she'd probably run away screaming. He needed to appear calm and confident, not like some horny teenager seeing a naked woman for the first time.

"Hi, yourself," he replied, the words coming out scratched even to his own ears. He cleared his throat and tried again. "You changed clothes."

She smiled, her dimples making an appearance. "I thought I would make myself comfortable. I hope you don't mind."

He laughed, a strangled sound full of appreciation and wonder. "Not at all. You've never looked better."

Darcy glanced down, fingering the hem of the worn flannel. She lifted her hand a bit, and Ridge couldn't look away from the edge of the cloth as it inched up her bare leg, going higher, higher, almost there...

She dropped it and his gaze flew to her face to find her grinning at him. She was taunting him!

"That wasn't very nice of you," he grumbled. She merely laughed, a musical sound that made his heart swell. He leaned forward to snag the soap and began working up a lather, then spread it across his chest. He glanced over to find Darcy's eyes glued to his hands as they passed across his arms and down his torso. The warm glow of satisfaction spread through him as he realized two could play at this game.

He deliberately slowed his movements, enjoying the way her muscles relaxed and her eyes took on the unfocused look of arousal. She took a half step into the bathroom without realizing it and he felt like yelling in triumph. But he stayed quiet, enjoying the seductive spell weaving around them both.

His body heated in a way that had nothing to do with the water. Darcy's eyes on him were better than any drug, erasing his aches and pains and making him feel like Superman. It was almost too good to be true, and that was before she'd even touched him. How much better would he feel with her skin against his?

He wanted to take things slow, to savor the moment and cherish every look, every smile, every sigh. But his body cried out for the release her hands would bring, and he found himself unable to appreciate the subtleties of the moment.

Darcy appeared to be running out of patience, as well. She stepped fully into the bathroom and used her foot to nudge the door closed. Even though there was no one else in the house, the added privacy gave him a little thrill, as if they were going to do something naughty.

Ridge swallowed hard as she moved forward. His self-control was fighting a losing battle and the closer Darcy got, the harder it was to stay seated in the tub and resist the temptation to grab her and pull her in there with him.

Darcy stopped at the edge of the tub and stared down at him, running her gaze from the tips of his toes to the top of his head and everywhere in between. Ridge forced himself to remain still, letting her look her fill. It would be his turn soon.

Her dark brown eyes warmed, reminding him of pools of melted chocolate. The steam from the bath made the tendrils of hair around her face stick to her cheeks and neck, and her skin glistened. She looked like a woman who had been well pleasured, which served only to arouse him further.

At last, she met his gaze. "You're bigger than I remember," she said, then blushed prettily, sending the remaining blood in his body straight to his groin.

"That might be the nicest thing you've ever said to me," he drawled, earning a laugh from Darcy.

"You know what I mean," she said, gesturing to her own frame. "You're taller, and your shoulders got bigger."

"Is that all?" he asked suggestively.

She bit her bottom lip. "I'll have to let you know."

His mouth went dry and he could only nod.

"So..." Darcy trailed off, eyeing him up and down once more. Her mouth curved up and her eyes sparkled. "Want me to wash your back?"

It was quite possibly the sexiest invitation he'd ever heard, and for a split second, Ridge lost the ability to speak as his brain imploded.

He grinned at her and spread his arms wide. "I thought you'd never ask."

* * *

Darcy couldn't take his eyes off Ridge.

He was truly a sight to behold, the lines and angles of his body stretched out in a glorious display. The water rippled as he moved, blurring and softening his edges but doing nothing to diminish his size.

She fingered the buttons of his shirt, knowing she needed to takc it off. But something held her back. She knew as soon as she joined him in that tub, it was all over—his desire for her was plain to see. And she wasn't quite finished looking at him yet. It had been so long since she'd seen him. She'd forgotten how nice it was to simply watch him. He was a large man, but his movements were so graceful, so controlled. The promise of power held in check.

Would she ever tire of the sight of him?

Ridge held out the bar of soap, a sexy smile on his face. "Change your mind?" His tone was light, but she saw the hint of vulnerability in his eyes. It always shocked her to realize that no matter how confident and tough he appeared, Ridge was a sensitive soul. More than that, though, Darcy was touched that he was giving her an opportunity to back out, despite having come this far.

"Not on your life," she said. "I'm just trying to figure out how I'm going to climb into this thing without falling. It's huge!"

Ridge's eyes were full of laughter as he looked up at her. "That's what every man wants to hear."

She groaned and shook her head. "When did your sense of humor become so juvenile?"

He cocked his head to the side, apparently considering the question. "When was it not?"

"Good point."

"Come on in, Darcy," he coaxed. "The water's just fine." His expression turned serious, those dark eyes drawing her in. "And you know I won't let you fall."

She shivered at the promise, recognizing the truth of his words on a bone-deep level. In a split second, they had gone from flirting to serious, and they both recognized his statement went beyond helping her into the bath.

"I'm ready." And it was the truth, on so many levels. She was ready to let go of the hurts and disappointments of the past, ready to start a new life here in Granite Gulch. Ready to make her dreams of family a reality with Ridge by her side.

She unbuttoned the shirt in record time, letting it fall to the floor in a puddle of fabric. Then she took his hand and stepped into the tub, lowering herself into the warm embrace of the water and Ridge's arms.

He leaned back, taking her with him so she rested with her back against his chest. His arms circled around her torso, locking her into place as he let out a deep sigh.

Darcy relaxed, her muscles turning liquid in his embrace. As they sat there together, she lost track of where her body ended and his began, feeling as if they had melted into one.

She felt him pressed hard against her lower back, but he made no move to change their position. After a moment, she sighed. "I thought I was supposed to help you get clean."

His answering chuckle vibrated from his chest into her back. "We've got nothing but time."

"Not too long, though, or the water will get cold."

"True." He sounded thoughtful. "Guess we should get started then." Without sitting up, he took the bar of soap and lathered his hands. Then he spread them across her stomach and began to move, sudsing her skin with every pass across her body.

Her breath caught in her throat as he moved up her stomach to graze the undersides of her breasts. He traced lazy circles on her skin, sending zings of sensation through her limbs that made her shiver.

She arched her back, seeking more contact. His frictionless touch ignited a firestorm of need within her, but did little to satisfy her desire. She needed more, and her body moved restlessly against him, instinctively searching for the satisfaction only he could provide.

Ridge spread his palms on her torso, effectively anchoring her in place. "Patience," he whispered, his breath hot in her ear. "Just feel."

"I need..." She trailed off, unable to put her feelings into words. But that didn't seem to matter.

"I know," Ridge soothed. "Soon."

Darcy let go, surrendering herself to his embrace. His hands swept over her, his touch everywhere, overwhelming her senses. It was the best kind of torture, and she wished it would never end.

Time lost all meaning as they explored, getting reacquainted with each other's bodies. Darcy had the strangest sense of déjà vu—Ridge's body was so familiar, and yet it was as though she was touching him for the first time, relearning the planes and lines of his body with each pass of her hand.

She didn't know how long they stayed in the water. Somewhere along the way her conscious thought fled, leaving her a creature of sensation. She dimly registered Ridge helping her out of the bath. They dried each other off, the big fluffy towels adding a new layer of feeling. Then he guided her into his bedroom.

"I wish I could carry you," he said ruefully.

It was a romantic notion, but Darcy didn't want his injury getting in the way of this moment. "Save your knee," she murmured, enjoying the play of the light on his muscles as he pulled down the bedspread.

"Next time," he promised.

Darcy shivered. There would be a next time. Many more next times, in fact. There was something so freeing about that knowledge. It filled her heart with joy and made her feel safe and secure for the first time in years. Ridge was her home, her center, her safe place. And she was never going to let him go again.

She pushed his shoulder gently until he stretched out on the bed. Then she joined him, careful to avoid his knee as she fit her body around his. Moving slowly, deliberately, she rose over him, then sank down with a sigh of completion. Ridge's own breath echoed hers but then he froze, his fingers digging into her hips.

"I'm not wearing—"

"Shh," she assured him. "I'm protected."

He relaxed. "It's not that I don't want—"

"I know," she interrupted. "Just not right now."

"Exactly." He sounded relieved. "I'm so glad we're on the same page."

"Ridge?" Darcy rotated her hips in a move that made his eyes roll back in his head.

"Yeah?" His voice was a strangled croak.

"Let's talk later."

He moaned as she picked up the pace.

"Later is good."

Chapter 17

Two weeks later...

Ridge threw the truck into Park and cut the engine, but made no move to get out. He'd put this visit off for as long as he could and now that the time was here, he was even more reluctant to go inside.

But he owed it to his siblings to talk to Matthew and get his clue. The old man was determined to play his little game, and since it was the only way they were going to find their mother's body, Ridge and the rest of his family were forced to play along.

That didn't mean he was going to enjoy it.

After a long moment, he climbed out of the truck. He might as well get it over with. The sooner he went inside, the sooner he'd be able to get back to Darcy. She was back at the cabin with Penny, baking and cooking up a storm. Flo was bringing little Sara over for dinner tonight, and he couldn't wait to see them. It was the bright spot in this day, and he couldn't wait to hold that baby girl again.

But first, he'd need a hot shower to wash off this visit. No way was he going to risk contaminating her innocence with the darkness of his father.

It didn't take long to check in. They were expecting him, after all. He signed in, walked through the metal detector and followed a guard down a series of corridors. The halls were wide and painted white, but Ridge still felt his shoulders tighten as they moved deeper into the prison. He was so used to being outdoors—the lack of windows in this place made it all the more depressing and triggered instant claustrophobia.

Finally the guard stopped in front of a door and opened it, gesturing for Ridge to enter. The moment had arrived. He was really going to do this.

Ridge took a deep breath, his stomach twisting hard. He hadn't seen Matthew Colton in twenty years, and in all that time, he'd tried his best to forget his father's face. Would he even recognize the man now?

He was about to find out. He stepped past the

guard with a nod. "Take all the time you need," the man said.

Ridge didn't respond. If he had his way, this visit wouldn't last long at all.

The room was a narrow rectangle, divided into individual stations by a series of partitions that gave the illusion of privacy for each visitor. Black phone handsets hung on a reinforced glass panel that revealed the room beyond. Ridge was the only one there, which meant he had his pick of seats. He chose one close to the door so he wouldn't have far to go when it was time to leave.

After a moment, the door in the adjacent room opened and a guard stepped in, followed by a thin, white-haired figure. Ridge sucked in a breath as he got his first look at his father.

The years had not been kind to Matthew Colton. Neither had the cancer. His once tall, powerful frame was now skeletal and gaunt, and he moved in a halting shuffle that suggested he was in pain. Ridge watched him approach with a curious sense of detachment. Had it been any other person, this graphic evidence of disease would have triggered his sympathy. But try as he might, Ridge could muster no sorrow for his father's ongoing demise.

Matthew sat down with a wince. Then he lifted his head and looked directly at Ridge for the first time, his piercing blue eyes full of rage. Ridge didn't know whether his father was angry at the cancer or upset over the fact he was going to die in prison. Either way, he couldn't bring himself to care. Matthew Colton's life had always been fueled by hate. Why should his death be any different?

Matthew's thin, gnarled hand reached for his receiver. Ridge picked up his end and was treated to the rattling sound of Matthew's breathing.

"Ridge."

"Matthew."

The man's mouth twisted in a cruel smile. "Don't you mean *Dad*?"

Ridge pretended to consider the question. "No. I really don't."

Matthew narrowed his eyes but gave no other sign of displeasure. "Well, now, that's a shame," he drawled. "Here I thought I was going to have a conversation with my son. But if that's not the case, I might as well just go back to my cell." His brow rose in challenge, and Ridge clenched his jaw. *Just play the game*, he told himself. *Let him think he's won something.* It made him physically ill to appease this monster, but he had to get his clue so he could help his mother rest in peace.

"That won't be necessary," Ridge ground out. "Dad," he added, almost choking on the word.

Matthew nodded, his expression triumphant. "That's more like it."

Ridge didn't bother to respond. After a moment,

Matthew shifted on his seat. "Tell me what it is you do again."

The question made the hair on the back of Ridge's neck stand on end. "That's not part of the deal." Even though there was no way Matthew Colton was ever getting out of prison, Ridge didn't want him knowing the details of his life. He didn't deserve to have that information.

"Guard!" Matthew called out, his voice surprisingly strong. The guard stepped into the room and Matthew cocked his head to the side in a silent question.

After a moment's hesitation, Ridge nodded. Matthew glanced over his shoulder. "Never mind. I don't need you yet."

The man frowned and glanced at Ridge, who shrugged an apology. Matthew waited until the door shut again before turning back to face Ridge. "Well?"

Ridge willed his jaw to relax. "I work search and rescue."

Something ugly flashed in Matthew's eyes. "You think you'll be able to find your mother's body?"

"Yes." Ridge refused to even entertain the thought of failure. They would find Saralee and lay her to rest. There was no other option.

A small, secret smile flitted across Matthew's face. "We'll see about that," he murmured.

The conversation had gone on long enough. "I believe you have something for me?"

"I do." Matthew straightened up, then started to cough. Ridge somehow managed to hold on to his patience while the other man hacked and gasped for what seemed like forever. When it was over, he raised a shaking hand to his mouth and wiped, trailing a small streak of bright red blood across his pale lips.

"The clue?" Ridge pressed.

"B."

Ridge frowned. *"B?"*

Matthew nodded. "That's right."

It didn't make any sense. "The letter, or the insect?"

The old man didn't answer right away, and for a moment, Ridge feared he wouldn't respond at all. Then he let out a sigh. "The letter."

Ridge added it to the short list of clues they already had: *Texas. Hill. B.* He turned the words over in his mind, searching for a connection that would help him find his mother. Was it the name of a town? A place of business? One of Matthew's old friends? But nothing jumped out at him.

Frustration welled in his chest at the futility of this visit. Was Matthew ever really going to tell them where to find Saralee? After all, it's not as if they could do anything to him if he didn't hold up his end of the bargain—the man was dying in prison. How much worse could things get for him?

"You don't look too happy," Matthew observed.

Ridge bit back a dozen retorts, knowing he had to play nice if he hoped to get more information out of the man. "The letter *B* isn't much of a clue."

"Oh, but it is," Matthew said, a smug note entering his voice. "More than enough, if you're clever. You just have to think like me."

Ridge's horror must have shown on his face because Matthew laughed, a harsh, grating sound that triggered another coughing fit, this one longer than the last. Finally, he wiped the tears of amusement from his blue eyes. "That's right, boy," he said, his voice rough. "You're going to have to get into my head if you ever want to find your mama."

"You're disgusting." Ridge didn't bother trying to hide his reaction. It was clear Matthew wasn't going to offer any additional help, not to him anyway. Maybe one of his siblings would have better luck. Like Trevor, for instance. He had made it his life's work to understand monsters like Matthew and he knew how to talk to them. Hopefully, he would be more successful at prying information out of the man. It wasn't a skill Ridge cared to acquire.

"That may be," Matthew replied. "But my blood runs through your veins, and don't you forget it.

Like it or not, I'm your father. I'm a part of you and always will be."

Ridge shook his head, thinking back to his time with little Sara. Taking care of that baby had made one thing very clear—fatherhood was more than just shared genes. "You're not my father. You're nothing more than a sperm donor." He stood and dropped the black plastic receiver back into its cradle, ignoring Matthew's muted shout of protest. Then he turned around and walked out, leaving the old man to rot in his own bitterness.

Annabel Colton pushed back from the table and allowed herself the indulgence of a jaw-cracking, eye-watering yawn. She'd risen with the sun to start her shift, then had come home to sift through the stacks of Matthew's mail that Trevor had dropped off.

"You're sure you don't mind?" Her older brother had seemed almost reluctant to part with the letters. She'd tried not to take it personally—none of her brothers were happy about her choice of career, but she was good at her job and even they had to admit it. Still, they tried to protect her from what they saw as the messier side of things.

"I'm happy to help." She knew Ridge had originally volunteered for the job, but he deserved a break. He'd been even more quiet than usual after his visit to the prison. Annabel didn't know if it was something Matthew had said or just seeing the man again that bothered him so much, but either way, he didn't need to trouble himself with Matthew's fan mail. Besides, he and Darcy were like two teenagers in love and Annabel didn't want to mar their happiness. Ridge had been alone for so long—it was nice to see him smiling again.

She pushed a stack of letters to the side and pulled another one forward. Sorting through Matthew's mail was harder than she'd anticipated. It wasn't the content of the letters—although that was pretty bad. Rather, it was the tangible proof that so many people admired him enough to go to the effort of writing. How many more out there looked up to Matthew but hadn't bothered to send a letter? It really made her worry about the state of humanity, that so many people wanted to connect with such an evil man.

Her eyes burned with fatigue, but she didn't stop. She had a meeting with her boss in—she checked her watch—just about an hour, and she wanted to report on her progress with this batch of mail. If she found something, it could really help direct the investigation.

Fortunately, there hadn't been any new victims of the Alphabet Killer of late. The police had held several press conferences to spread the word that women with long dark hair should take extra precautions, and it seemed the message was getting through. Annabel had seen women in Granite Gulch walking in groups, and she personally knew several women who had taken to wearing a wig to hide their hair when going out in public. It was a shame people needed to alter their lives so drastically for the sake of safety, but it was a small price to pay if it prevented additional deaths.

Of course, if the Alphabet Killer really had gone to ground it was going to be that much harder to stop her. But Annabel wasn't going to give up. She would see this case through to the end, no matter what.

With a sigh, Annabel pulled out another letter and began to read. It seemed familiar somehow, and when she got to the end, she realized why.

What she had initially mistaken as an ink blot was actually a crudely drawn red bull's-eye.

Chills raced through her limbs, chasing away her fatigue. She sat up and read the letter again, this time paying more attention to the handwriting. Was it the same as the other letter from their killer?

She pushed aside piles of paper, searching frantically for the photocopy of the killer's letter that Trevor had given her to use as a comparison in case she found something. Excitement bubbled in her veins as she realized she had probably just discovered the proverbial needle in a haystack.

At last, she found the page and held it next to

the letter. A wide grin split her face as she verified it was indeed the same handwriting.

But the best part of all?

This letter had a signature.

Regina Willard.

"Gotcha," Annabel whispered. Now they had a solid lead, after weeks of guesswork and circumstantial clues.

She stuffed the letter and the photocopy back into the original envelope, noting with a small shock the return address in the upper left corner. *Blackwood.* As in the next town over.

"You've been here the whole time, haven't you?"

It was almost too good to be true—the killer's name and a location all at once. Annabel glanced at her watch. It was still early, but this news was too exciting to sit on for long. She grabbed her keys and phone and hopped in the car, dialing Trevor as she drove.

I'm coming for you, Regina, she thought, stepping on the gas to beat a yellow light.

You can run, but you can't hide.

* * * * *

SPECIAL EXCERPT FROM

HARLEQUIN

ROMANTIC SUSPENSE

One night of passion with Marcus Jones led to a pregnancy Chloe Ryder didn't expect. And when a serial killer they captured launches a plan for revenge, Chloe wonders if she'll survive long enough to tell Marcus about their child...

Read on for a sneak preview of The Agent's Deadly Liaison, *the latest book in Jennifer D. Bokal's sweeping Wyoming Nights miniseries!*

"You think this is a joke? I wonder how many pieces of you I can cut away before you stop laughing."

On the counter lay a scalpel. Darcy picked it up. The handle was still stained with Gretchen's lifeblood. Chloe went cold as she realized that she'd pushed too hard for information.

Knife in hand, Darcy slowly, slowly approached the bed. Chloe pressed her back into the pillow, trying in vain to get distance from the killer and the knife. It did no good. Darcy pressed Chloe's shackled hand onto the railing and drew the blade across her palm. The metal was cold against her skin. She tried to jerk her hand away, but it was no use.

Darcy drove the blade into Chloe's flesh.

HRSEXP0522

The cut burned, and for a moment, her vision filled with red. Then a seam opened in her hand. Blood began to weep from the wound. She balled her hand into a fist as her palm throbbed, and anger flooded her veins.

Chloe might've been handcuffed to a bed, but that didn't mean that she couldn't fight back.

"Damn you straight to hell," she growled.

With her free hand, Chloe pushed Darcy's chin back. At the same moment, she lifted her feet, kicking the killer in the chest. Darcy stumbled back before tumbling to the ground. Had Chloe been free, she would have had the advantage.

But shackled to the bed? Chloe had done nothing more than enrage a dangerous person.

Standing, Darcy brushed a loose strand of hair from her face. She smiled, then scoffed before echoing Chloe's words. "Damn me to hell? Hell doesn't frighten me, Chloe. Nothing does—especially not you."

HRSEXP0522

Get 4 FREE REWARDS!
We'll send you 2 FREE Books plus 2 FREE Mystery Gifts.
KENTUCKY CRIME RING
JULIE ANNE LINDSEY
TEXAS STALKER
BARB HAN
FREE
Value Over
$20
UNDER THE RANCHER'S PROTECTION
ADDISON FOX
OPERATION WHISTLEBLOWER
JUSTINE DAVIS
Both the Harlequin Intrigue® and Harlequin® Romantic Suspense series feature compelling novels filled with heart-racing action-packed romance that will keep you on the edge of your seat.
YES! Please send me 2 FREE novels from the Harlequin Intrigue or Harlequin Romantic Suspense series and my 2 FREE gifts (gifts are worth about $10 retail). After receiving them, if I don't wish to receive any more books, I can return the shipping statement marked "cancel." If I don't cancel, I will receive 6 brand-new Harlequin Intrigue Larger-Print books every month and be billed just $5.99 each in the U.S. or $6.49 each in Canada, a savings of at least 14% off the cover price or 4 brand-new Harlequin Romantic Suspense books every month and be billed just $4.99 each in the U.S. or $5.74 each in Canada, a savings of at least 13% off the cover price. It's quite a bargain! Shipping and handling is just 50¢ per book in the U.S. and $1.25 per book in Canada.* I understand that accepting the 2 free books and gifts places me under no obligation to buy anything. I can always return a shipment and cancel at any time. The free books and gifts are mine to keep no matter what I decide.
Choose one: ☐ Harlequin Intrigue Larger-Print (199/399 HDN GNXC)
☐ Harlequin Romantic Suspense (240/340 HDN GNMZ)
Name (please print)
Address
Apt. #
City
State/Province
Zip/Postal Code
Email: Please check this box ☐ if you would like to receive newsletters and promotional emails from Harlequin Enterprises ULC and its affiliates. You can unsubscribe anytime.
Mail to the Harlequin Reader Service:
IN U.S.A.: P.O. Box 1341, Buffalo, NY 14240-8531
IN CANADA: P.O. Box 603, Fort Erie, Ontario L2A 5X3
Want to try 2 free books from another series? Call 1-800-873-8635 or visit www.ReaderService.com.
*Terms and prices subject to change without notice. Prices do not include sales taxes, which will be charged (if applicable) based on your state or country of residence. Canadian residents will be charged applicable taxes. Offer not valid in Quebec. This offer is limited to one order per household. Books received may not be as shown. Not valid for current subscribers to the Harlequin Intrigue or Harlequin Romantic Suspense series. All orders subject to approval. Credit or debit balances in a customer's account(s) may be offset by any other outstanding balance owed by or to the customer. Please allow 4 to 6 weeks for delivery. Offer available while quantities last.
Your Privacy—Your information is being collected by Harlequin Enterprises ULC, operating as Harlequin Reader Service. For a complete summary of the information we collect, how we use this information and to whom it is disclosed, please visit our privacy notice located at corporate.harlequin.com/privacy-notice. From time to time we may also exchange your personal information with reputable third parties. If you wish to opt out of this sharing of your personal information, please visit readerservice.com/consumerschoice or call 1-800-873-8635. Notice to California Residents—Under California law, you have specific rights to control and access your data. For more information on these rights and how to exercise them, visit corporate.harlequin.com/california-privacy.
HIHRS22